BOOKSTORE GIRLS

Kei Aono

BOOKSTORE GIRLS

*Translated from the Japanese by
Haydn Trowell*

MACLEHOSE PRESS
QUERCUS · LONDON

First published in Japan as 書店ガール (*Shoten girl*)
by PHP Institute, Inc. in 2012

First published in Great Britain in 2025
by MacLehose Press, an imprint of Quercus
Part of John Murray Group

1

Copyright © 2012 by Kei Aono
English translation copyright © 2025 by Haydn Trowell
The edition arranged with PHP Institute, Inc. through
Emily Books Agency LTD. and Casanovas & Lynch Literary Agency

The moral right of Kei Aono to be
identified as the author of this work has been
asserted in accordance with the Copyright,
Designs and Patents Act, 1988.

Haydn Trowell asserts his moral right to be identified as the translator of this work

All rights reserved. No part of this publication
may be reproduced or transmitted in any form
or by any means, electronic or mechanical,
including photocopy, recording, or any
information storage and retrieval system,
without permission in writing from the publisher.

This book is a work of fiction. Names, characters, businesses, organisations,
places and events are either the product of the author's imagination or are
used fictitiously. Any resemblance to actual persons, living or dead,
events or locales is entirely coincidental.

A CIP catalogue record for this book is available
from the British Library

TPB ISBN 978 1 52944 633 3
Ebook ISBN 978 1 52944 635 7

Typeset in Scala by CC Book Production
Printed and bound in Great Britain by Clays Ltd, Elcograf S.p.A.

Papers used by Quercus are from well-managed forests and other responsible sources.

Quercus
Carmelite House
50 Victoria Embankment
London EC4Y 0DZ

John Murray Group
Part of Hodder & Stoughton Limited
An Hachette UK company

The authorised representative in the EEA is Hachette Ireland,
8 Castlecourt Centre, Dublin 15, D15 XTP3, Ireland (email: info@hbgi.ie)

BOOKSTORE GIRLS

1

The performers on stage swapped out. The next act was about to start – a musical number, apparently. A few seconds later, the master of ceremonies introduced a congratulatory song by some of the groom's old university friends. They were tuning their guitars and bass, getting ready to play, when one of them grabbed the groom, Nobumitsu Obata, hoping to make him sing.

At first, Nobumitsu put on a show of reluctance, but with a little nudging from the people around him, he allowed himself to be guided to the centre of the stage. His hesitancy, however, was just for show. His face lit up, radiating confidence, and there was no mistaking that he knew his way around a song. As soon as he grabbed the microphone, he went straight into a quick vocal warm-up, rearing to go.

"And now, Ayaka and Kobukuro's 'Winding Road', performed by the groom for the bride!" one of the band members announced with a wide grin.

"What? I can't sing *that* on my own!" the groom protested.

It seemed no-one had run this by him beforehand.

But, as if waiting for this exact moment, his university

buddies closed in on the bride, Aki Kitamura, gently nudging her up onto the stage. The song was a duet, so they must have planned all along to have the bride and groom sing it together.

Aki, however, gave her head a firm shake – and *that* was no act. Even as her friends tried to coax her forward, she froze, her face stiff, refusing to budge. The delay fed into the crowd's restlessness, the hum of chatter growing louder.

Finally, Nobumitsu stepped down from the stage, walked over to her, and gently put an arm around her shoulders. A second later, the emcee hurried over and whispered something in her ear.

Whatever they said, it left her breathing a resigned sigh. Reluctantly, she climbed up onto the stage.

Oh? Are they really going to make her sing? This *should be interesting.*

Riko Nishioka, until that moment deep in conversation with a salesman going on and on about ebooks, stopped mid-sentence and turned her attention to the stage. The wedding party was being held in a rented-out Italian restaurant, and it was packed to the brim with guests – at least a hundred of them. The groom was a manga editor at the publishing house Hitotsuboshi Press, and the bride was a well-known bookseller at Pegasus Books, a major bookstore chain. The crowd was mostly industry folks, with more than a few sales representatives openly exchanging business cards while barely bothering to so much as glance up at the stage.

They were shameless. This wasn't a business event. They could at least have the decency to pretend to be enjoying the wedding. It was like they were trying to recoup the cost of their gifts by squeezing in as much networking as possible.

Riko was Aki's supervisor, and the assistant manager of

Pegasus Books' Kichijoji branch. She lived for her work, and at forty, she was still single. She had a sharp, well-defined, intelligent look about her, and could pass for a woman in her mid-thirties. Tonight, she wore a chic wine-red dress, impeccably tailored to highlight her figure.

"You look amazing, Riko. You always do, but you're especially stunning tonight," a salesman weaving his way through the tables said, tossing out this over-the-top compliment on the fly.

"Thank you, Ashida. You don't know how happy I am to hear you say that," she replied, offering him her brightest professional smile – enough to make the man flush in embarrassment.

Oh, please. He doesn't actually think I fell for that, does he? I'm way past the point of getting suckered by his empty compliments. Acting flattered is just part of the job. Not that I'm about to spell that out for him. Honesty only gets you so far, Riko quipped to herself.

On stage, the keyboard player hit the opening note, signalling the starting pitch for Aki. The sound rang out, gradually quietening the hum of the audience. With everyone's eyes locked on her, Aki gripped the mic, steeling herself. Taking a deep breath, she began to sing the first line.

"*On this winding road ahead of me, tiny lights are shining faint but free.*"

The bookstore clerk sitting next to Riko snorted and quickly clamped a hand over her mouth, while across the table, a sales rep choked on a piece of fried chicken, letting out a loud cough.

The pitch was unmistakably off. Since she had started a cappella, there was no hiding it.

"*Though they're far and hard to see, I'll take each step and let it be.*"

From there, the band joined in with a soft accompaniment meant to complement her singing. But even with the backing music, the pitch issues went unresolved. A glance at the band members revealed awkward expressions – they clearly hadn't expected her to be this tone-deaf. Even the emcee was stunned, standing there slack-jawed in disbelief.

The audience, however, loved it.

"So, Aki's got an Achilles' heel, huh? Who would've guessed?"

"Makes sense. Now we know why she never comes to karaoke night."

Everyone in the room was watching the stage, fighting to suppress their laughter. Even the business-card exchanges had ground to a temporary halt. Riko was struggling to keep her own mirth in check – not because of Aki's singing, but because of the chaos erupting around her.

You really should've done your homework and made sure she could sing first.

This event was supposed to showcase the bond between bride and groom, but now the poor bride was being turned into a spectacle.

And yet, despite everything, Aki, up on stage, remained stunningly beautiful. She was always gorgeous, but today, in her bridal attire, she looked especially radiant. Her casual mini wedding dress was worlds apart from the formal gown she had worn at the ceremony, highlighting her long, slender legs, the graceful curve of her neck, her shoulders, and her toned arms. Her fair cheeks were flushed, and her long lashes drooped shyly, giving her an air of delicate femininity. Hers was a figure that no man could possibly resist.

Just as long as you never hear her sing.

"Kindness so great it overflows, nothing can ever bring it down..."

A tragic pattern had begun to emerge – the more earnestly she sang, the further off-key she went. But then, something changed. Aki shot Nobumitsu a pleading look – and he met her gaze with steady reassurance, his expression all but saying, *Leave it to me.*

"Though they're far and hard to see, I'll take each step and let it be."

Everyone in the room thought the same thing – *He's good.* His rich, resonant voice carried the melody perfectly. Then, led by Nobumitsu's singing, Aki gradually started to find her notes.

"More than the days I tried to hide, more than all these tears we've cried..."

The two of them locked eyes, desperately pushing themselves to match the other's voice. The audience's laughter slowly melted away as they watched the pair's tender interaction, replaced by warm, admiring smiles.

So, in the end, it's just a sentimental harmony. How dull.

Riko turned away from the stage and downed a glass of wine.

Here I am, freshly dumped, and now I have to watch some happy couple act all lovey-dovey. Why did they have to have their wedding now? *I feel like curling up in my room and losing it.*

Up on stage, the song was building up to its climax. Nobumitsu wrapped his arm around Aki's shoulder, the two of them pressing their cheeks together as they sang the final lines in unison.

"Down this winding road I go, where the me of my dreams waits below."

As soon as the song ended, the crowd erupted into cheers.

"Alright, you two!"

"Looking hot!"

The groom's friends, the ones who pressured them both up onto the stage in the first place, were now throwing cheesy shout-outs. Whether out of relief it was finally over or guilt at embarrassing the bride, they were going way over the top. Sure, it had turned out a little different than planned, but in the end, the duet served to showcase how madly in love the two newlyweds were. What started as a disaster – or rather, a terrible off-key performance – had somehow turned into a win.

"Let's give a huge round of applause for the happy couple!" the emcee, Kazuhiro Iwata, a salesman at Hitotsuboshi Press, called out to the audience. "She's a knockout beauty with a stunning figure, and she's tough as nails at work, always going toe-to-toe with us salesmen and never backing down. Aki sure has been blessed with more than her fair share of gifts – but, as they say, even the gods have to draw the line somewhere . . . and when it comes to singing, well, I think we can all agree she's not quite a natural."

A burst of laughter erupted from the crowd. Aki forced a smile, though one that was clearly strained.

"Life's unpredictable, isn't it? You never know what's coming your way. Sometimes, you're stuck doing something you're terrible at. But hey, even the hardest stuff is easier when you've got someone to face it with. When push comes to shove, I'm sure Nobumitsu here will have her back."

All eyes turned to Nobumitsu. He gave the crowd a sheepish smile, dipping his head in a quick bow.

"Let's hope you both remember this day and keep working to tackle life's ups and downs as a happy couple. Now, let's give a big round of applause for this wonderful bride and groom and their equally wonderful duet!"

Once more, the room filled with applause. Nobumitsu slipped an arm around Aki's waist, waving at the crowd. Aki managed a stiff smile, while Nobumitsu wore a grin so wide it looked like his face might melt off.

He really stepped up to the plate, huh? No wonder he's in such a good mood. Not so sure about her, though.

Riko knocked back another glass of wine.

Ugh. I feel sick just looking at that lovesick puppy face. Just like the day he told me we were over.

"Looks like it turned out alright in the end. I was worried it would all go sideways when Kitamura started singing."

The voice belonged to Takanori Nojima, Riko's boss, seated beside her. Nojima was about five years older than her, but he still looked sharp – slim, with jet-black hair and a youthful air. Years in customer service had given him a polished, easy-going manner.

The hall was filled with tables, each one a little hub of acquaintances chatting together. Riko's table was occupied by Aki's co-workers from Pegasus Books.

"Obata's singing is top-notch. I haven't heard him belt out a tune since that press event, but he's really good," one of them commented.

Aki is still unbearable, though. Or so Riko wanted to say. But even she had her limits.

"Oh yeah. We all went to karaoke afterwards, didn't we?" someone else chimed in.

Nobumitsu and Aki met almost a year ago at a signing for the manga artist Nao Agachi. Nobumitsu had come along to oversee the event as Agachi's editor, while Aki, being in charge of Pegasus Books' comics section, was running the show. After the session wrapped up, everyone went out for drinks, and then karaoke – where, at Agachi's insistence, Nobumitsu let loose with an anime theme song like his life depended on it.

Back then, Aki flat-out refused to sing, even though Obata kept urging her.

Did Obata know she couldn't hold a note to save her life? Then again, he's so smitten, he probably thinks it's endearing.

Nobumitsu was still wearing that ridiculous, goofy grin as he chatted with the guests.

"I hear the honeymoon's in Hawaii. I've always wanted to go," said Ryosuke Tsujii with more than a hint of envy. Tsujii, seated at Riko's table, was in his mid-thirties and supervised the fourth floor at Pegasus Books. Tall, tanned, and lanky, he seemed to use his every vacation day to go hiking, surfing, or whatever else. Work definitely wasn't his top priority.

"I heard they're staying at the Halekulani," chimed in Yoshio Hatakeda, the group's self-appointed trivia expert. "Most tourists stick with places like the Sheraton or the Royal Hawaiian on Waikiki Beach, but the Halekulani's on a whole other level. The décor, the restaurants, the service – it's all first-class."

He said it like he had stayed there himself, but knowing Hatakeda, that was unlikely. He was as cheap as they came, and he hated travelling. He must have read about it online. Even if he did go to Hawaii, there was no way he would splurge on a luxury hotel.

Though similar in age to Tsujii, Hatakeda was his polar opposite – short and stocky, with a perpetually sleepy look on his face. The only time he perked up was when he got to flaunt some random piece of knowledge.

At that moment, a loud voice interrupted the conversation. "Well, well, if it isn't Pegasus Books' finest – the manager and assistant manager, no less!"

"Ah! Iwata! Wonderful job hosting tonight," Riko gushed with polite insincerity. "I had no idea you were such a natural. Those ad-libs were perfect."

"Nah, you're too kind," he said, clearly basking in the compliment.

Built like an athlete – tall, broad and loud – Iwata was Nobumitsu's colleague and Pegasus' sales liaison at Hitotsuboshi.

"It's a packed house tonight," said the teetotalling Nojima, raising his glass of iced oolong tea for a toast.

Iwata clinked his glass in return. "Yeah, I hear more than a hundred people turned out. Obata's got tons of work connections, and Kitamura's really popular with everyone's sales teams. I've seen people from all kinds of publishing houses here."

"Yes, I can see. There's a huge turnout from Hitotsuboshi, as well. I think their whole sales team showed up."

"Funny you mention that," Iwata said with a smirk, clearly trying to hold back laughter. "Their deputy manager, Shibata, *didn't* come. He's Kitamura's biggest fan, too. There's a rumour going around the office that he scheduled a business trip just so he wouldn't have to see her in a wedding dress."

"But Shibata just got married himself last month, didn't he? To a woman seventeen years his junior. She went to Sacred Heart University." Hatakeda threw in another unnecessary fact.

Where does he dig this stuff up? Riko thought. *If only he'd put that energy into something useful.*

"Well then . . ." Iwata let out a low chuckle. "Maybe he skipped the party out of respect for his wife?"

The quip wasn't even funny, but the men at the table all burst out laughing.

This again? Riko thought, rolling her eyes. The topic of Shibata's young wife was a running joke for them lately. The *seventeen years his junior* part seemed to be their favourite detail. Hitotsuboshi's sales team hadn't been able to shut up about it.

"So, the infamous Shibata can't stand up to his young wife, huh?" Nojima chuckled.

A self-proclaimed devoted husband, Nojima was clearly envious of the other man's young wife. Why did men go so crazy for younger women?

"Exactly! Ever since he got married, Shibata's been so antisocial. There was a meeting in Shinagawa just the other day, and instead of coming out for drinks with everyone afterwards, he went straight home! And guess what time the meeting ended – five o'clock! Five! Can you believe it?"

"Wow. And he used to call himself nightlife royalty. His wife must have him wrapped around her little finger."

"Totally! And get this, the other day he . . ."

Riko forced a polite smile as the others continued talking, but deep down, she couldn't care less about their banter. She merely nodded along while downing another glass of wine.

Seriously, this is not *the kind of conversation to have in front of a single woman in her early forties. Have some tact, people. No wonder you guys don't have any luck with young women.*

Riko was fuming, but the men didn't seem to notice. They carried on, gleefully swapping stories of other men's wives, until—

"Oh, shoot. I've got to announce the next act. Be right back!"

Iwata bolted off towards the emcee stand, ending the conversation. Riko breathed a sigh of relief and poured herself another glass of wine. On stage, Nobumitsu's old classmates were still performing – a slow, soulful ballad.

"Still, I never thought Kitamura would get married so soon," Tsujii murmured, silent up till now.

"They only dated for, what, six months?" Hatakeda replied.

Tsujii and Hatakeda couldn't be more different in looks and personality, but maybe because they were so close in age, they got along surprisingly well. They were practically inseparable – they had even come to the wedding together.

"Young people these days move so fast," Riko remarked. "I guess they're just more practical about things – and quick to move on."

Yep, they're quick to move on, alright. Like shedding old skin. But it's not just young women who do that.

Riko took another sip of wine, thinking back to how quickly *he* had moved on. Men didn't hesitate at all when they knew what they wanted.

"Hey, come on, that's a bit much, don't you think? Are you drunk already, Nishioka?" Nojima, ever the peacemaker, tried to keep things light.

"Drunk? On a couple of glasses of wine? No way! Anyway, everyone's thinking it," she insisted, slurring her words.

Yep, drunk as a sailor.

Nojima shook his head with a resigned look, glancing at Tsujii and Hatakeda as if to ask, *What do we do with her?* Tsujii returned his gaze with a weary, *What can you do?* while Hatakeda remained stony-faced.

"You've had enough, Nishioka. What's got into you today?"

"Sorry. I might have gone a bit overboard. But it's true, the girls at the store are pretty shocked. Look – none of them showed up tonight except for me."

Before Aki started dating Nobumitsu, she had been seeing her co-worker Takahiko Mita, breaking things off once her now-husband came into the picture. Everyone at the store knew about it.

"Now that you mention it, none of the girls are here. It's just you, Nishioka?"

"I saw Hagiwara helping out at the desk," Nojima replied, as nonchalant as ever.

Mami Hagiwara was a part-timer who handled the textbook section. She was the only woman at work Aki was close to, and not only was she helping at the front desk tonight, she was also one of the party organisers.

"Ah, Hagiwara. But the invites went out to everyone, didn't they?"

On stage, the band finished their set and started clearing out. The next act was to be a harp performance by one of Aki's cousins. The harp was already being carried onto the stage, and the performer began setting up.

"Well, yeah," Tsujii said. "But after all that drama, it wouldn't exactly be easy for them to show up even if they *did* want to."

"By the way, did anyone send Mita an invite?" Riko asked, realising her mistake a moment too late.

Her voice had carried further than she intended, practically echoing across the hall. The timing couldn't have been worse – the harpist had just finished setting up, and the whole room had quietened down in anticipation of the performance.

For one long, awkward moment, Riko's question hung in the air.

A moment later, however, the harpist began to play, and the guests turned their attention to the music as if nothing had happened. It seemed her slip-up hadn't caused any noticeable ripples.

Phew. I guess no-one heard me. Or if they did, they probably thought it was just casual chit-chat.

After all, Aki and Mita's past relationship wasn't common knowledge outside their bookstore.

Slowly, Riko downed another glass of wine in an effort to calm her nerves.

Riko's hunch had been on the mark – most of those in the room *hadn't* paid any attention to her irresponsible comment. A few people sitting nearby shot her annoyed looks, no doubt wondering why she was being so loud when the performance was just about to begin, but that was about it.

Well, almost. There was one person who *had* heard her, and who definitely *hadn't* brushed it off – the bride herself. To her, Riko's words dripped with malice, poisoning the entire night. It didn't matter that this wasn't Riko's intention – Aki had decided it was.

Why is she mentioning Takahiko at a time like this? Did she do it on purpose? Did she want me *to overhear? Is she trying to get under my skin?*

Aki was already angry. She had sworn to herself she would never sing in front of a crowd, yet she had been dragged onto the stage to be humiliated. But knowing Nobumitsu and his friends hadn't meant any harm, she had been left with no clear outlet for her frustration.

Now, the perfect target had presented itself.

I'll give her a piece of my mind later. I don't care if she's the assistant manager, she's ruined the party.

Aki, with her straightforward, no-nonsense personality, was the kind of person who wore her emotions on her sleeve – but that also meant she was prone to jumping to conclusions, and quick to pick a fight. Once she had decided Riko had rubbed her the wrong way, her anger only snowballed.

I know she doesn't like me. She's never liked me, not since I first joined the store. She wants everything her way, so of course she hates anyone who pushes back.

I knew it. She's the reason I was forced up onto that stage. She must have goaded Iwata into setting me up.

After all, when she had refused to take part, the host had leaned in and whispered, "I hear you're a great singer, Aki. Your boss told me. Come on, let everyone see how much you and Nobumitsu love each other."

Only now did it hit her. *Your boss told me.* He must have meant Riko – she had deliberately set her up to crash and burn.

To be fair, Aki's assumption wasn't entirely unreasonable. In her mind, the words "your boss" could refer to only three people – the fifth-floor supervisor Hatakeda, the assistant manager Riko, or the store manager Nojima. And all three of them knew she was hopelessly tone-deaf. Hatakeda was too aloof and indifferent to bother telling Iwata something like that, and Nojima was far too kind-hearted. That left only Riko.

Yet as it happened, the boss Iwata was referring to wasn't Riko at all, but the jokester Tsujii. From an outsider's perspective, Tsujii would have been considered her superior even if he wasn't her direct supervisor.

A few weeks earlier, Iwata had run into Tsujii while out on

a sales call, and he had used the opportunity to fish for information without mentioning the upcoming wedding reception.

"What would you say Aki's good at?"

"Singing, of course. Yeah. Kitamura's singing voice is *definitely* worth a listen."

Tsujii had meant it as a playful quip, but Iwata took it at face value. Having focused solely on judo from grade school through to university, Iwata was the quintessential sports guy – not the type to get a joke. In fact, he thought it was a great idea. After all, Nobumitsu was proud of his karaoke skills, so why not sneak in a duet for the happy couple as a surprise?

Now, why did Iwata decide to consult Tsujii about this? The reason was simple. Riko, the assistant manager and third-floor supervisor, was always swamped with work and wasn't the type to waste time on small talk, while Hatakeda, the fifth-floor supervisor, was the silent, brooding kind, and difficult to approach. So, by process of elimination, that left only Tsujii. The fourth-floor specialist books section was the store's quietest, so as the floor supervisor, Tsujii had plenty of time on his hands. On top of that, he loved to chat, and with the right nudge, he would happily spill all kinds of information. As far as Iwata was concerned, he was practically a goldmine. Of course, Tsujii himself had completely forgotten ever offering this particular piece of advice.

On stage, the harp performance continued. Aki pretended to listen, but inside, she was fuming, her pent-up frustrations with Riko bubbling over.

"Kitamura? Er, I mean, Obata?" sounded a voice, pulling her back to reality.

She looked up to see Nojima, the store manager, standing timidly in front of her.

"Ah, Nojima. Thank you for coming today."

"No, no, thank *you* for inviting me. Actually, I have somewhere to be right now, so I'm afraid I have to go."

"Oh, okay. Let me grab Nobumitsu."

She glanced around, finding her husband on the other side of the room chatting with a group of old classmates.

"No need for that – don't want to dampen the mood when everyone's having such a good time."

"Are you sure?"

"Absolutely. Really, though, it was a wonderful party. It warms the heart to see you two so happy."

"Uh, thanks."

Happy? The whole party had been a nightmare – first she was outed as a terrible singer, then her ex's name had been shouted across the room for everyone to hear.

Watching Aki's face darken, Nojima rushed to smooth things over. "By the way, I'm sorry not everyone could make it. It's such a shame."

Aki's smile froze. She had sent invites to everyone at the store except for Mita, and yet only the managers had bothered to show up.

She had even rescheduled the wedding to coincide with one of the store's rare maintenance days, when everyone would have the day off. All that planning had been for nothing.

"The girls – honestly, they're being a bit childish. It's a wedding, for crying out loud. Shouldn't they be here to celebrate? And Nishioka saying you moved on too fast? That wasn't fair at all."

Moved on too fast? Aki's anger flared. *Like she knows what really happened.*

"I'm sure things will have settled down by the time you

get back from your honeymoon. Everything changes once you tie the knot," Nojima continued, unaware he was only adding fuel to the fire. "You'll be back in a week, right?"

"Yes. We're back on the fifth of July."

"Well, have fun! I'm looking forward to hearing all about it."

"Thank you."

She saw him off at the exit.

When she returned to the main room, the harp performance had just wrapped up. Next, Nobumitsu was supposed to give a thank-you speech. Prompted by the host, Aki took the stage beside him. Nobumitsu began by cracking his usual jokes to get the crowd laughing. From up on the stage, Aki could take in the entirety of the room.

What is she even doing here? If she didn't want to celebrate my marriage, she shouldn't have bothered to show up.

A loud burst of applause brought Aki back to her senses. Nobumitsu had finished his speech, it seemed. Flustered, she hurried to follow his lead with a deep bow.

"Alright, the bride will now share a small piece of her happiness! Get ready, ladies – it's time for the bouquet! Who will the lucky one be?"

Just as Aki was about to leave the stage, the emcee's next words stopped her in her tracks.

"Single ladies, are you ready?"

Squealing in excitement, a group of young women gathered in front of the stage, stretching their hands into the air as if to say *Pick me!*

Aki couldn't fail to notice Riko deliberately turn her back to the stage, engrossed in a conversation with a salesman as if the day's events had nothing to do with her.

Don't worry. I wouldn't dream of giving you my bouquet, Aki thought, clutching the bundle of white roses tightly in her hands.

"Alright, Aki, whenever you're ready!"

At the emcee's cue, she threw the bouquet with all her might – deliberately aiming away from Riko. The bundle of flowers soared high, scattering a few petals as it went, only to smack into the ceiling. The impact sent it veering off course, into an empty part of the room. A disappointed *Aww!* sounded all around, and a hand shot out to toss it back into the air, sending it flying with greater force until it landed squarely on Riko's head.

Startled, Riko instinctively reached up and caught it before it hit the ground.

"Well, well! Pegasus Books' very own Riko Nishioka has caught the bouquet! Congratulations!" the emcee's voice boomed.

The entire hall seemed to swarm around her.

"Congrats!" someone said, clapping her on the shoulder.

"You're next, Nishioka," Tsujii grinned, clearly enjoying the spectacle.

Riko's face flushed a deep crimson.

Is this some kind of joke? she fumed. *So what if I'm still single at forty? Do they think that's funny?*

Meanwhile, Aki bit her lip in frustration.

Of all people, why did it have to be her?

The bouquet was a once-in-a-lifetime gesture, supposed to go to a close friend, someone she could genuinely wish happiness for. Not someone like *her*.

Both women were rendered speechless, but meanwhile, the party carried on without a care. The emcee launched into his closing speech, and before long, it was time for everyone to leave. Aki and Nobumitsu were ushered to the door to thank the guests as they exited. Mami Hagiwara, one of the staff packing up at the reception desk, spotted Aki and hurried over.

At twenty-three, Mami was four years Aki's junior. Her fair skin, rosy cheeks and deep dimples gave her a striking charm. Today, she wore a silver sleeveless dress paired with a black handbag and shoes, giving her a sophisticated look.

"Aki! Um, I've collected all the participation contributions," she said in her usual babyish tone. "I figured it'd be safer if I held on to them until everything's wrapped up, you know? I didn't want to leave them in the waiting room or anything."

She opened the paper gift bag in her hands to show Aki the contents. Since the party had an attendance fee, most guests had just given cash directly, but a few had gone the extra mile and wrapped their contributions in ornate envelopes. The name *Riko Nishioka* was visible on one of them. Aki's simmering frustrations began to bubble over.

"Can I borrow that for a second?" she said, pulling out the envelope from Riko and marching back into the hall.

"Wh-what are you doing?" Mami stammered, trailing after her like a duckling chasing its mother.

"Aki!" Nobumitsu called, but she ignored him, weaving through the crowd until she came across Riko, still chatting with a group of salesmen in the middle of the room with the ill-fated bouquet cradled in her arms.

"Nishioka. Do you have a moment?" Aki asked, her tense face at odds with her wedding dress.

Riko raised a puzzled eyebrow, then flashed the group of salesmen a polite smile and excused herself. By the time she had stepped aside to join Aki, that smile was nowhere to be seen.

"What is it?" she asked with more than a hint of annoyance.

"Not here," Aki said, gripping Riko's arm and pulling her along.

Several guests tried to stop Aki as they moved through the dwindling crowd, either to congratulate her or to strike up a chat, but she hurried on, ignoring them.

"What's this about, Kitamura? Isn't the bride supposed to be at the door to see everyone off?" Riko asked.

"I'll do that later," Aki replied curtly, ushering her into the waiting room, Mami slipping in behind them.

The room mustn't have been air-conditioned, as the temperature inside was stifling. The drab, cramped space, no bigger than four-and-a-half tatami mats in size, was cluttered with two long tables covered in bags, boxes of decorations, and a myriad of other wedding-related items.

Once the door was closed, Aki turned to face Riko.

"I'm disappointed in you, Nishioka."

Here we go, Riko sighed inwardly. *Drama.*

"Disappointed? Over what, exactly?"

Riko had had more than a few drinks, and with the sting of her recent break-up still lingering, seeing someone else so happily in love only fuelled her resentment. The fact that it was Aki, her brazenly self-confident younger colleague, just made it worse.

"If you have a problem with me, come out with it. Don't hold back just because I'm your superior."

Watching on the side, Mami's eyes widened.

Is this one of those catfights, like in manga comics? I've never seen one in real life before. I should pay attention – this could come in handy later!

Mami, an aspiring manga artist, had taken a part-time job at Pegasus Books as a stopgap until she realised her dream. She had never, however, finished so much as a single manuscript, always abandoning her drafts halfway through. In truth, she was more of a manga enthusiast than an actual artist.

"You clearly don't like the fact I'm getting married, Nishioka. Nojima told me what you said – about me being *quick to move on*."

"Huh? What are you talking about?" Riko asked.

After all she had drunk, she had completely forgotten what she might or might not have said. At the time, her bitterness towards her ex-boyfriend, who had dumped her for someone else, had overshadowed any thoughts of Aki.

"Don't play dumb. You made sure to say Mita's name loud enough for the entire room to hear."

"Yes, I also heard it!" Mami chimed in, eager to back Aki up – though in her mind, she was stepping in rather than choosing a side.

"Uh . . . Well . . ." Riko vaguely recalled saying *something*, but the precise details escaped her.

To Aki, however, Riko's hesitance came across as evasion, which only incensed her further.

"If you don't like me, that's fine," Aki snapped. "But bringing it up at a time like this – that's just childish. I'm disappointed."

Riko wanted to argue back, but since she couldn't quite remember what she had said or done, she realised she had no firm ground to stand on.

"Here. You can have this back," Aki said, thrusting something into Riko's hand.

Riko looked down, stunned to see the gift envelope she had given Aki earlier. *What the . . . ?*

Her drunken haze began to lift as a cold wave of clarity swept over her.

"If you didn't want to celebrate with me, you didn't have to come," Aki said, staring back at her in disdain.

That's it, Mami thought from the sidelines. *Aki just landed the finishing blow.*

Riko, on the other hand, was incensed by that unnecessarily dramatic remark.

"Fine!" she shot back, shoving the bouquet into Aki's chest. Several white petals fluttered to the floor. "If that's how you feel, I don't want this stupid thing, either. You threw it at me on purpose, didn't you? You wanted to make a spectacle of me – remind everyone that I'm still single!"

Riko had been mortified when the bouquet landed on her earlier. At her age, being seen catching it felt like a public confession that she still dreamed of marriage.

"That's not true," Aki insisted. "Why would I waste my wedding bouquet on something so petty?"

"Then why did you throw it at me? You could have given it to someone who actually wanted it!"

"I *wasn't* aiming for you! It just . . . ended up over there!"

"Oh, come on. What, you're saying it has a mind of its own?"

"You're so full of malice. It must have been drawn to all your negative emotions!"

"Malice? What's *that* supposed to mean? *You're* the one who threw this at me, so if anyone's full of malice, it's you!"

"No, it's you!"

Aki and Riko locked eyes, their gazes sharp enough to send sparks flying.

Wow. This is incredible. A front-row seat to an actual catfight! Mami could barely contain her excitement.

The two women remained frozen in their stand-off, each determined not to break first.

At that moment, the door swung open.

"Ah, there you are, Kitamura. Everyone's looking for you. They can't leave without saying goodbye to the bride and groom," sounded Tsujii's laid-back voice as he came to collect his belongings.

Aki blinked, jolted back to her senses. "Oh, right. Now isn't the time for this," she muttered, finally tearing her gaze from Riko.

She turned to leave the room, only to stop and glance at Tsujii. "Here, *you* can have this," she said, abruptly shoving the bouquet into his arms. "Give it to your girlfriend or something."

"Huh? I don't have a girlfriend. I've been single for a year and four months now."

But Aki continued out of the room without bothering to listen to his response.

"You can have this, too," Riko added, pressing something else into his hands. "Use it to take your future girlfriend out on a date."

"Wait, what? Nishioka? I just told you, I don't have a—"

Tsujii stopped there, only then recognising the item he was holding in his hands.

"Wait, is this . . . a wedding gift envelope? Why would you give this to *me*?"

Riko, however, had already slipped past him, slamming the door shut on her way out.

The room fell into silence, leaving only a dreamy-eyed Mami and a bewildered Tsujii.

"What was *that* about?" Tsujii asked, turning to Mami.

Mami, overcome with a look of unbearable emotion, shook her head. "You wouldn't understand, Tsujii. Women can be . . . complicated. This was very educational."

"*Educational?*"

"It's too deep for you. You wouldn't get it, not when you don't have a girlfriend."

Tsujii rolled his shoulders in exasperation. Mami, meanwhile, continued to stare wistfully at the door Aki and Riko just exited through.

2

"I heard what happened, Nishioka. I can't believe Kitamura was so rude to you," commented Shiho Ozaki, who worked alongside Riko in the third-floor literary fiction section, as soon as she walked in.

"Honestly, who even thinks of returning a wedding gift? It's unbelievable!" added Shoko Yamane from the comics section. There was no mistaking the excited lilt in Yamane's voice, though whether that was due to the thrill of badmouthing Aki or simply the drama of the situation itself, even she probably couldn't say.

"Can you believe she's already twenty-seven? She really has no common sense," said Minako Makihara, a part-timer from the comics section. Barely in her early twenties, she spoke with the confidence of a woman far more experienced.

The three of them, it seemed, had been eagerly discussing yesterday's incident in the staff break room before opening time.

Figures. Riko slumped her shoulders in resignation.

One night's sleep had sobered her up, and by morning, she deeply regretted letting herself get dragged into a fight with

Aki. But by then, it was too late – word of their confrontation had spread like wildfire.

With both Tsujii and Mami as witnesses, there was no covering up what had happened. She already had a hangover, and all this gossip was only adding to her headache.

"Maybe she took it out on you because she couldn't handle everyone seeing how tone-deaf she is?"

"That's definitely what happened."

The women were clearly enjoying themselves. Aki had never been popular among the store's female staff. Her good looks and ability to attract male attention already made her a target, and her headstrong, uncompromising nature only made things worse.

In the end, Mita gave into that steamroller attitude of hers, too, didn't he?

There was no end to the gossip when Mita first started dating Aki. A contract worker in the specialist books section on the fourth floor, Mita was tall, handsome and effortlessly charming – a natural favourite among the female staff. He was so popular he even had his own small fan club.

That fan club was more of a light-hearted affair than anything serious, but it came with an unspoken rule – no-one was to *jump the line*. When Aki disregarded that and started dating him, her audacity earned her the ire of her co-workers.

The only reason it didn't spiral into a major issue at the time was because Aki was one of the store's few full-time, permanent employees. Most of Pegasus Books' female staff were part-timers or contract employees, and the only other female full-time employee was Riko. If anything, the girls were resigned to what happened, convinced they were unable to compete. The real breaking point came when Aki broke up with Mita three years later and immediately started dating Nobumitsu Obata, an editor at a major publishing house.

Unforgivable.

The women promptly banded together to form an unofficial anti-Kitamura alliance, and that was when the passive-aggressive harassment began. Women have a knack for rallying against a common enemy, and this was no exception. Now, with this latest incident, they felt vindicated – and they couldn't be happier about it.

This is bad. I really didn't want to get involved in this kind of drama.

While Riko wasn't particularly fond of Aki herself, as the store's assistant manager she was supposed to stay out of petty emotional disputes. If she took the others' side, it would only justify their hostility and make the situation even worse.

"I did warn you, Nishioka. It would've been better if you hadn't gone," said Shiho Ozaki, Riko's direct subordinate.

She seemed genuinely sympathetic, but Riko could only respond with a vague smile.

This whole mess is my own doing. There's no use complaining now. If I don't keep a low profile, I'm going to be cast as the ringleader of this anti-Kitamura movement . . .

"Don't you think Kitamura was way out of line, Nojima?" Yamane called out as the store manager passed through. "She was so rude to Nishioka, even though she went out of her way to attend on her day off."

"Ah, well, yes. Kitamura – er, Obata – could stand to be a bit more considerate towards her seniors," Nojima stammered, clearly caught off guard.

Nojima was conflict-averse, especially when it came to personal disputes among the staff.

"Exactly! She's acting like a spoiled little girl."

"Honestly, now that she's married, she should just quit and focus on being a housewife."

The women eagerly piled on, but while they didn't hesitate to criticise Aki for returning Riko's congratulatory gift, they carefully avoided all mention of the bouquet.

Tsujii lived for gossip, and Mami was famously loose-lipped, so there was no way they hadn't spilled that part of the story. There was only one possible explanation – the girls didn't want to remind Riko of her age or single status.

Do they think I'm that fragile? I'm not even bothered about my age – it's their pity that's exhausting.

Was getting older really so terrible? She had worked hard to build her career, and she took pride in the life she had carved out for herself.

But she couldn't say any of this out loud. Young people tended to see ageing as a kind of sin. She used to be no different on that score. If she spoke up, the others would likely dismiss her words as the bitter ramblings of an older woman who had lost out.

Speaking of which, what's that bestseller called again? The Howling of the Defeated?

"Alright, everyone, it's almost time for the morning meeting," Nojima said, bringing an end to the discussion.

Riko breathed a sigh of relief as the girls filed out.

Riko pulled the row of books slightly forward, just a few centimetres, then gently pushed it back with both palms, stopping when the spines lined up evenly about five millimetres from the edge of the shelf. Then, as a finishing touch, she smoothed her hands over the spines, making sure there were no bumps.

She repeated this process from one end to the other, until the row of books was perfectly straight – and then again at each and every shelf in the store's literary fiction section.

"About five millimetres out from the edge – that's the way to do it," a colleague told her when she first started working at Pegasus. "It makes the spines look nice and even, and it's easier for customers to hook their fingers on a corner to pull them out."

Back then, there wasn't any debate. You just did as you were told, no questions asked.

"Don't cram the books too tightly together. But don't leave too much space, either. You want to leave just enough room to slide a finger in between them when you pick one up."

These days, hardly anyone seemed to care how the books were arranged. Sure, some bookstore clerks kept an eye on the stock itself, but few seemed to bother lining the books up properly. It was rare to find another store where the books jutted out from the shelves like this. More often than not, they were shoved all the way in, so their edges were flush with the back of the shelf. To Riko, such haphazard displays looked more like someone's home library. That wasn't how it was supposed to be. But the younger staff didn't seem to care. Even when she tried to teach them, they wouldn't bother to follow through.

She remembered a conversation with Aki Kitamura from when her younger colleague first joined the team.

"I get what you're saying," Aki had said, her tone light and matter-of-fact. "But that's a lot of work, isn't it? I mean, it's not like it helps sales. Can't we just, like, do that when we've got free time, after everything else is finished?"

Yes, that was the moment Riko decided she didn't like Aki. *Doesn't help sales? Give me a break.*

If a bookstore didn't take the time to display its books properly, what was the point? What they did was like a fishmonger arranging fish or a greengrocer laying out vegetables. When the shelves were lined up nicely, the books all but screamed, *I'm ready, come pick me up!* People liked to fuss over the display tables, but the shelves mattered, too. The spines were supposed to make a perfect line five millimetres from the edge. Bookmark ribbons couldn't hang down over the spines. Slip sheets needed to be tucked neatly into the back pages, not sticking out. Attention to detail was what being a bookstore clerk was all about.

Riko enjoyed the process, as well – carefully lining up each row, feeling the weight and texture of the books under her palms. There was something calming about it. If she let a shelf go untended for too long, the space seemed to get ... stale, somehow.

While adjusting the books, she would also tweak their arrangement a bit.

Maybe I should move the Byatt from the far left to the middle? It's a good book, but it's been sitting here forever. Hmm ... Actually, it looks better over here – goes with the colours of the covers next to it. It might catch someone's eye now.

It was funny – sometimes, a book that hadn't sold in weeks would fly off the shelf as soon as she rearranged it. Books that didn't get any attention on the display tables would sometimes sell when they were properly tucked into the right shelf. There was something intangible at work – something you couldn't figure out just by looking at sales data on a computer, like Hatakeda did. That was what made the job so interesting.

Pegasus Books was located in Kichijoji – a neighbourhood often ranked in magazine surveys as Tokyo's most desirable place to live – about twenty minutes from Shinjuku on the JR line. Kichijoji was both a bustling shopping district popular with young folks and a wealthy residential area with old money, and Pegasus Books was its most longstanding bookstore, occupying the third, fourth and fifth floors of an old building near the roundabout in front of the station. With a thousand square metres of floor space, Pegasus Books' flagship store had once been the largest bookstore in the suburbs of Tokyo, and the chain had since expanded to close to twenty other locations in the Tokyo area. Riko had worked at this one since she first joined the company, and she liked to think she knew everything there was to know about it.

It was while arranging the shelves that she felt most like a bookstore clerk. She didn't mind helping customers – chatting with regulars about books was fun and sometimes even educational, and fortunately, the store had a good clientele. Yes, younger customers had largely switched to the new bookstore in the station building, but Pegasus still had its share of loyal, local book lovers. Academics, authors, translators – they all knew their stuff, and she often learned things from them that she couldn't pick up online or from magazines. But organising the shelves was what made her feel truly grounded. Running her fingers along the spines, getting a feel for the books, was what ultimately helped her start shaking off her frustration with Aki.

Honestly, the things she does, Riko thought with a sigh.

The staff had taken to calling Aki "the princess", a nickname that stuck after someone commented on her shoes. After all, footwear was a big deal for bookstore clerks, who were on their feet all day long. Pegasus didn't allow sneakers, so they all had to wear leather shoes. Aki had smiled, casually replying, "Oh, these? They're custom-made. I have my own shoe mould, so I always get them made to fit. My feet are narrow with low arches, so off-the-shelf doesn't work for me. Ferragamos fit me perfectly, but I can't wear those every day, so I usually go with these."

She hadn't meant any harm, but that didn't stop the rest of the staff from feeling put out. Custom-made shoes? Ferragamos? Most of them were just scraping by. Aki, however, was the only child of a wealthy family, plus she still lived at home. Custom footwear might not have been such a big deal for her, but a little awareness would have gone a long way. And so, ever since the situation with her shoes came to light, the others had referred to her as "the princess".

But there was more to the nickname than just that. Aki wasn't just any employee – she was the granddaughter of the chairman of a major stationery company with ties to Pegasus Books. Everyone knew that was how she had landed a full-time position straight out of university – and why headquarters reached out to check in on her from time to time. Riko, on the other hand, had started as a part-timer and spent five years working her way up. It had taken even longer for anyone at headquarters to remember her name.

Still, it might not have been so bad if Aki just kept her head down. But she was brash, spoke her mind to her superiors, and acted overly familiar with the publishers' representatives. When Riko or anyone else tried to correct her, Aki brushed them off. She was one of the few full-time, permanent staff members in the store, yet she lacked any basic sense of decorum.

For those reasons and more, Riko was shocked when Aki announced her plan to continue working at the store after getting married. "Are you serious?" she had blurted out at the time.

Most female clerks quit after getting married or having kids. The hours were long, the pay wasn't great, and Pegasus didn't offer much in the way of support for working mothers. Riko had seen plenty of capable women leave over the years. She couldn't imagine the carefree, privileged Aki sticking it out.

Her relationship with her co-workers was strained, and her husband made a good salary, so she shouldn't have felt any pressure to remain in the workplace.

And yet, Aki said cheerfully, "My husband's super busy, and he doesn't get home early. He even works Sundays sometimes. I'd be bored out of my mind if I didn't have a job!"

Bored, huh?

So, this was just something to fill her time. Riko couldn't help but feel bitter. Aki's life was worlds apart from her own. After all, she was single and had to work to make ends meet.

"That would mean it should be on the fourth floor . . ."

"But my daughter said she saw it here on the third floor. I double-checked with her!"

A young part-timer and a customer were arguing near the magazine section. Overhearing the commotion, Riko walked over to see what was going on.

"But this floor is for fiction and magazines," the young man explained awkwardly. "Anything about penmanship would be in the practical books section, which is on the fourth floor."

The customer, a middle-aged woman, probably a housewife, refused to back down. Riko didn't recognise her, meaning she was either an infrequent visitor or a first-time customer.

"What seems to be the problem?" Riko asked brightly as she approached them. She couldn't risk leaving a bad impression, especially if this was someone new.

It was the flustered part-timer, however, who rushed to answer her. "This lady's looking for a penmanship book. I told her we don't have it on this floor, but she doesn't believe me."

Kids these days. They don't have the first clue how to address customers politely. And calling her this lady? Not a good look. I'll have to give him a lesson in customer service later.

"Well, I saw it on TV the other day!" the woman said, clearly annoyed. "And then my daughter said she saw it on the third floor here. I know I'm not wrong."

She was being stubborn – probably because she didn't want to go to another floor. In her defence, the store had a rather confusing layout – the third floor was for fiction and magazines, the fourth floor was for practical and specialist books, and the fifth floor housed comics, children's books, study guides and textbooks, along with the office. The problem was that the building was old, and there were no escalators, just a lift and stairs. Even the staff found it inconvenient.

"What kind of book are you looking for, exactly?" Riko asked, keeping her tone friendly as she met the woman's eyes.

"The one they showed on TV. It's about penmanship and writing out classic texts, or something like that."

The woman's description sparked something in the back of Riko's memory.

"Could it be this book, ma'am?" she asked, mentioning the title.

"That's it! That's the one!" The woman's face lit up. "I heard it's really popular."

"Yes, it is. In that case, it's right here on this floor. Please, follow me."

Riko led the woman to the bestseller table near the registers.

The book was tucked at the edge of the display because they were running low on stock – only four or five copies were left. Riko picked one up from the top of the pile and handed it to the woman.

"Thank you," the woman said, flipping through the pages. Then, apparently satisfied, she added, "Wonderful!"

But instead of taking the book Riko handed her, the woman placed it back on the pile and grabbed a fresh copy from the bottom.

"I'll take this one to the register," she said.

Oh well. The book Riko had given her wasn't damaged, but some people just wanted the one at the bottom.

Keeping her smile intact, Riko said, "Thank you very much," and bowed slightly.

After the woman left, the young part-timer turned to Riko with an apologetic look. "Sorry about that. Thanks for stepping in."

"You need to make sure you listen to what the customer is saying," Riko advised. "And try to memorise the titles of the current bestsellers. Stop by and see me after your shift – I'll give you some pointers."

She made a mental note to give him some proper training later. Just as she was about to head back to her tasks, another voice called out.

"Um, excuse me."

This time, it was a university-aged man.

"Do you have light novels on this floor?" he asked.

"I'm sorry. Those are on the fifth floor, next to the comics section," Riko answered.

"Huh? But you've got Nisio Isin's books here," he said, looking confused.

"Those are the hardcover editions, which are kept here with the new titles. The paperback versions are on the fifth floor."

"Hah? Why don't you just put them all in the same place?" he grumbled before heading towards the stairs.

He wasn't wrong – it *was* a strange way to organise them. With so many different formats and publishers, simply sorting by genre or label didn't always work. Sunako Kayata's books, for instance, stuck out like a sore thumb among all the serious titles in the Chuko Shinsho line-up.

Riko's thoughts drifted for a moment before snapping back to something else entirely.

What happened with that gift money? Did Tsujii really spend it? He hasn't said a word all morning.

What a waste. And I can't ask for it back now . . . I shouldn't have tried to show off.

Her thoughts were interrupted by a cheerful chime, a signal that the registers were getting busy. Any available staff were expected to help out.

Pushing all thought of the gift money aside, she made her way to the cashier. Each floor had one near the stairs. Unusually for this time of day, a line of five or six customers had already formed.

"Welcome," she said, slipping behind the counter.

She positioned herself next to a part-timer already working at the register. Picking up a paperback sitting nearby and willing her face into a soft smile, she asked the next customer, "Would you like a cover for this?"

3

The honeymoon was amazing. Aki had her reservations about Hawaii, always considering it a romantic cliché, but she had gone along with the plan because Nobumitsu insisted. Nonetheless, the moment she stepped off the plane, she was hooked. The warm breeze, the sweet scent of flowers drifting in the air. Hawaii struck her as a laid-back resort with all the convenience of a bustling city. The high-end hotel Nobumitsu had picked was in a prime location, just a stone's throw from the main street in Waikiki – yet it felt like a different world, so quiet, with the ocean visible right below their window. And the service was top-notch, as well.

She and Nobumitsu were on the move from day one – swimming, shopping, driving around the island. They both had the same approach to travel – waste no time, pack as much in as possible. If they hadn't been on the same page about that, the trip would have turned sour fast. That kind of mismatch was how couples ended up fighting their way to an early divorce. Luckily, Nobumitsu was proving to be a solid travel partner on their first overseas holiday together.

Then, out of nowhere, Aki found herself wondering – what if it had been Takahiko?

Takahiko Mita. Her ex. The guy behind the drama at the wedding. He was never the active type.

"If you want to go shopping, Aki, you go ahead. I'll just be on the beach reading."

That was exactly what he would have said. He wouldn't argue with her, but he wouldn't try to match her energy, either. More than the six-year age gap between them, it was that detached attitude of his that made him feel so much older. If she pushed, if she really insisted, he would breathe a tired, conflicted sigh and eventually tag along. Sometimes, she would act stubborn on purpose just to see his reaction.

If there was anywhere he actually wanted to go, it would probably be a bookstore – Borders, Barnes & Noble, something like that. Honolulu had a few big ones. She and Nobumitsu had avoided them completely because they didn't want to think about work. But Takahiko? He would have insisted on checking them out. *Research*, he would call it. She remembered him boasting about reading Vonnegut in the original English, so he was definitely into foreign books.

Come to think of it, in the three years they were a couple, they had never really travelled anywhere together. The farthest they went was an aquarium, maybe an art museum. But still, she had really loved that quiet, mature side of him.

The first time Aki noticed Takahiko Mita was in the staff break room, unloading magazines around the end of her first year at Pegasus. It was the release date for the women's magazines, and since they were all special New Year's editions, they were all thicker than usual and came with bulky bonus items. More shipments than usual meant more hassle. On top of that, the magazines were heavy, and stuffing the extras inside was a pain. Aki couldn't believe her bad luck, getting stuck with magazine duty. How long was this going to take? There were only three of them on shift – her, Mita and a university kid working part-time.

"This is ridiculous," Aki grumbled as she struggled to tie a bundle of magazines neatly. "Why do they have to pack in so many freebies?"

She pulled at the string to adjust it, but the motion made the paper slice her fingertip. Paper, she had learned, could be surprisingly vicious.

"Ouch!" she yelped.

"Are you okay? Here, use this." Mita pulled a Band-Aid from his pocket and handed it to her.

"Thanks," she said, wrapping it around her finger.

She could already see blood seeping through the tape. Working at a bookstore had wrecked her hands – always covered in tiny cuts, fingers constantly dry and rough.

"Do you think the people who come up with these freebies realise we have to bundle them all by hand?" she complained.

Some of the bonus items were bigger than the magazines themselves – giant boxes, thick pouches, you name it. Sometimes, it felt like the freebie was the main product and the magazine was just thrown in as an afterthought.

"I don't mind it," Mita said calmly, continuing to work at a steady pace.

Aki barely knew Mita – he worked on the fourth floor, handling the specialist books section, so they didn't interact much. But she knew he was well-read and knowledgeable, someone the store manager and assistant manager trusted implicitly.

"Seriously?" she blurted out.

In her surprise, she pulled too hard on a rubber band, snapping it and smacking her hand.

"With books, at least you have the fun of discovering new releases," she said, rubbing her stinging fingers. "But magazines? Every issue is basically the same as the last. And these stupid freebies are such a pain in the neck. What's there to like about them?"

Aki had a habit of voicing whatever thoughts popped into her head. If she had said that to Nishioka, she would probably have been scolded on the spot: "It's your job, so do it." But she had a feeling Mita would take the time to answer her silly questions.

"Well, maybe this is just me," he began, still focused on his work, "but when magazines first arrive, they don't feel like magazines. They're just bundles of paper."

"Bundles of paper?"

"Yeah. When they're fresh out of the shipment box, they feel lifeless. Just stiff, untouched paper. Like they haven't become real magazines yet."

"Huh."

Aki didn't quite get it. She had never thought about it like that before.

Mita didn't seem to mind her muted response, continuing, "But once we handle them – bundling them up, adding the freebies – then, they start to feel more like actual magazines. Like they're coming to life."

"Hmm . . . That's an interesting way to look at it."

Mita gave a slightly sheepish smile. "The same goes for books, really. A book or a magazine only becomes *real* when someone takes an interest in it, when it's actually read. Until then, it's just printed paper. And we're the ones who help bring them to life – getting them ready, putting them on shelves. That's why I don't mind this kind of work. Because it feels like it has a purpose."

"Wow. You're a romantic, huh?"

Aki meant it as a light tease, but deep down, she was moved. She had never thought of her job that way before. To her, handling magazines had always felt like a tedious chore. But Mita genuinely loved working as a bookstore clerk.

After that, she started paying more attention to him. The way he patiently dealt with customers, how he treated junior staff with kindness, his deep knowledge of books – everything about him impressed her. And soon, she realised it wasn't just admiration. She actually liked him. She realised that for certain when she overheard the other female employees gossiping about him, their idle chatter irritating her more than she wanted to admit.

She didn't overthink it. She went up to him and said straight out, "I like you, Mita. Will you go out with me?"

He looked surprised – probably caught off guard – but he didn't turn her down. And just like that, they started dating.

Aki was never the type to play mind games. She didn't have the patience for it. She wasn't the kind of girl who would subtly nudge a guy into confessing first or wait around hoping he would take the hint. If she liked someone, she would just say so. If it didn't work out, so be it. It wasn't in her nature to dwell on things out of her control.

But after they started dating, the atmosphere at work changed. It took one of her male colleagues to pull her aside and clue her in before she understood.

"You know, a lot of the girls here are into Mita," he said. "They're kind of bitter about it."

That was the first time Aki realised how popular he was. He might have just been a contract employee, but he was more capable than most of the full-timers. On top of that, he was nice to everyone – including the part-time girls. No wonder they all liked him.

The cold shoulder from the other female employees started subtly at first. Then, after she broke up with Mita six months ago and started dating Nobumitsu, it got that much worse. They barely spoke to her unless it was work-related. They had stopped inviting her to drinks after work. Some outright avoided her. And when news of her marriage broke, the passive-aggressive pettiness escalated even further.

Her indoor shoes went missing. She wasn't told about meeting schedule changes. She once showed up for a late shift, only to find out she had been switched to an earlier one without anyone bothering to tell her.

"Again?" she muttered whenever it happened. She wasn't angry – just exasperated. It was so childish, like something out of a middle-school drama. Thumbtacks in ballet shoes, that kind of thing. And to think, Mita had just broken up with her. If they liked him so much, now was their chance. Why harass her when they could use this time to try their luck comforting him?

She did her best to remain unfazed. If anything, she made a point of acting cheerful. Letting it get under her skin would be to give them exactly what they wanted. Besides, not everyone had turned against her. Mami Hagiwara, along with some of the male staff and part-time guys, were still on her side. She figured the drama would die down, eventually.

But she was wrong.

Besides the managers and Mami, not a single co-worker showed up to her wedding. She liked to pride herself on being thick-skinned, but even she was shaken by that.

Do they really hate me that much? she asked herself again while staring out the window of the rental car.

"Aki, can you check the map?" Nobumitsu's voice pulled her back to her senses. "We turn right up ahead, yeah?"

"Uh – just a sec."

She hurried to unfold the map. They were heading to the North Shore, driving west out of Waikiki. The city skyline had faded, giving way to scattered houses and open roads.

"Yeah, right turn here. Left goes to the airport."

"Got it."

"After that, it's just straight ahead."

"Good." Nobumitsu waved his hand in a little *no more talking* gesture. He was an unusually cautious driver, especially here, driving on the opposite side of the road. He had already warned her not to distract him too much.

Left to her own thoughts, Aki felt herself drifting again.

"Can you grab me a mineral water?" Nobumitsu asked, eyes still on the road.

"Sure."

She reached into her bag for a bottle.

No more pointless thoughts. She was here, in Hawaii, on her honeymoon. No need to let the past ruin it.

Handing him the bottle, she smiled. "Hey, let's take a break at the Dole Plantation when we get there."

With that, she pushed the memories aside.

Apart from that one brief moment, their honeymoon passed smoothly. When they told restaurant staff they had just got married, they were treated to champagne and cake. On their cruise, dancers gathered around their table to congratulate them. Nobumitsu, always ready for a good time, even got up and joined them in a hula dance, earning himself a round of applause from the other passengers.

They had only been dating for a short while, and they were both usually busy with work, so they hadn't spent a lot of time alone together before this trip. With each day, she was surprised to learn new things about him – like the fact that he couldn't stand coriander, or that he was picky about his toothpaste brand. But every little discovery felt fresh and exciting.

And so, she had completely forgotten about work by the last night of their five-day, four-night trip – until dinner, that was. They were in a romantic restaurant with a view of the city, and she was cutting into her lobster when it happened.

The only light in the restaurant came from the flickering candles on the tables, making the nighttime skyline outside stand out even more. The soft glow set the perfect mood. She probably looked pretty nice in this lighting, she thought. Her foundation was a little off because of her tan, but no-one would notice that here.

She was wearing a brand-new muumuu she had bought earlier that day – sleeveless, with plenty of ruffles near the hem, and long enough to skim her ankles. The creamy fabric was covered in bright hibiscus flowers. Nobumitsu, on the other hand, was wearing a vintage aloha shirt patterned with surfboards. He wasn't particularly tall – just over one metre seventy – but years of swimming had given him broad shoulders and an athletic build. Plus, the fun, colourful shirt suited his easy-going personality perfectly. They must have looked like the ideal honeymoon couple, she thought with a thrill.

Maybe he was tired from all the swimming and sun during the day, as Nobumitsu had been eating in silence. Then, out of nowhere, he said, "I think I'll head straight to the office from the airport tomorrow."

"What? Seriously?"

Their flight out of Honolulu was early in the morning, but with the time difference, they would arrive in Japan before noon. Strictly speaking, it wasn't impossible for him to make it to the office by two or three in the afternoon.

"Do you have to? You'll be exhausted. Wouldn't it be better to take the day off to rest?" Aki asked, disappointed.

She was going back to work the day after they got home, so she had been looking forward to one last relaxing afternoon together.

"Yeah, but I want to check in with the editorial team. I mean, I'm the acting editor-in-chief now," he said with more than a hint of pride.

Nobumitsu had been a deputy editor at a men's comic magazine, but after discovering a breakout hit by a new manga artist, he was promoted and tasked with launching a new comic magazine of his own. Within six months, once it was officially up and running, he would be given the title of editor-in-chief for real.

"Well, I suppose it can't be helped," Aki sighed. "In that case, you should keep the gifts for your co-workers in your carry-on bag."

"Good point. Better to hand them out right away."

"What did you end up getting?"

"Chocolate-covered potato chips from Neiman Marcus.

Stuff like that always goes down well with my team. And I picked up some liquor for my boss."

"Safe choices."

"What about you?"

"I got something, but to be honest, I don't even want to think about work. There's too much going on at the moment."

"Don't stress about it," Nobumitsu said breezily. He signalled the waiter for another beer. "Your co-workers are just bitter because they're all single. Now that you're married, they'll get over it."

"It's not that simple. Some of them hold a grudge against me . . . And I kind of threw Nishioka's wedding gift back in her face."

She set down her knife and fork, suddenly uncomfortable. Looking back, she knew she had overreacted. The wedding reception had her on edge, what with her being forced to sing in front of everyone, and she had let her emotions get the better of her. Nishioka was her boss, after all, so now she found herself wondering if she should seek her out to apologise.

"Well, what's done is done," Nobumitsu said without looking up, still focused on his lobster.

"I was *so* mad. I mean, can you believe it? They didn't even respond to the invitations."

"Forget about it. It's over." His tone was casual, unconcerned.

"I just . . . I'm dreading going back. And—"

She was about to ask whether she should apologise to Nishioka when Nobumitsu cut her off.

"Come on, Aki, let's drop it." He finally looked up, his knife frozen in his hand. "It's our last night in Hawaii. Let's not ruin it talking about this stuff."

"I suppose . . ."

"Work has its ups and downs for everyone. If you start dwelling on it now, you'll never stop. I want to enjoy myself when I'm with you. I don't want to be brought down by all this depressing stuff."

"Yeah . . ." she answered in reluctant agreement.

She knew this wasn't the time to bring it up. But still, she had wanted his advice.

"You know what? Let's make a rule – no talking about work at home. Funny stories are fine, but no complaints. No stressful conversations. That'll be our household pact." He smiled, clearly pleased with his own idea.

"Our household . . ."

The word felt foreign to her. She wasn't used to thinking of them as a married couple yet. And a family that only ever talked about fun things? It sounded fake, though she kept that thought to herself.

She glanced out the window. The city lights were supposed to be the restaurant's signature romantic touch, the perfect ending to their trip. But now, they just looked ordinary.

Tokyo's skyline would have been just as good.

Her lobster felt dry in her mouth. Without chewing, she washed it down with a swig of champagne.

4

Riko stepped off the subway and headed towards Exit A3. Then, at the top of the stairs, she turned right, finding herself at the entrance to the community centre. It was already past eleven at night, and the doors were long since locked.

In front of the building, there was a small, triangular space with a few benches and a flowerbed. The ground was tiled with a mosaic of flowers. It was too small to be called a park, but it was probably meant as a waiting area – a way to make use of an awkward bit of leftover land.

She pulled out a handkerchief, wiped down a damp bench and sat. It was already July, but the rainy season was still dragging on. It had rained until mid-afternoon, and even now the air remained hot and clammy. The cool surface of the bench felt nice against her skin. From here, she could see all the faces coming and going from the subway.

Less than ten minutes from Ginza by train, this area used to be filled with old wooden houses and factories. Now, however, redevelopment had changed the face of the town, and high-rise apartments – some reaching thirty storeys – dominated the skyline. Perhaps that was why there were more people climbing up the station stairs than she had expected – mostly office workers on their way home.

She knew he would pass through here. She had come this way with him often enough to be sure of that. When was the last time? Now that she thought about it, he hadn't invited her to his place at all in those last few months. He had always made excuses to avoid seeing her, and when they did meet up, it was always some neutral space, never his apartment.

She hadn't questioned it at the time. He always insisted he didn't like having people over, that hotels were more comfortable. She just took his word for it. But looking back, he had always been in a hurry to leave.

She should have paid more attention. But back then, she simply didn't have the bandwidth for it. Work had been busy, and there had been a million little things to take care of – house repairs, errands, obligations.

And so, right up until the very end, she hadn't so much as a clue.

They went out to dinner as usual that night, then had a few drinks at their regular bar. She assumed they would go to a hotel afterwards. But then, out of nowhere, he said, "We need to break up."

She didn't understand at first. She couldn't process the words. Maybe she just refused to.

She remembered thinking his tie was unusually gaudy that night.

Then the rest of it came out.

He had been seeing someone from work. One of his subordinates. She was pregnant. He wanted to do the right thing, take responsibility, marry her. She was twenty-seven.

It took another few minutes for it all to register.

"It wasn't supposed to be like this," he kept insisting. "She's younger, and she works under me. And of course, there was you. But she was the one who wanted . . ."

So that was it. He had been two-timing her, and now she was being tossed aside. That was all.

". . . I feel terrible about this," he went on. "But we were never really talking about marriage, right? We're both adults, we . . ."

She tuned in and out, his voice coming in broken fragments.

God, what a cliché. This is the sort of thing you'd expect from some cheap TV drama. Couldn't he at least come up with better lines?

". . . I was really surprised when she told me . . . But this might be my last chance. I *do* want kids. At my age, it's starting to feel more urgent . . ."

Ah. That old trick. Using a baby to lock a man down. It probably works best on guys in their forties.

He had always been so adamant that he wasn't interested in marriage – that he had already been through one divorce, that being single was easier. He had practically warned her off the idea.

And now, here he was, rambling on and on, trying to justify himself.

She wasn't even listening anymore.

Had the other woman known about her? Some women got even more single-minded when they had a rival. Had she set her sights on him, determined to win?

Riko's eyes drifted to his shirt. She didn't recognise the colour. And it hadn't been sent to the cleaners – the starch was gone, the cuffs had faint, uneven wrinkles. Someone had ironed it by hand, someone who wasn't used to it.

That was when it clicked.

They were already living together.

The other woman was washing his clothes, ironing them. Marking him as her own.

He's mine. Stay away.

The thought hit her like a punch to the gut.

"So, it's over, then?" she said at last, unable to stand the feeling any longer. She just wanted to get out of there.

"You understand, right?" he said, relief washing over his face. His brows unknitted, the lines on his forehead smoothing out. He even smiled, ever so slightly.

How obvious could he be?

Had he always been this transparent?

No – she had liked that about him. He was easy-going, straightforward. No emotional baggage, no deep wounds to nurse. At her age, delicate, complicated men were more trouble than they were worth. She had liked his confidence, the way he carried himself, how work had always seemed to come easily for him.

But men like that could be oblivious. They had no problem flaunting their advantages, completely unaware of the people around them.

". . . We'll still see each other through work, and I'd really like for us to stay friends. You're a good person, and . . ."

God. He was still talking.

Did he really think they could be friends? That she would just nod along, give him her approval after the fact?

No. He just wanted an easy exit. No guilt, no mess, no bad blood. That was all he cared about.

"Let's go," she said, cutting him off.

She had had enough.

That was three months ago.

"Forget about him. He got played by some younger woman, and he's too dumb to realise it."

Her friends all said the same thing. Like her, they were all hitting their forties while still single, and they were always ready to rally around their own when one of them got hurt.

"You're right," she said, forcing a smile.

I'm a grown woman. This kind of thing doesn't get to me. It's not like I haven't been through break-ups before. I'm not going to crumble over a little heartbreak.

But everyone in their group knew the truth. At their age, when would the next relationship even come along? Their standards had got higher, and they had their pride to think of. They weren't about to settle for just anyone. Most decent men their age were already taken. Affairs? Things like that only ended with the woman getting hurt. They were all too smart to fall into that trap. And younger men? What would they even talk about with them? Could they really be with someone without constantly feeling insecure about their own age?

And so, dating – falling in love – was far from simple.

Maybe that's why I can't let go.

It was over. Nothing she said or did would change that.

He wasn't coming back. There was no returning to how things were.

She understood that, in her head.

Her heart, however, wouldn't play catch up. It hurt. She couldn't breathe. She was only now realising how much she loved him.

She just wanted to see him one more time.

It can't end like this. It's too cruel.

But there had been no contact. Nothing. It was over for him.

He didn't even show up to the wedding – the one she had gone to just to see him, convinced he would be there.

Is he avoiding me? Can he really not stand for us to be in the same room?

And so, here she was.

She didn't tell him she was coming. She didn't even know what time he would be on his way home, what with his schedule being all over the place. There was no guarantee she would see him.

He was probably already back at his apartment, with his new, younger partner.

Maybe it was better she didn't see him.

If she did, she would probably end up saying something resentful. What would it accomplish apart from leaving a bad taste in her mouth?

But maybe that was what she needed. Maybe it would be better to feel *something*, even if it was ugly.

Trying to be the bigger person, keeping things clean and mature – that was why she was stuck like this in the first place. If they had had a proper fight, maybe she would have been able to hate him. Maybe she would have found the energy to move on.

But instead, time had just stopped. Her heart had felt frozen since the day they broke up.

It was late enough at night that she could tell exactly when a train arrived – people would spill out of the subway entrance all at once.

The trains heading into the city were largely empty by now. The ones going out still let off a few passengers – ten, maybe more – trickling up the stairs.

She had been sitting on the bench for over an hour. The temperature had dropped noticeably. Even in summer, the night breeze could carry a chill. It wouldn't be long before the trains stopped running.

Just one more, she told herself. One more train, and she would go home.

Another one must have arrived, as a small group of people emerged from the station.

He wasn't there.

He never liked taking the train this late at night. Even if they were still running, he preferred to take a cab home. "That's the whole point of living downtown," he used to say. *It must be nice to have such a big salary,* she remembered thinking.

Enough. Time to go home.

Maybe they were never meant to be.

She stood up, brushed off her skirt, and turned towards the subway entrance. Just as she was about to head down the stairs, a figure started climbing up.

Riko froze.

It was him.

His slightly thinning hair. That familiar tweed suit.

His head was tilted downwards as he climbed, but he must have sensed someone standing there, as he suddenly looked up.

They locked eyes.

"Shit."

His face twisted like he had just seen something horrifying. And then – he shoved her.

She stumbled, slamming into the wall and barely catching the handrail as he bolted up the remaining steps.

And then he *ran*.

Not the half-hearted, awkward shuffle of a middle-aged man trying to avoid a conversation – no. Full sprint. Like a rabbit running for its life.

She just stood there, gripping the railing, watching him go. She was still off-balance from being pushed, her side pressed against the wall. He turned a corner, disappearing. Gingerly, she planted her feet on the stairs, let go of the railing, and took a deep breath. Pain shot through her right elbow where she had hit the wall. That was going to leave a bruise.

A second later, something cold slid down her cheek.

Oh. Tears. So many of them.

The moment she realised it, a sob tore out of her. And then, she was full-on crying.

5

"Oh. Sorry."

Aki was just returning from her break when she nearly bumped into Takahiko Mita, who was coming out of the office just as she was walking in. The moment she saw his face, her heart skipped a beat.

"Oh, you're back today?"

Mita's tone was as calm and friendly as ever.

"Yeah, pretty much."

"You got some sun, huh? How was Hawaii? It rained the whole time here."

"It was great. But the moment we landed in Narita, we got hit with this awful humidity. Part of me wanted to turn around and fly right back," she joked.

She breathed an inward sigh of relief. She could feel her co-workers staring at them, but truth be told, the person she had really been dreading facing wasn't Riko – it was Mita. It didn't matter what that awful woman thought of her, but the idea of being avoided by him? That stung.

"I'm back now. Starting today, I'm all in," she said with a determined nod.

She had braced herself for the worst – and yet, now that she was actually here, her shoulders felt somehow lighter. Maybe this was a good sign. With a spring in her step, she headed up to the office on the fifth floor.

"Thanks for putting up with my absence," she said, handing her manager two boxes of assorted Godiva chocolates – one for the office and another for the part-timers in the break room.

"You didn't have to go to all this trouble on your honeymoon. But thank you." Nojima grinned as he took the boxes. "So, how was Hawaii? You've got a nice tan!"

"It was amazing. We spent practically every day at the beach, so I got pretty sunburned. And this is with tons of sunscreen on."

She pulled up her sleeve a little to show him.

"Looks great on you! It was raining non-stop here. Business was slow, as you'd expect. Oh, by the way, we got a call from Shibata at Hitotsuboshi yesterday. He said he was sorry he couldn't make your wedding."

"Oh, he didn't need to worry about that. He's always so considerate."

Of all the publishing reps Aki knew, Shunsuke Shibata was the one she liked best. He had been genuinely happy about her marrying a co-worker from his own company, but a last-minute business trip had kept him from attending the wedding.

"He said he'd call again after you came back."

"Did he? I'll give him a call later."

"Well, I've got a meeting at headquarters, so I'd better get going. Can you pass these around to everyone?"

With that, Nojima handed the chocolates to a nearby employee and headed out the door.

*

"I'm back."

After greeting the manager, Aki headed to the staff break room.

"Ah, Kitamura – no, wait, it's Obata now," called Ono, one of the part-timers, remembering her new family name. "Welcome back."

"We've been waiting for you, Obata," added another. "The comics have piled up like crazy – there's barely any space left in here!"

"Huh? What do you mean?"

Pegasus Books had a large storage room on the third floor where most of the sorting and bundling of magazines took place. Deliveries were brought there first before being distributed to the individual floors. The fifth-floor staff break room wasn't particularly big, and it was mainly used as a temporary storage area or a workspace for quick tasks. The comic shelves, she couldn't fail to notice, were overflowing with unopened packages.

"What's this?"

"All the comic orders that came in while you were away. I went ahead and put out the bestsellers, but that's about it."

"Huh? What happened to Makihara? I asked her to organise everything."

Minako Makihara was a part-time university student assigned to the comics section. She was in law school at a prestigious university and usually worked four days a week.

"She's on a seminar retreat."

"What? Since when? Nobody told me."

"Uh . . . I think it was last Thursday? The day after you went on honeymoon."

"When's she coming back?"

"No idea. Hatakeda might know."

"Did somebody say my name?"

Just then, Yoshio Hatakeda poked his head into the staff break room. He was in his late thirties and single, with shaggy hair that covered his ears and a long, parted fringe that almost fell into his eyes. It looked like he hadn't had a haircut in weeks, though Aki had heard this style of his was intentional – apparently, he was imitating some anime director he admired. He was more of a computer person than a book guy, preferring to work at his desk rather than deal with the shelves. As Aki's direct supervisor, he wasn't that ambitious, and nor did he micromanage the staff. In many ways, he was an easy boss to work under.

"When is Makihara supposed to be back?"

"Hmm . . . I think she's off until the end of next week."

Hatakeda's speech was always oddly polite, no matter who he was talking to.

"So . . . Does that mean no-one's touched the comics that came in last week?"

"Well, we had Ono and Hagiwara put out the big new releases, but there were a few other shipments, too . . ."

"What about Yamane?"

Shoko Yamane was another part-timer in the comics section.

"She's been helping out with the literature fair. The third floor requested her. I heard she told everyone not to touch the comics because you'd want to handle them yourself when you got back."

Ah. So that was it. They had just let everything pile up for her to deal with on her own.

Makihara and Yamane might technically have been Aki's

subordinates, but they were much closer to Riko. In fact, Yamane used to joke that she was the president of the unofficial Mita Fan Club, making her one of the more vocal members of the anti-Aki faction.

"I never expected much from Yamane, but I always took Makihara to be more responsible. Nobody told *me* she was taking time off," Aki said with a resigned sigh.

"I – I didn't know anything! I'm just passing on what I heard," Hatakeda stammered, clearly wanting no part of this mess.

Seeing the nervous look on his face, Aki softened her tone and flashed him a bright smile. "I'm not blaming you, Hatakeda. I just got back, and I'm already buried in work. It's a little overwhelming, that's all."

"They sure are mean – Yamane and Makihara both," Mami remarked while shrink-wrapping the seemingly endless stack of comics so customers couldn't flip through them.

At Pegasus, every comic – new or old – was shrink-wrapped. Mami didn't technically belong to the comics section, but since she worked on the same floor, she would pitch in whenever she had a free moment. She wrapped them, and Aki shelved them. With five carts' worth of books to go through, Aki was beyond grateful for the help.

"Well, it is what it is. It's not like I didn't see this coming."

Makihara had been pushing to rearrange the Boys' Love section to appeal to a younger audience, and Aki had given her advice on how to reorganise the stock. Now, a ridiculous number of back issues had arrived. Aki had assumed Makihara would handle it, seeing as it was her section, but no. She never would have guessed she would be doing this on her first day back. She hadn't even given any thought to how to arrange the books or which to return to the publishers.

Boys' Love – or BL, as the fans called it – was a genre of fiction depicting romantic relationships between young men, mostly aimed at female readers. It came in the form of manga comics and light novels filled with manga-style artworks. While the covers were often cute and innocent, the contents could be surprisingly explicit. The fanbase was also broader than one might expect, and there were quite a few girls at the store who were into it – including both Makihara and Mami.

"Hmm . . . This one's been here forever. It's probably time we returned it."

Aki grabbed a few volumes and stacked them on the empty part of the cart.

Mami let out a dramatic shriek, prompting a nearby customer to turn around in alarm.

"What? You're sending *these* back? No way! Nene Katsura is *huge* right now! Her *Don't Leave Me Alone* and *Love Machine* series are blowing up online! The lead is so well written! I'm telling you, she's gonna be a big name by the end of the year! You *can't* send her stuff back!"

"Alright, alright. Those are already wrapped, you know?"

"Crap!"

Mami scrambled to hit the stop button and pull the lever at the front of the shrink-wrap machine, sending a bundle of three or four neatly wrapped comics tumbling out.

"Whoops. I did it again . . ."

Shrink-wrapping wasn't particularly difficult. So long as you kept feeding comics into the machine at a steady pace, there shouldn't be any issues. And yet, Mami somehow managed to mess it up almost every time. Sometimes she would accidentally wrap multiple books together, which wasn't the worst mistake, but other times, she would jam the machine and damage the covers, rendering them unsellable. If that happened, even brand-new books had to be sent back to the publishers.

"You should pay more attention to what you're doing."

"I know . . ."

Mami wasn't just a BL fan – she was also into fan culture and self-published comics. When she was first interviewed to work at Pegasus, she asked to be assigned to either the comics or the light novel sections, and she apparently gave a long speech about wanting to expand the BL selection, referring to it throughout as *healing fiction*.

She had her own personal BL theory. Girls who grew up in all-girls schools never experienced gender-based discrimination first-hand. But once they entered university or the workplace, reality hit them hard – inequality in relationships, double standards, everything. BL, with its fantasy of two men in a perfectly equal relationship, was a soothing escape.

Nojima found her enthusiasm amusing, but Nishioka didn't like her at all. And so, despite there being an opening in the comics section, Mami was assigned to textbooks.

"She's too biased. People like that shouldn't work in sections they're passionate about."

That was Riko's logic. But Mami wasn't the type to give up easily. She hung around the comics section whenever she could and constantly threw her own opinions into the mix. Aki, who wasn't personally invested in BL, usually just let her comments slide. But Makihara, who shared her interests, seemed to find it annoying – like Mami was overstepping her bounds.

Aki didn't really get it, but apparently, their tastes were

different enough to cause friction. More than once, Makihara had snapped, "You're not even in charge of this section, so stop interfering." She wasn't wrong, but Aki couldn't help but feel bad for Mami. She didn't mean any harm.

"Well, which of these *can* we return?"

Since Makihara wasn't around, Aki had no choice but to fall back on Mami's knowledge.

"Hang on a sec." Mami paused her shrink-wrapping and scurried over. "Hmm . . . This *At His Mercy* series can go. It used to be popular, but it's outdated now. Look at the art – it's kinda cringe, right?"

She held up a volume, but Aki honestly couldn't tell. BL art styles were surprisingly varied – some characters had unnaturally long faces, others were super round. Despite her efforts to study the genre, she still couldn't tell the difference between trendy and past-its-sell-by-date.

"Anything else?"

"Hmm. Miki Amano and Umi Hiroi's stuff can probably go."

Aki pulled out the books as instructed, utterly indifferent. Within minutes, the towering pile of BL comics was gone.

"Thanks. That was a great help."

"No problem! This kind of work is fun – let me know anytime! But I should probably get back to my section."

Just then, Aki's work phone buzzed in her apron pocket.

"Hello?"

"*Obata. You've got an outside call. Shibata from Hitotsuboshi Press.*"

It was Hatakeda, calling from the office.

"Thank you. I'll take it."

She switched to the external line.

"Hello, Shibata?"

"Kitamura? Or maybe I should call you Obata now?"

"Either is fine."

Shunsuke Shibata was the deputy sales manager at Hitotsuboshi Press. Someone at his level wouldn't normally bother with a lowly bookstore employee like her, but he had taken her under his wing when she first started, inviting her to drinks parties and treating her to meals from time to time.

"Sorry I couldn't make it to your wedding. Got saddled with a business trip. Give Nobumitsu my regards, would you?"

"Don't worry about it. Work comes first."

"Well, I sent you a little wedding gift to make up for it. Didn't want to leave it with your husband, you know?"

"Huh? Where did you send it?"

"To the store. I didn't have your home address. It hasn't arrived yet?"

"I've just come back to work today, so I haven't checked the mail yet. It must have arrived. Thank you," Aki said quickly, though a bad feeling had taken root inside her.

She *had* checked her mail earlier, and there was no package.

After chatting with Shibata on the phone for a bit, she made her way to the office on the fifth floor.

She checked the mail area again to make sure. Nothing.

"Excuse me. Has anyone seen a package for me? It should have arrived by now."

She asked a few people nearby, but no-one seemed to know anything.

"Maybe it's in the break room?" someone suggested.

She went next door.

Since it wasn't break time yet, there wasn't anyone around. She scanned the storage area in the corner, checked under the shelves – and then, out of the corner of her eye, spotted something in the bin. Her stomach clenched.

A gold Godiva box – the one she had given everyone as a gift this morning.

She pulled it out of the bin, pieces of chocolate tumbling onto the floor. Hardly anyone had touched it before it had been thrown away. Her note was still stuck to the lid – *From Kitamura*.

"Seriously?" she cursed.

Someone clearly wanted to mess with her. Such a waste. If they didn't want it, they could have just left it alone.

She put the box back in the bin and stepped out of the break room – only to run into Hiromi Kumazawa.

Hiromi worked on the fourth floor in the business books section. Mid-thirties and married, she never joined the team for drinks except for leaving parties, and she refrained from gossiping with the other women. Because of that, she was on neutral terms with both Aki and Riko.

"Ah, Kitamura! You're back. What are you doing in here?"

The break room was mostly for part-timers and contract employees. It was an unspoken rule that full-timers didn't use it.

"I'm just looking for something. A package, addressed to me."

"Who from?"

"Shibata from Hitotsuboshi Press. He sent a wedding gift, but I can't find it anywhere."

Hiromi's expression darkened. "Oh. Are they giving you trouble again? Honestly, some people . . ."

Aki blinked. "You know about it?"

"Well. When Ozaki goes around badmouthing you at full volume, it's hard *not* to hear it. You've been through a lot."

"Yes, well." Aki sighed. "I keep hoping things will settle down with time."

Hiromi gave her a sympathetic look. "You know what they say – people move on eventually. Try not to let it get to you."

"Thank you. But I still have no idea what happened to the gift."

"Ah!" Hiromi let out a sudden gasp, raising a hand to cover her mouth.

"What?"

"It's probably nothing . . ."

"Please, just tell me."

"Alright, but don't tell anyone you heard this from me."

"Of course."

"This morning, I saw Nishioka with a package near the back dumpster. And, well . . . She isn't on cleaning duty, is she? I *thought* it was odd."

As assistant manager, Nishioka was exempt from cleaning duties. She had no reason to be putting out the trash.

"I hope I'm wrong . . ."

"I get it," Aki said. "I need to go check."

Aki hurried out of the break room, took the lift down to the first floor, and slipped out the back door.

The shared refuse area was behind the building. The moment she stepped outside, a wave of heat from the air conditioning units hit her. She glanced over at the space sectioned off behind a concrete wall, divided into areas labelled *Burnable Waste* and *Non-Burnable Waste*. Only a few plastic rubbish bags sat inside.

Further back was the spot for bulky waste. One thing in particular stood out – a small package haphazardly wrapped in department store gift paper, with a shipping label attached to it.

The sender was listed as Shunsuke Shibata, the recipient as herself.

There was no doubt about it – this was the package she had been looking for.

When she picked it up, the wrapping paper slipped off easily. Inside was a red box wrapped with decorative gift paper bearing the kanji character for *congratulations* – a Baccarat box.

Lifting the lid, she saw two crystal glasses nestled inside. Or at least, that was what they were supposed to be. The glasses had shifted out of their paper moulds, like they had been carelessly tossed in. Aki picked one up.

"Unbelievable."

One glass had a clean crack running straight down from the rim. The other had a chunk missing from the base.

Whether it was an accident or deliberate, both glasses were broken. And instead of reaching their intended recipient, they had been dumped outside.

"How could anyone do something like this . . .?"

Her hands trembled as she picked up the shard from the corner of the box.

"I don't know what to tell you," Riko said, exasperated. "I'd love to help, but this really isn't my thing. It's not worth making a fuss over me."

"Come on now," the sales rep pressed. "My boss has told me we absolutely *have* to get a quote from you, Nishioka."

"Do you realise the position you're putting me in? You know I've never done anything like this before, right?"

Over in the store's literary fiction section, Riko was locked in a bitter back-and-forth with a visiting sales rep who wanted to prominently feature an endorsement from her in the advertising campaign for an upcoming paperback release. Knowing she would resist, he had come prepared, bringing the book's editor along for support.

In recent years, it had become commonplace for booksellers to give interviews and let themselves be quoted in magazines and newspapers. It was surely one of the most media-exposed retail jobs out there. Riko didn't mind sharing a few comments when appropriate, but she had always avoided having her name printed on book covers or in ads.

The relationship between bookstores and publishers was a two-way street. When a book became a hit, it benefited both sides. She did her part – participating in market research meetings, giving feedback on advance copies and offering opinions where she could.

But letting them use her name for marketing? Absolutely not. She wasn't a critic or a literary expert – just a bookseller. She didn't want to be responsible for a book's success or failure, and she definitely didn't want her name being used as a sales tactic.

"Come now, Nishioka," the editor chimed in. "This paperback edition was only made possible because of your recommendation. You're practically its godmother. We *need* your support."

That gave her pause.

Technically, they weren't wrong – she *had* played a part in the book's success. But it wasn't some grand, deliberate effort. It had just happened to come up in a casual discussion with her ex. That was all.

*

Her ex worked in sales at a publishing company, so whenever they were together, work inevitably crept into the conversation.

One time, he started talking – half enviously, half complaining – about a recent surprise hit in paperback. Originally, the book had been published by a children's publisher. Then, a major publishing house picked it up and re-released it as a paperback for adults. Most in the industry assumed it wouldn't sell – children's books rarely did when rebranded for an older audience. But against all expectations, it took off to become one of the biggest hits in years.

"Donguri Books had the original, huh? They must have it good right now."

Her ex's frustration came from the fact that his own company's paperbacks weren't selling well. The entire book market was in decline, and paperbacks were no exception.

"Well, Donguri specialises in children's books," Riko said. "Maybe that's why literary editors overlooked it."

She didn't mind this kind of shop talk – she actually found it kind of interesting.

"Well, yeah," he answered. "It's not just children's books, though. A lot of hit authors these days start out in light novels. Even the editors say they have no idea where the next big writer will come from. And there are so many light novels being published, it's impossible to keep track of them all."

"Then maybe you should listen to young women more?" Riko suggested. "They've got great instincts when it comes to fashion, music, pretty much everything. Including books."

"You mean the girls working in bookstores?"

"Them too. But also the ones who read *Book Club*."

"What's *Book Club*?"

"It's basically a book guide for women who love to read. But its main audience is, well, fangirls and the like."

"Fangirls?"

"The kind of woman who reads Boys' Love novels."

"Ah, BL fans. But that's a niche market. We need books that appeal to everyone."

"You shouldn't underestimate them," Riko said. "They have a knack for sniffing out good stories. When they back a book, it sells. You know Atsuko Asano and Shion Miura? Their earliest fans were BL fangirls."

"Huh? But those authors don't write BL."

"That's the thing – they don't *need* it to be BL. They just like books that have that kind of style. Actually, they prefer finding those elements in books that weren't originally intended to be BL. It's like a game to them. But the books they latch on to aren't just about the style – they're high quality, too. And once they start talking about a book, the mainstream starts taking notice. That paperback you mentioned a minute ago – *Book Club* did a feature on it long before it became a hit. I wouldn't be surprised if some editor spotted it there and decided to re-release it."

"Huh. You think so?"

Her ex had a conservative mindset, and he saw BL as nothing more than a fringe trend. The idea that a book's success could be driven by that kind of readership hadn't remotely occurred to him. But the truth was, a solid percentage of serious female readers *did* have those interests. And unlike male light novel fans, who tended to stick to their niches, fangirls liked to read widely. They loved all kinds of books, and they also had a habit of reading between the lines, finding subtexts the author never intended, and delighting in interpreting male friendships as something more. It wasn't just about being a fan – it required a certain level of reading skill. In a way, BL fandom was an advanced form of literary analysis, a kind of high-level game for literature-loving women.

"That's why I pay attention to what they're excited about when I'm deciding which new books to stock," Riko continued. "For example, their latest hot pick is *Until Your Voice Reaches Me* from Natsugumo Press. So, I ordered some copies – and sure enough, it's selling really well. It's already a four-book series. I'm sure it'll do great if they release it in paperback."

"What's it about?"

"It's set in a boys' choir, and it follows these young professional singers. The level of research is impressive – it really gets into the details of how those choirs work. Plus, you know how a boy soprano's voice is only beautiful for a short time? There's something really poignant about these boys putting everything they have into something so fleeting. The character dynamics are great, as well. The classic rivalry-turned-friendship is kind of predictable, but it works."

Riko wasn't a BL fan herself, but she had grown up reading girls' manga comics, so she understood why some women gravitated towards those kinds of stories.

"Interesting," her ex said. "Maybe I should mention it to our editors. Natsugumo should be easy enough to negotiate paperback rights from. What was the title again?"

That conversation had taken place nearly six months ago, and Riko had completely forgotten about it. To her, it was just a casual chat – she had no intention of influencing his work decisions.

But he *had* mentioned it to the editors. After that, one of them read the book, loved it, and successfully secured the paperback rights. The editing work was already done, and now the sales team was gearing up for a major marketing push. Given how well a similar book had performed for one of their competitors, they expected this one to be just as big, and they were pouring an unprecedented amount of money into advertising.

And now, not only was the sales rep asking if they could include Riko's name in the book's marketing materials, but he also wanted to conduct an interview with her about how the paperback deal had come about.

"Oh, man. This is a problem. We were counting on having you with us for this, Nishioka. We even lined up a feature article in *Vintage*."

Riko snapped back to reality. *Vintage* was the publisher's flagship magazine – an upscale men's lifestyle publication that still managed to sell over 500,000 copies each month in an age when magazines were struggling. Landing a feature there would be a huge deal in terms of promotion.

"I appreciate that, but I haven't really—"

Before she could finish, Aki cut in, clutching a red box in her hands.

"Care to explain *this*, Nishioka?" she demanded, thrusting the box towards her. "What the hell were you even doing with it?"

"What do you mean?" Riko frowned.

Aki's face was flushed, whether from anger or something else.

"Enough," Riko snapped. "We can talk about it later."

The last thing she wanted was to get into a scene in front of the sales rep. She shot Aki a warning look, but the younger woman refused to back down.

"Oh, what? You're running away?"

Aki was incensed. At this rate, things were only going to escalate.

Riko turned back to the sales rep and his associate. "I'm sorry. Can we continue our conversation later?"

She didn't want these two to see whatever *this* was.

"Please, Nishioka. We're counting on you."

"We really hope you'll agree to help."

The sales rep and the editor both bowed deeply.

"Yes, yes. Let's talk later."

"Thank you! We'll follow up tomorrow with the details," the sales rep said with a look of relief.

Just like that, Riko had been roped into the promotional efforts. But right now, she had a more pressing problem to deal with. She grabbed Aki and steered her into the staff break room.

"This was *you*, wasn't it?" Aki demanded, yanking open the red box to reveal a pair of broken glasses.

"What are you talking about?" Riko answered.

"If it wasn't you, then it was one of your underlings. First the chocolates I brought back get thrown in the bin, and now *this*? Who does something this petty?"

"Lower your voice," Riko said coolly. "The customers can hear you." She eyed the pair of broken glasses. "Where did this come from? Is it yours? Did you leave it lying around somewhere?"

Aki hesitated for a second, thrown off by Riko's questions.

"It was a gift from Shibata at Hitotsuboshi," she finally said. "He couldn't make it to the wedding, so he sent this instead. But I never got it. Someone chucked it out."

Her voice had lost some of its heat.

"I see," Riko said. "And what makes you think *I* broke it? Why would *I* do something like that?"

"Because – someone saw you. They saw you carrying the box near the refuse area."

"Me? You're sure? I *did* go to the security desk this morning to discuss delivery logistics, but I never went near the refuse area."

"So . . . you're saying you don't know anything about this?"

"Of course not."

Aki stared at her, trying to gauge her reaction. Riko held her gaze, unflinching.

"Do I seem like the kind of person who would do something so childish?" she asked. "And if I *were* going to pull a stunt like this, don't you think I'd be a little smarter about it? I wouldn't leave the evidence lying around – I'd make sure it disappeared completely."

"Like . . . how?"

"Maybe I'd hide it somewhere. Like in my locker. That way, no-one would ever find it, and you wouldn't know if it was an accident or deliberate."

Aki's eyes flickered with doubt. She fell silent for a moment, then she shook her head.

"But what if whoever did this *wanted* me to see it? What if they wanted to make sure I knew? To hurt me."

"That's possible," Riko admitted with a slight shrug. "I can't say what their motive was. I was just pointing out the flaws in your theory. Whether it was an accident or deliberate, I have no idea."

Aki's face twisted in frustration, like she wanted to argue but she wasn't quite sure how.

"And another thing," Riko added. "I'm your superior. If I

really wanted to make your life miserable, don't you think I'd have better ways to do it than *this*? Why would I take such a stupid risk? Now, who says they saw me there?"

Aki stared at her for a long moment. Then, finally—

"I'm sorry. Maybe I jumped to the wrong conclusion."

"Next time, don't go around accusing people without proof."

Aki flinched.

"And more importantly, that little outburst of yours on the sales floor was unacceptable. Customers were watching. Did you even stop to think about how that must have looked to the publishers? You know how much they love to gossip."

Aki paled. She finally seemed to grasp the damage she had done. Word of this incident was going to spread like wildfire.

"I'm sorry your gift got broken. But this is a workplace, and you're a bookseller. Keep your personal emotions out of the job. Showing your private face here is a huge mistake."

"I'm sorry," Aki mumbled, shoulders slumped.

Without another word, she turned and walked back to the sales floor.

Once Aki was gone, Riko let out a long breath.

Did that seem natural?

Did Aki really buy it?

She hadn't thought anyone had seen her on the first floor.

But now that it had come to this, her only option was to stick to her story.

Even she didn't know why she had done it. The moment she saw the sender's name, she had simply lost control.

That man – Shunsuke Shibata – had shoved her away like he was disgusted by the mere sight of her. People's true feelings always show in moments of shock – and that push made it painfully clear what he thought of her. He didn't even want to see her face.

And yet, the very next day, she saw his name on a package – for *Aki*.

He couldn't stand to look at *her*, but he cared enough about Aki to send her a gift?

She couldn't stop herself. She took the package and slipped out to the back of the building, where no-one was around. She knew she was acting crazy, but she had to know. After all, there was something about the shape, the size of the box – it felt too familiar.

Then she saw it. That unmistakable Baccarat red.

Her heart pounded as she lifted the lid.

She was right. She had hoped she was wrong, but of course, she wasn't.

A set of crystal wine glasses – the exact same ones Shibata had given her for her birthday after they started dating.

Out of all the things he could have picked, why *this*?

At that moment, the door slammed shut in the wind. Caught off guard, her hand slipped, the box fell, and the impact sent the two delicate glasses flying out, cracking on the concrete floor.

Riko froze, her blood turning to ice.

Before she could even process what she had done, she heard someone coming. The hum of a lift, footsteps approaching.

Without thinking, she left the broken glasses right there in the refuse area and hurried away, promising to come back for them later.

Riko now breathed a tired sigh.

She and Aki always had the worst possible timing.

She made her way to the changing room next to the office and opened her locker. Inside sat an identical Baccarat glass set – the one she had rushed out to buy during her lunch break. If that sales rep from Hitotsuboshi hadn't held her up, she would have been able to swap out the damaged glasses before Aki arrived for her late shift.

But it was too late. She couldn't switch them now.

"This whole thing feels cursed," she muttered under her breath.

Her relationship with Aki was only going to get worse.

6

"This is just the *worst*," Aki complained to her husband.

It had been a while since he had got home this early. Lately, he had been swamped with work preparing for the launch of his new magazine, so it was rare for Nobumitsu to get back before midnight. She couldn't even remember the last time they had eaten dinner together on a weekday.

"That old bat Nishioka completely ruined my day," Aki grumbled as she cooked.

Nobumitsu was sitting at the counter table facing the kitchen, sipping at his beer. On the table, he had laid out some salami, a jar of homemade pickles and a wheel of Camembert he had picked up on his way home.

"Wait, Nishioka? You mean your assistant manager? The one you gave the wedding gift back to?"

"Yeah. Her. You think she's trying to get back at me?"

She wasn't expecting Nobumitsu to come home early, so she hadn't planned for anything fancy. But seeing as he had already started drinking, a light meal should be fine. There was some basil pesto in the fridge, so she figured pasta would do.

"But she denied it, didn't she?"

"Of course she did. Like she'd ever admit it. But she was so weirdly calm about it – she wasn't even mad. That just makes her *more* suspicious. I'm telling you, *she's* the one who smashed it."

Aki kept talking as she worked. Their kitchen was designed so that the counter and sink were at the same height, seamlessly connected, rather than hidden behind a wall like in most open kitchens. The design was meant to make the kitchen a central feature of the living space, not just a room for cooking. The kitchen had been one of the main reasons she had agreed to move into this apartment, and the marble countertop and stylish faucets made it perfect for entertaining.

"Whoever did it, that's messed up. Breaking someone's personal stuff? That's workplace harassment."

"Workplace harassment . . ."

Hearing it put that way, she couldn't help but agree. Up until now, she had just thought of it as petty bullying or mean-spirited pranks. But looking back at all the things Nishioka had done, *harassment* definitely seemed like the more accurate term.

"If this keeps up, maybe you should think about changing jobs?" Nobumitsu suggested.

"Changing jobs?"

Aki was startled. She hadn't so much as considered that before.

"I can't do that. I got that job through family connections, so I would need a good reason if I'm going to quit."

"Then say it's because you got married. People quit for that all the time."

"Give me a break. Seriously? If I left like that, there's no way I'd be able to get another bookstore job. My parents would never let me hear the end of it."

"So what? There are plenty of other jobs out there. It doesn't have to be a bookstore. You're young, you can start over," Nobumitsu said, trying to be encouraging.

"No. It *has* to be a bookstore," Aki all but shouted.

She couldn't imagine doing anything else.

"Why are you so hung up on bookstores? The pay sucks. And it's not like you'll be able to keep working there once we have kids, right?"

"Because I love selling books. I don't want to do anything else."

"Huh? Seriously?"

Nobumitsu looked genuinely surprised. He clearly hadn't pinned her for the kind of woman who cared about her job, or about being a bookstore clerk.

Aki was surprised at herself, too. When had she become so attached to her work?

Ever since her student days, she had always known she wanted a job in sales or customer services. She liked meeting people, and she preferred fast-paced activities where she could see immediate results. Sitting at a desk all day would drive her crazy. She chose a bookstore simply because she loved books, and her family connections helped her land the job without too much effort. There had been no deeper reason than that.

Once she actually started working, however, she realised she was more suited to it than she had expected. No other retail job had such variety – new books came in every day, and bestsellers changed constantly. It was perfect for someone as easily bored as she was. She also loved seeing customers' reactions in real-time. If she changed a display, she could immediately see the effect on sales. It was very rewarding.

If I'm going to do this, I want to make a real impact. I want to create a bestseller all on my own. That was what she had thought at the time, and it was a sentiment that still held sway inside her.

These days, even small, local bookstores could gain national recognition through social media. If they worked hard enough, they could even get featured in newspapers, magazines and on TV.

If she was going to do this job, she wanted to be one of those success stories. If she quit before making any serious achievements, it would all have been for nothing.

"I had no idea you were so committed to selling books," Nobumitsu said. "Alright. I won't tell you to quit. But you *are* going to stop working when we have kids, right?"

He sounded almost uneasy.

"I don't know . . ."

Balancing a bookstore job with raising a child would be nearly impossible. None of the female employees at Pegasus Books were working parents. Nobody had even taken maternity leave before. It was something she would eventually have to consider, but she wasn't ready to deal with it yet.

"Is that what you want?" she asked. "For me to quit my job and be a full-time housewife?"

"Not forever. But when they're little, yeah, I think a mother should be at home with them."

"But you always said you were fine with me working after marriage."

Aki felt a twinge of disappointment. She had thought

Nobumitsu was understanding about her work. In fact, that was one of the reasons she had felt comfortable marrying him.

"I *am* fine with it – before kids come into the picture. I mean, I work crazy hours, and things will be even more difficult once we launch the magazine. You'd be bored out of your mind at home all by yourself, right?"

Silently, Aki took out a glass and poured herself a beer. She felt a vague sense of unease building inside her. Sure, working at a bookstore and raising kids would be a difficult act to balance, but the idea of becoming a stay-at-home mum didn't sit right with her. Waiting at home for her husband to come back late every night was so not her.

She downed her drink in one gulp and turned to face Nobumitsu.

"Even if we have kids, I want to keep working. I need to keep working at a bookstore."

Those were her honest feelings. She *might* leave her job at Pegasus when she had children, but she wanted to continue working at *a* bookstore.

"That's not realistic," her husband said. "You're not home until ten after your late shifts. And with what you make, you wouldn't even be able to afford a babysitter. You'd end up working just to pay for childcare. Why put yourself through that?"

There it was – the unspoken *I make enough for both of us*.

It was true – his salary *was* ridiculously high. She had been left stunned the first time she saw his monthly pay cheque. He made more than twice what she did, and it would go up again if he got promoted to editor-in-chief.

Publishing houses paid more than bookstores, she knew that. But she had never expected the difference to be so staggering. After all, they were both dealing with books. She was happy his salary was so high, but she didn't like thinking about how different it was from her own.

Even more frustrating was the way he was acting – like he thought he was better than her just because he made more money, even though they were both working full-time.

"You could always go back part-time once the kids are older," he said. "Plenty of bookstores are short on staff, and they'd jump at the opportunity to hire someone with experience. You'd have flexible hours, less responsibility – it'd be way easier."

"Maybe. But I don't like the assumption that women should just quit their jobs when they have kids. I didn't think you were that old-fashioned."

"It's not about being old-fashioned – it's just reality."

"I thought you liked that I have a career? That's what you said. For me, working isn't just something to pass the time until we have kids," Aki said firmly.

Nobumitsu sighed. "Okay, okay. I get it. Can we not fight about something that hasn't even happened yet?"

"But—"

"Come on, this is getting nowhere. All I said was that if work's getting too much for you, you can always quit. I only said it for your sake. I don't want you stuck in a place where you're constantly being bullied. I hate seeing you so down all the time."

He was clearly trying to cut the conversation short, and with a statement like that, Aki had no choice but to fall silent.

"You're right. It's my fault," she murmured.

Of course, that didn't make her feel any better. If anything, she felt like she had just uncovered Nobumitsu's true feelings.

"See, this is exactly why I hate talking about work at home," he grumbled, reaching for his beer.

Was that his third? Or his fourth?

"Ah, right. Speaking of which. I got an email from Agachi today," he said, bringing up a different topic in an effort to change the mood.

"Agachi? What did he say?"

Aki placed the pot on the stove and poured herself a second beer. Drinking while cooking didn't faze her – she could hold her liquor just fine.

"He said he was sorry for bailing on the wedding. He really wanted to be there."

"Well, he's a manga artist. Deadlines come first."

Nao Agachi used to be one of Nobumitsu's authors. He had switched magazines, so someone else was his editor now, but to Nobumitsu, he was still a special writer. Back at his old job, Agachi's action-comedy *Fly High!* was the biggest hit Nobumitsu had ever worked on. Agachi had been struggling to gain traction at another publisher, and it was Nobumitsu who approached him and got his new series started. The two of them must have had good chemistry, because it wasn't long before *Fly High!* became a massive hit, even getting a TV adaptation. That success played a large role in Nobumitsu's promotion. More than that, though, the signing event at which Nobumitsu and Aki first met was for *Fly High!* as well.

Agachi was thrilled when they got engaged, telling everyone in the industry he was their Cupid. He was supposed to be the guest of honour at the wedding – but two hours before the ceremony, he called Nobumitsu in a panic. Apparently, if he didn't submit his latest manuscript by the following morning, it would miss the magazine's deadline. And that magazine just had to be Nobumitsu's old workplace. There was no way he could force Agachi to attend.

"Anyway, now that his schedule's calmed down, he wants to bring us a wedding gift and check out our new place. Do you have time?"

"Saturdays work for me. But what about you?"

Aki placed a bowl of salad on the table – just some lettuce, onions and cucumbers she had lying around. The French dressing, however, she had made herself – she could whip that up in no time at all.

"Well, I think I can make time this month," Nobumitsu said. "It's a nice gesture on his part."

"In that case, should we invite some other people, too? It'd be more fun with a crowd."

"Yeah, that could work. Takezaki and Seina Miwa both said they wanted to meet you. Agachi's apparently been telling everyone you're a total knockout."

"A *knockout*? He said that?"

Aki burst out laughing. Who even used that word anymore?

"Those guys don't have much luck with women, so they're jealous. Of me. Getting married."

"Maybe I'd better dress up and play the part? I'll cook up a feast. Might as well let them think you landed a gorgeous wife *and* a great cook," she teased, trying to lighten the mood.

Hearing Nobumitsu's true thoughts had left her in a dark mood, but there was no point arguing about it now. The issue of kids could wait.

"What should I make? Maybe Italian? You think Agachi likes pasta?"

In her head, she was already preparing the menu.

"Trust me, those guys will eat anything. Just make sure

there's plenty of it. The fact that it's homemade will be enough to impress them."

"No, no, I'll make something really good and rub it in. Let those poor single guys get properly jealous."

She flashed Nobumitsu a bright smile. She didn't want things to get awkward with him. They had just got married, after all. She had to try lifting their spirits, even if it felt forced. They could take it slowly with all that talk about kids. They had time.

With that thought, she shoved the emotions swirling inside her down and locked them away.

"I'm home," Riko called out as she shut the front door behind her.

Her house was in a quiet suburban neighbourhood around twenty minutes on foot from Musashi-Koganei Station, a short ride down the Chuo Line from Kichijoji. The cluster of nearly identical houses packed together on equal-sized hundred-square-metre lots had been developed in the late 1970s. Most of the residents had moved in during their thirties and forties, raised their children there, and stuck around after their kids had left, meaning the average age in the neighbourhood was well past sixty. The place felt lifeless to Riko, weighed down by its elderly population.

She noticed her father's shoes scattered around the hall. With a sigh, she lined them up neatly. Had he gone out today? A light had been left on, casting a shaky glow. A scattering of bugs hovered beneath it.

I forgot to buy a new bulb again, she thought. *I had better get one tomorrow.*

In the past, her dad would have replaced things like that without being asked.

She stepped into the kitchen on the left and peeked into the aluminium pot on the stove. The simmered chicken wings and potatoes she had made that morning were still there. She had told her dad again and again to put any leftovers in the fridge, especially in this summer heat. She brought the pot close and sniffed – probably still okay. Her father wasn't a big fan of chicken, so he had barely touched it. But chicken wings were cheap, and she couldn't always cater to his preferences. She was too tired to cook anything else tonight.

Was he already asleep?

She climbed the stairs and glanced to the right. The tatami-floored room on that side was her dad's. The one on the left had been her bedroom since childhood. She slid the door open.

Her father, Tatsuto, was slumped over his floor table, mouth slightly open, fast asleep. The TV in the corner was still on, an NHK announcer droning on about one thing or another.

"Dad. Hey, Dad," she called, shaking him gently. "You can't sleep here. You'll catch a cold."

"Mmm . . .? Ugh . . ."

He was dozing off like this more often these days. Ever since he retired from his last job three years ago, he had had too much time on his hands. He didn't have any real hobbies, or much of a social life, so he just pottered around all day. Sometimes, he did a little gardening in their tiny garden, but even that probably felt like a hassle. Mostly, all he did was sit around watching TV. He had just turned sixty-eight, but lately, he seemed to be ageing all at once. The ashtray on the table was overflowing. His smoking had picked up – probably out of sheer boredom.

"Look at all this," she muttered, gathering up the cigarette butts. "You know it's dangerous to fall asleep while you're smoking."

He blinked blearily. "Welcome home. What time is it?"

"Past eleven. I'll lay out your futon. Go to bed already."

"Yeah . . . Yeah, alright."

She turned off the TV, pushed the floor table to the side of the room, then laid out his futon. It was too hot for a blanket, so she pulled out an old, threadbare towel sheet. The thing had been blue once, but after years of washing, it had faded to a dull greyish white. The fabric was frayed, practically falling apart. She had been meaning to replace it for years, but her father refused. He had always been stubborn, but now he resisted even the smallest of changes.

"Alright, go brush your teeth and change," she said.

Is this what it's like to have to nag a child?

Lately, her father couldn't even be bothered to brush his teeth properly. "Most of them are dentures now, so what's the point?" he would say. His breath had got worse, too. As if the stench of cigarettes wasn't bad enough.

"Ugh. Why's it got to be such a pain?" he grumbled.

"Don't say that. It would do you good to move around a little."

She knew he didn't want to go downstairs to the bathroom – it was too much trouble. She had thought about installing a small sink and toilet upstairs, but she knew full well he would never accept that.

About six months ago, she had read in a city bulletin that there were government grants available for making homes more accessible. She had jumped through every bureaucratic hoop to apply – consulted with a contractor, got a preliminary quote, filed the paperwork, even received the necessary permits. Everything was set. And then, at the last minute, her father shut it down.

"*I* built this house," he protested. "So long as I'm alive, I want to keep it the way it is."

She had pleaded, reasoned, even tried guilting him into it. She insisted it wouldn't be a major renovation, just a small change in the flooring and walls, but nothing worked.

"You can do whatever you want with it after I'm gone. But not while I'm still here."

His sheer stubbornness drove her crazy. Did he have any idea how much time and effort she had put into the process? She had spent hours running around, dealing with paperwork, talking to officials, all for his sake.

And in the end, all for nothing.

Riko went back to the kitchen and put the pot on the stove. She opened the rice cooker – empty. No miso soup, either. Clicking her tongue, she pulled open the freezer. Fortunately, there were two frozen rice balls left. Good enough. She wasn't about to start cooking something from scratch just for herself. Besides, it had been so long since lunch that her hunger had already settled into a dull nothingness.

There were two pieces of mail on the table – a credit card statement and a flyer for a discount suit sale. Staring at them, she tossed the rice balls into the microwave and set the timer. When she opened the fridge to grab some barley tea, she spotted a half-eaten pack of fish sticks. Checking the expiry date, however, she found it was more than a month past.

When was the last time I cleaned out the fridge? God knows what else is lurking in there.

She sank into her chair at the table, exhaustion settling into her bones. The soles of her feet were swollen and achy, like she had got frostbite. She was used to the strain of standing on her feet all day, but today, it weighed on her heavier than usual.

She knew exactly why she hated Aki Obata so much – because happy people were unbearable when you weren't one of them.

The effortless way Aki radiated happiness made Riko feel like she was being crushed.

Why hadn't she just quit her job? It wasn't like she needed the money. There were rumours going around that she and her husband had bought a luxury condo for fifty or sixty million yen. Meanwhile, Riko had been working for twenty years and still couldn't scrape together anything close to that.

Here she was, still living with her father because paying rent felt like such a waste.

The microwave beeped. She pulled out the rice balls and carried them to the table.

Aki had been such a smooth talker with Shibata – "I don't mind older guys at all! Men in their forties are totally in my range."

She was so fake. But Shibata had looked pleased. For a young woman like her, wrapping an older man like him around her fingers must have been all too easy. Come to think of it, Shibata's wife had been twenty-seven when they got married, the same as Aki. What kind of tricks had she used to reel him in?

None of this is fair. It's always the savvy women who come out ahead.

And then there were those wine glasses . . .

Just thinking about it made her blood boil. It was even more infuriating than when Shibata had pushed her away and disappeared up the subway stairs.

Why did it have to be those glasses?

Baccarat had plenty of other designs to choose from.

She suddenly stood up, walked to the cabinet and pulled out a pair of wine glasses – identical to the ones she had inadvertently broken. She gripped one tightly and just stood there.

Maybe she should smash these as well? There was no point keeping mementos from a man who was long gone.

She stepped towards the sink, raised the glass high—

And froze.

She couldn't do it.

She could still see the way Shibata had looked when he had given them to her, embarrassed but at the same time pleased. She couldn't bring herself to break them.

She set the glass back on the table. Then, reaching up to the top shelf, she pulled down the bright red box the pair had come in. It was too nice to throw away – that was why she had kept it. She carefully placed the glasses inside. They were still in perfect condition. After a long pause, she let out a pained sigh and closed the lid.

It felt like she was filing away a finished chapter of her life.

Holding the box close to her chest, she walked to the back door. The non-burnable rubbish bin sat just outside. She opened it and placed the box inside, gently, before shutting the lid.

Her eyes stung.

Back in the kitchen, the pot on the stove was boiling over. She turned off the gas and reached for a plate – then stopped.

No. Why make more dishes to wash? No-one was watching.

Why am I the only one trying to do things the right way? she thought, her mood still sour.

She usually made a point of setting the table properly, even when eating by herself – right down to laying out a chopstick rest and coaster. But tonight, she just didn't care. Everyone else did whatever the hell they wanted, so why couldn't she?

She pulled the pot off the burner and set it on the mat on the table. Then, sitting in front of it, she grabbed her chopsticks and started shovelling chunks of potato into her mouth.

7

"Why not?" Aki demanded, gripping the paperwork as she confronted Riko. "If it's a no, at least give me a real reason!"

"How many times do I have to explain this? That event just isn't a good fit for our store. You know what kind of customers we have, don't you? They come here because we're well established. They're older, relatively well off, and, if we're being honest, fairly conservative."

"Which is exactly why we should be expanding our customer base! We *need* events like this if we want to bring in a younger crowd."

The paperwork in Aki's hands was a proposal for an event – a signing for Nene Katsura, a rising star in the BL manga scene. But the moment Riko saw that the author specialised in BL, she shut it down.

"Even if we *were* to hold a signing, why pick an author with such a niche audience? Someone like her would be a better fit for a speciality comic shop, not us. If we're going to do a manga signing, it should be with a more big-name author."

"But she *is* a big name! Her sales have been skyrocketing

lately, and this would be her first ever signing. I *know* fans will show up."

Even though Pegasus Books was the largest bookstore in the area, when it came to manga sales, they lagged far behind the nearby comic shop. Which was why, if a manga artist was going to hold a signing event in Kichijoji, that store would usually be the first choice. Aki found that incredibly frustrating. Given the floor space, there shouldn't have been such a big difference.

"How do her sales stack up, Hatakeda?" Riko asked.

Hatakeda, who had been scrolling through sales figures on his computer, hesitated before answering. "Let's see . . . Looks like she sells about 120,000 to 150,000 copies per volume. Her first print runs have been increasing lately, so she must be gaining traction."

"For a manga artist, that's borderline. Even for BL, those aren't necessarily impressive numbers. Do you think she'll draw a crowd?"

"Yeah . . . At that level, a signing might struggle to pull in enough people," Hatakeda agreed.

The two of them exchanged sceptical looks. Aki knew the numbers weren't exactly in her favour, but she had her own reasons for wanting to push ahead.

"I get that it's a bit of a gamble. But that's exactly why we should do it. This is our chance to put ourselves ahead of the curve, to show her fans we're paying attention to her before anyone else is."

She couldn't back down. Since she had reorganised the shelves to feature more BL titles, sales had seen a noticeable uptick. She had even overheard customers praising the store's BL selection. That being the case, why not go all in? She had started studying BL herself so she could make the section even stronger. Hosting Nene Katsura's first signing event would cement their reputation.

"I get that you're passionate about this," Riko said, folding her arms. "But don't you think it's too soon for a signing? If it flops, it won't just hurt the store – it'll be a blow to the author as well."

A poorly attended signing was humiliating for everyone involved. The store would have wasted time and money, sure, but the biggest damage would be to the author's confidence. Of course, if things looked bad, they could always pad the numbers – have the publisher or store employees pose as attendees. Such practices were an open secret in the industry.

Even so, Riko had seen it happen before. A decade ago, *she* had planned a signing event for an author she adored. But when the day came, barely anyone showed up. It had been unbearable, watching the author stand there, awkward and crestfallen. She swore to herself she would never let that happen again.

"But this will be different. People *will* come – I'll make sure of it!" Aki insisted.

To her, this wasn't just about a signing. It was about the future of Pegasus Books itself.

"Even if they do, is it worth it? We're talking about cheap manga volumes here. Can we really make enough profit to justify the cost?"

Signings weren't just about exposure – they were supposed to boost sales. That was why bookstores usually held them for high-priced hardcover releases, or at least books with strong tie-in merchandise. Manga comics, on the other hand, had razor-thin profit margins. On top of that, hardcore fans would already own past volumes, so there wasn't much hope for additional sales. Riko knew that from experience.

"The publisher is fully backing this," Aki argued. "They'll handle the tickets, and they've assured me the store won't have to worry about anything."

For the publisher, book signing events had a different meaning. Yes, a single store might see a spike in sales for one day, but in the grand scheme of things, it would just be a minor blip. The cost–benefit ratio wasn't great. What really mattered was strengthening the relationship with the bookstore. It wasn't really about any one event – it was a way to build a lasting business relationship.

From an editorial perspective, a signing was also a way to support the author. It gave them a chance to meet their fans, and it reminded them they were popular enough to warrant an event. Sometimes, these things were organised just to keep authors motivated.

But in the end, those were the publisher's concerns. Riko didn't see why *their* store had to get involved.

"Holding a signing means we'd have to promote it and bring in extra staff for the day. Even if we're not paying the author a formal fee, we'd still have to provide some kind of gift. If we can't make enough profit to justify all that, what's the point? Let's say a comic costs 560 yen. The store's cut is twenty per cent, so 112 yen per book. Even if we sell a hundred copies, that's only 11,200 yen. The numbers just don't add up. Can't you see that's a terrible return on investment?"

Aki bit her lip. When Riko laid it out in hard numbers, her argument suddenly felt a lot weaker.

"As you said, long term, there might be some value in it.

But if this single event puts us in the red, it's a loss we just can't afford. We're not running this store as a hobby."

As Aki slumped in defeat, Riko pressed on.

"You said this author has a strong niche following, right? In that case, people might well come from all over. But how many of them are actually going to become regular customers? Most of them will probably just want an autograph. Once they get it, they'll never set foot in here again. Instead of catering to those one-time visitors, wouldn't it make more sense to focus on events that appeal to our existing customers?"

The more reasonable Riko sounded, the more Aki wanted to push back. No matter how logical her arguments were, it still felt like she was making excuses.

"If we think like that, we'll never do anything new. So long as it doesn't put us in the red, why not try, at least? It'd be good for staff morale, as well."

"Staff morale?"

"Yes! It's not every day they get to meet an author. Some of them are huge fans of Katsura. They're looking forward to it."

That argument was a red flag for Riko. Bringing personal interests into work was unprofessional. A real bookseller should put the customers' preferences first, not their own – and being a professional bookseller was a point of pride for her.

"Sorry, but that's not how we do things. We're not running events just because the staff think it would be fun. That's not a valid reason."

This time, it was Aki's turn to bristle. She wasn't suggesting this *just for fun*. *She* wasn't into this BL stuff.

"Isn't part of our job to keep the staff motivated? What's wrong with that?"

"Nothing. But this isn't the way to do it. You don't rope in an author just to indulge your own interests."

"That's not what I'm doing."

"Really?"

Riko stared Aki down. Aki refused to look away.

"Alright, alright, let's not get worked up," Nojima interceded to break the tension. "But Nishioka does have a point. With these numbers, a signing might be a little tough . . . We'd be putting the publisher in a bad spot if it flopped."

"But—"

"It's not a hard no. If her sales pick up a bit more, we can revisit the idea. You're not wrong to want to think ahead."

"But that's exactly why we should do it *now*. If we do it now, it'll get the BL community talking."

"Alright, that's enough. And if it fails? Are you going to take responsibility for that?"

Riko's words hit hard. Aki clenched her jaw.

That wasn't fair. She wasn't *in* a position to take responsibility, so what was she supposed to say?

Meanwhile, Riko was growing more irritated by the second. At the end of the day, Aki was just a regular employee. She wasn't responsible for the store's overall performance. She only had her own little section to worry about. But there were bigger priorities to consider.

"You don't get to push your ideas through without taking responsibility for them."

With that, Riko spun around and marched back to the sales floor.

"Let's revisit the idea once the author gets a little more traction. Okay?" Nojima said, patting Aki on the shoulder.

Aki was too frustrated to respond. She just glared at the

door Riko had disappeared through, her hands clenched into fists.

"She shot it down *again*?"

Mami let out a sigh of deep disappointment from behind the register.

Aki nudged her with her elbow – talking like that at the counter was a surefire way to attract customer complaints. Sure enough, the customer in front of them, who had just been about to pay, glanced up curiously. Aki quickly flashed him a polite smile.

The young man, clutching a manga comic with an illustration of a half-naked girl on the cover, blushed and quickly looked away.

"Thank you," Aki said smoothly as he paid and hurried off.

For the time being, there were no other customers. Mornings could be like that – little pockets of downtime between mad rushes.

"Ugh. She's impossible," Aki grumbled, making sure no-one else was within earshot before heaving a dramatic sigh of her own.

Each floor of the bookstore had its own checkout counter, and today, Aki was working with Mami and a new part-timer, Anna Nakamura. Anna had just joined the team in the comics section – hired last-minute after Minako Makihara cut back her shifts to focus on full-time job hunting. She was an old friend of Mami's and, more importantly, a fellow BL fan.

"I don't know, Nishioka seems kind of hysterical. Think she's going through the menopause or something?" Anna whispered under her breath, a little too gleefully.

That was the kind of cruel remark only a young person

could serve up, never considering that one day, they would be that age, too.

"Could be," Aki replied, indulging in the petty spitefulness.

Lately, Riko Nishioka had been increasingly open about giving her the cold shoulder. Given that the wedding reception mishap and the wine glass incident were still unresolved, that wasn't exactly surprising, but all the same . . .

"She's such a pain. And that whole recommendation display thing? Did she really have to go that far?" Mami chimed in.

Practically every bookstore maintained its own recommendation displays to boost sales. Most of the time, they consisted of handwritten cards with catchy blurbs about specific books. A well-placed, well-written display could significantly increase sales. Lately, with the publishing industry in a slump, handwritten recommendations had become an essential tool for driving sales.

"It *was* a bit over the top, wasn't it?"

Anna, eager to prove herself in her first week, had enthusiastically made a whole bunch of recommendation cards for her favourite comics – on her own time, unpaid. Aki had appreciated the effort and put them up right away. But Riko wasn't impressed. She yanked them all down the very same day, dismissing them as *too messy*.

Sure, Makihara, who had done most of the recommendation displays before, had the neatest handwriting in the store, along with a great eye for design – and compared to that, Anna's work was definitely rough. But she had passion. You could see how much she cared about the books, and that kind of enthusiasm mattered. At least, Aki thought so.

Riko might be good at her job, but she sure as hell doesn't understand people.

"Welcome!"

A customer walked up to the register with a book, and Aki put on her best professional smile to ring it up. Once they left, the conversation continued where it had left off.

"You know, she's never really been a fan of recommendation displays," Mami said.

"Really?" Anna stared back wide-eyed.

With bookstore recommendations practically everywhere these days, it was hard to imagine a bookseller who didn't like them.

"Think about it – there are hardly any in the literary fiction section, right?"

"Now that you mention it . . ."

Anna, being new, hadn't really paid attention to the other floors yet.

"The only ones down there are the ones publishers send over," Mami continued.

"She'd rather not have them at all," Aki added, pulling a stack of wrapping paper out from under the counter and neatly folding the sheets for later use.

Anna followed suit, while Mami continued sorting return slips.

"She says recommendation displays block the books behind them and make them harder to see."

"But they *do* work," Mami insisted. "With so many new releases coming out all the time, customers don't know what to buy. A good recommendation gives them that little push to make a purchase."

"The assistant manager thinks they look tacky," Aki said, her voice dripping with sarcasm.

If she wanted to get hung up on appearances, there was

no way they would be able to run a normal bookstore. By that logic, they shouldn't even be selling BL novels packed with steamy homoerotic scenes.

"She's so old-school," Mami groaned. "Recommendation displays are just standard now."

"How are we supposed to promote books without them?" Anna nodded.

Aki understood their frustration.

"And then she said we only want to do that Nene Katsura signing event for ourselves, not the store."

"Well . . . yeah," they both admitted without hesitation.

Unlike Aki, Mami and Anna were indeed fans of the author. Naturally, part of why they wanted the signing event to go ahead was so they could contrive a chance to meet her.

"What's so bad about that?" Mami asked in all seriousness.

"We get paid next to nothing here," Anna added. "Shouldn't we at least get *some* perks?"

Given her position, Aki couldn't exactly agree outright, but she saw their point. Booksellers – whether part-timers or full-time staff – certainly weren't big earners. Even compared to other retail jobs, their pay was on the lower end. If they couldn't count on financial rewards, why *shouldn't* they find motivation in other ways? If you enjoyed your work, you put in more effort – and that, in the end, benefited the store as well.

"Honestly, what does she even enjoy about working here?" Aki muttered.

"She should lighten up," Anna agreed.

"I'm so *bored*. Let's do something fun, Mami."

"Seriously."

"No recommendation displays, no author events. What *are* we allowed to do?"

"Other bookstores do this stuff like it's totally normal."

"We want to do something big, too! Get some real sales going."

"Right? And have the authors appreciate us for it."

"And maybe even get some signed copies . . ."

"Or have a magazine do a feature on us."

Mami and Anna were so caught up in their fantasy that they had completely forgotten about folding the wrapping paper.

"Well, she'd never allow it," Aki said bitterly. "Her policy is that bookstore staff shouldn't stand out too much."

"Come on," Mami huffed. "Just because *she's* like that doesn't mean she should force it on the rest of us."

"Exactly! These days, you can't just sit back and wait for books to sell themselves," Anna agreed.

They weren't wrong. Aki herself wanted to push the envelope and be more proactive.

"As long as she's in charge, it's probably not happening. She's too inflexible."

With a sigh, Aki shoved the neatly folded wrapping paper back onto the shelf.

8

"Hello."

"Ah, Riko! Welcome. Do you have the day off today?"

The elderly bookstore owner, sitting behind the register with a book in hand, looked up and gave her a warm smile. The store, about the size of a small apartment, was devoid of customers.

"Yes. I spent the morning cleaning and taking care of things at home, so I thought I'd take a little break."

Yesterday, she had had a heated argument with Aki Obata, and it had been weighing on her ever since. On top of that, she still felt guilty about the wine glass incident. The exhaustion from fighting with Aki was hitting harder than usual lately. Needing a change of pace, she went out for a walk, and she ended up here.

"You're really something, Riko. You could go literally anywhere on your days off, yet you go out of your way to visit this tiny bookstore."

The shop, called Isshindo, was just a ten-minute walk from her house, and she had been coming here since elementary school. Being an only child with parents who both worked full-time, she had spent a lot of time alone as a kid, and naturally, she became a bookworm. Her parents were always generous when it came to pocket money, so she had practically lived in this store growing up.

"I just wanted to see you, Uncle ... Oh! You've still got copies of Yoko Ogawa's new book? You're on top of things. We sold out right away at my store. We have to wait for the next print run."

The owner's name was Shimizu, but Riko had called him *Uncle* ever since she was little. At this point, there was no changing that old habit.

"I have a few regulars who'll be looking for it, so I made sure to stock up."

"Did you pick it up in Kanda?"

"That's right. A small shop like mine is at the bottom of the list when it comes to bestsellers."

Everything in this store was handpicked by Shimizu himself – either ordered directly from the publishers or bought in person from the wholesalers in Kanda. It was a stark contrast to her own store, where new releases arrived in bulk from distributors whether she wanted them or not.

"Would it be okay if I bought one?" she asked. "I wanted a copy for myself, but we always let the customers have first dibs at our store."

"Of course. You're not the assistant manager here – you're a valued customer. I can restock for the others."

"Thanks. But let me browse a little more first."

"Take your time. Not like I have anything else to do, and there's no-one else here."

She started with the literary fiction table. It was small, and there weren't many books on display, but every single one of them was a brand-new release. The selection wasn't overly pretentious, but it also wasn't just the usual bestsellers. Tucked in the corner, she spotted a couple of books that only true book lovers would appreciate. It was a well-curated collection.

Behind the literary fiction section were the paperback and non-fiction shelves – not a huge area, just four small back-to-back bookshelves. At her store, they got every new paperback release from every publisher, but it was different here. Everything on these shelves had been deliberately chosen. Even though she had been coming here ever since she was a child, she only realised the difference after she started working at a bookstore herself.

"Uncle. Do you pick out the paperbacks yourself, too?"

Back when she first started in the industry, she assumed that major publishers automatically shipped paperbacks to every store, whether they asked for them or not. But here, even major imprints like Shincho or Kodansha only had a couple of new releases on display.

"Of course. Who else is going to do it?"

"Couldn't you ask the publishers' sales reps . . .?"

"They don't bother with stores as small as mine. And even if they did, I can't stock everything – I'd never sell it all," he said with a hearty laugh.

That made sense. At Pegasus, publishing reps from companies big and small dropped by on a daily basis. Sometimes, when she was swamped, she wished they would just leave her alone. Despite them both being in Tokyo, her store and this one operated in completely different worlds.

Looking back, the reason she had never noticed the lack of automatic shipments here wasn't just because she didn't understand the industry. And Shimizu had always stocked the books she needed. Unlike other small bookstores that just took whatever bestseller sets the publishers bundled together, this store only carried books that were actually relevant. No forgotten, once-popular titles collecting dust. Yes, big-name authors like Keigo Higashino and Miyuki Miyabe were here, but so were hidden gems that only true book lovers would appreciate. And not a single one of them had a sun-faded spine.

There were even some translated books – not many but a few. She picked one up – *The Haunted House* by Rebecca Brown. She had been meaning to read it for a while but never got around to buying it.

Because of her job, she tended to prioritise books that were currently trending. After all, customers expected her to be knowledgeable about them. Her personal favourites, like translated fiction, often got pushed to the back of the queue.

But here, time seemed to move at a different pace. Instead of chasing fleeting bestsellers, she felt like picking up books she could truly savour.

"I'll take this one."

When she brought it to the counter, Shimizu's face lit up.

"Ah, I was hoping you'd buy that."

"Really?"

"I know how much you loved *The Gifts of the Body*. I figured you'd want to read this, too."

"Wow, you have a good memory."

She barely remembered telling him about that. Yes, she had loved that book, but it had been years ago.

"It's all part of the job. That said, you usually buy from your own store, so I wasn't entirely sure. But I figured I'd stock it, just in case."

"You really put that much thought into what your customers might want to buy?"

"Of course. Every book here is chosen with someone in mind. This one's for you, that one's for another regular, and so on."

"That's amazing. I wish I could be that thoughtful. I mean, sometimes I put books on the shelves thinking, *Oh, so-and-so might like this,* but not to that level."

"That's because your store is much bigger and gets a lot more customers. My business is mostly deliveries and regulars. It's on a different scale."

It was true – this shop was far from the station, tucked away near a supermarket and a tiny shopping district. The only people who came in were locals.

"Still, I'd love to run a store like this one day."

She was half joking, half serious. This was what bookselling was supposed to be – understanding customers and finding the perfect book for them, not just pushing whatever was popular.

Customers no doubt appreciated the special treatment, too.

At a busy store like hers, though, where just keeping up with the rush at the registers during peak hours was a struggle, there would be no way they could pull this off.

"Don't be ridiculous. You're the assistant manager at a big chain store. My place is barely scraping by. The only reason I can keep going is that I don't pay rent – I built this store on my own land. We manage because it's just family running the place. Let me tell you, I'd love to try running a massive store like yours. I could stock all the bestsellers, and I could also squeeze in a few books related to my own interests."

"Oh? What kind of books would you stock?"

"Railway ones, of course."

"Ah, that makes sense. You do love trains."

Railway photos were casually scattered here and there throughout the store, all taken by Shimizu himself. A model train sat quietly beside the register – a D51, if she remembered correctly. His favourite locomotive. But despite his passion, there were hardly any railway books on the shelves. He did have some in the past, but since no-one showed any interest, he had stopped stocking them.

"If I had more space, I could indulge my niche tastes," he said with a sigh. "But with a store this size, I just don't have the room."

"Yes, I can understand that," she replied.

Her own store was three times as big – about a thousand square metres. And she took pride in having a well-stocked world literature section – not just because she loved it, but because her customers appreciated it, as well. Compared to this quiet suburban town, Kichijoji was practically the big city. Being near the station meant they attracted all kinds of readers. She was fortunate in that regard.

"But I've got used to this laid-back pace," Shimizu continued. "I don't think I could handle it if my store ever got as busy as yours. I certainly wouldn't be able to read on the job anymore! I might not make much money as things are, but at my age, this pace is just about right."

He always spoke in a slow, deep voice – calming, almost soothing. Riko knew the relaxed atmosphere wasn't just because of the low foot traffic. It was his personality on show.

"Maybe I should open a store like this when I get older," she mused.

"I'd love to have someone like you take over one day," he said.

"You don't have anyone to give it to?"

"Nope. My kids gave up on this unprofitable business a long time ago. They all got jobs at big companies. This place will close when I retire."

"I see . . . But you're not planning to retire anytime soon, right?"

"Not for now, no. I've still got regulars who rely on me."

"Keep it going for as long as you can. I'll drop by again."

She felt a lot calmer than when she first arrived. Coming here had been the right choice. This place was like a secret little oasis for her.

As she stepped outside, she glanced back at the register. Shimizu caught her eye and smiled. He always watched his customers leave, right until they were out the door. That had never changed – not since she was in elementary school.

Riko smiled back. She already knew she would be coming again soon.

9

"What's this one for?" manga artist Nao Agachi asked as he casually peeked into the room next to the living room.

"Hey, don't just open random doors!" Nobumitsu protested. "We're using that as storage space."

Agachi and the other writers, however, ignored him and barged straight in.

"Relax," Agachi said, glancing around. "It's way tidier than my place."

"Wow, you really are an editor, huh?" his fellow manga artist Seina Miwa added, impressed. "The entire wall is covered in books."

The room was lined with sliding bookshelves on every wall except for the one with the window – probably around ten cases in total. Half were filled with novels, the others with comics.

"Huh, let's see what you've got . . . Oh, hey, mine's there!" Miwa said with a pleased grin.

Tonight, Aki and Nobumitsu were hosting a home party, inviting Agachi, a handful of other manga artists, and friends from Nobumitsu's publishing company who couldn't make it to the wedding. It was the middle of the Obon holiday, so there were no looming deadlines for anyone. In other words, it was an easy time for the writers to step away from their work. Everyone invited was able to make it.

"Oh, what's this? Pretty sure this one's 18+," Agachi said, pulling out an adult comic with a smirk. "Your wife's not gonna scold you for this?"

Agachi was skinny and small in stature – nothing like the bold, intense linework of his drawings. But despite his frail appearance, Nobumitsu knew he was as stubborn as they came.

"That's not mine. It's my wife's," Nobumitsu said casually.

Miwa's eyes widened. "Wait, seriously? Your wife's into this kind of stuff?" he said loudly.

Despite his feminine-sounding pen name, Seina Miwa was a giant – easily one metre eighty tall and probably more than a hundred kilos. He had thick eyebrows, large, piercing eyes, and an overall tough look. Yet the work he produced was delicate, almost like a female artist's. Since he never showed his face publicly, rumours often swirled that he might actually be a woman.

Overhearing Miwa's loud reaction, Aki poked her head in from the living room.

"Oh. I'm not really interested in that sort of thing. It's for work," she said smoothly, quickly grabbing the comic from Miwa and putting it back on the shelf. "That one was in our store's top ten bestsellers, so I figured I should read it."

"There you have it." Nobumitsu paused for a second, gesturing around the room. "By the way, most of the books in here are Aki's, not mine."

Agachi scanned the shelves again. "Now that you mention it, the comics section is all over the place – you've got boys' manga, teenage manga, BL, even some adult stuff. This doesn't look like someone's personal collection."

"Yeah, well, I *am* in charge of the comics section at the store. But I barely read any manga when I was in school," Aki admitted. "So now, I'm making up for lost time. I try to check out anything that's trending."

Saying it out loud felt a little embarrassing – like exposing her work process.

"Oh wow, even this super niche one?" Miwa had pulled out a book from the top shelf. "You don't usually see this in regular bookstores."

"Yeah," Aki nodded. "It was getting a lot of buzz online. I figured if it was good, I might stock it in our store, so I bought it from a specialist shop."

"That's real dedication," Agachi said, sounding genuinely impressed.

"Okay, okay, enough snooping around," Nobumitsu interrupted. "Let's get out of this cramped room."

One by one, the group shuffled back to the living room.

Once they were settled on the sofa again, Agachi turned to Nobumitsu. "So, if all those books belong to Aki, where's your bookshelf?"

"I don't have one."

"What? You're an editor, though!"

"I'm not the type to keep books. Anything I need for work is at the office. Besides, Aki buys plenty, so I just read whatever she brings home," he answered defensively.

"But don't you read outside of work?" Agachi pressed. "Don't you at least check out the bestsellers to stay on top of recent trends?"

Nobumitsu sighed. "Alright, let me be real with you – booksellers read way more than editors do."

"Huh? Seriously?"

"Think about it. When you work as closely with manga artists as I do, you're too busy to sit around reading books. I mean, obviously, I read reference materials when I need to, but that's about it. When deadlines start creeping up, I'm pulling all-nighters back-to-back. If anything, watching movies is way more useful for work than reading books, so they're what I try to keep up with."

The drinks were loosening Nobumitsu's tongue more than usual. Aki wondered if it was really okay for him to be saying all this in front of his own authors.

"So that's how it is," Agachi said, sounding unconvinced.

"But it has to be different for literary editors?" Miwa chimed in.

Before Nobumitsu could answer, another editor who had been quietly listening to this exchange, Satoru Konno, jumped in.

"I have a friend in the books division, and he actually reads less now than before he got the job," Konno said. "Between editing manuscripts, screening submissions for the rookie awards and keeping up with what his authors publish at other companies, he barely has time to read anything for fun."

Konno was two years' Nobumitsu's junior and had a somewhat highly strung air about him. He had recently transferred into the comics division from the accounting department, and he was still struggling to find his footing. Nobumitsu had handed some of his work over to him, but he was worried that Konno and Agachi weren't getting along. In fact, part of the reason he had organised tonight's gathering was to help smooth things over between them.

"Is that really how it is?" Agachi pressed. "You guys still check out promising new writers from other publishers, right?"

As Aki half-listened in from the sidelines, she started wondering if it was time to bring out the main dish.

"Of course," Konno nodded. "They even have regular book club meetings at the office. But from what I hear, they only really care about authors with the potential to become bestsellers. So, essentially, they only focus on living Japanese writers who do commercial fiction. Our company doesn't invest much in literary fiction since it doesn't sell. One of my old classmates loves classic literature, especially foreign novels, but he got assigned to edit mystery and action novels instead. Do you know how many mysteries get published every month? He's constantly trying to keep up, and he always complains he never has time to read the books he actually likes."

"Huh. I always thought editors were big book lovers who read all the time."

"Well, sure, we *do* read more than the average person," Nobumitsu admitted. "But we prioritise what's necessary for work. It's more about depth than breadth. And that alone is a massive amount to get through. Besides, just because you work at a publishing company doesn't mean you have to be a hardcore bookworm. Our company isn't even famous for literary fiction – most people join because they want to work on magazines. Lately, more and more applicants specifically want to get into the comics division. I wasn't even asked about my reading habits during my job interview. Honestly, I don't know how many true bookworms there are in publishing. A lot of people just wanted a media job with a decent salary."

By now, Nobumitsu was completely drunk. The manga artists, on the other hand, weren't drinking at all – apparently, none of them could handle alcohol. And so, the editors had taken on all the drinking for the night.

"For the record, I *do* love books," Konno interjected. "I was a bit of a literature nerd at school."

Now that he mentioned it, Konno did have a bookish, intellectual air about him.

"Yeah, right," Nobumitsu scoffed. "I've never seen you actually reading anything."

"Because I don't read at work."

The two drunken editors started bickering playfully.

This is disappointing, Aki thought with a sigh.

She had always assumed that editors – at least compared to the general public – were voracious readers. Was that just a misconception? Or was it only true for literary fiction editors?

"Honestly, I think booksellers are way more passionate," Nobumitsu continued. "Whenever I go drinking with them, they're always fired up about one title or another. But when I drink with my co-workers, we never talk about books. Zero. I don't get it – why are booksellers so into this stuff? Maybe *I* should be the one asking *them* that."

Now that Aki thought about it, her husband never talked about books at home, either.

Agachi, who had been quietly snacking on cakes and sweets – probably to make up for his not drinking – perked up.

"Speaking of booksellers," he said, "they've been doing all these campaigns to boost certain titles, right? Like that Booksellers' Award thing. If they push a book and it sells well, do they actually make extra money off it?"

"As if," Aki snorted.

The Booksellers' Award was run by volunteers. Sure, it benefited the bookstores when a title sold well, but the people organising the award and the booksellers who voted didn't get paid for it.

"*That's* dedication," Nobumitsu said. "I mean, the booksellers buy all the nominated books themselves, right? That's got to be a lot of reading. I don't know how they do it."

"I know, right?" Aki nodded. "To vote, you have to buy and read every single nominated book. That alone is a huge commitment. But if I were in charge of the literary fiction section, I'd probably take part, too."

"Huh? So only fiction staff can vote?"

"Technically, anyone can. But reading all those books is a huge task. I think about giving it a shot each year, but I just don't have the time to read that much."

At Aki's store, Ozaki from the literary fiction section and Mita from the textbook section voted in the Booksellers' Award every year. Strangely enough, Riko, though well-versed in literature, didn't take part. Maybe she just didn't like the festive chaos.

"Oh, that reminds me," Miwa said all of a sudden. "Didn't a bunch of booksellers form manga fan club once?"

Years ago, when the girls' manga *Honey and Clover* was first released, comics staff from several bookstores got together to promote it, actively working with the publisher to launch a joint campaign across different stores. The book went on to become a massive hit, even getting a movie adaptation – all thanks to the passionate efforts of those booksellers.

"That's the dream, isn't it?" Konno said with a sigh. "The publisher wouldn't even have to do anything if the booksellers promoted titles on their own. Back then, they even paid out of their own pockets for T-shirts and other merchandise. There isn't a comics editor alive who doesn't wish for that level of attention."

"Editors, sure, but we manga artists want that even more," Miwa said, turning to Agachi.

He nodded, too busy stuffing his mouth with popcorn to say anything.

"Well," Aki said, bringing everyone back down to earth. "It has to be a really special book for that to happen."

It was rare for a comic to inspire that kind of cross-store movement. The book had to be so good that staff wanted to rally behind it, regardless of whether the author was famous or whether the publisher had a big budget. That said, comics were easier to get into than novels, and they had a larger readership. They attracted a lot of attention online, too, so word tended to spread faster. In general, good books naturally found their audience.

"Still," Nobumitsu pressed, "if we editors can get a hit, it directly benefits us. It boosts our reputation, helps our careers, and maybe even wins us an award. But what's in it for the booksellers? Why put in all that effort?"

"Well . . ." Aki thought for a moment. "It's rewarding when an author appreciates it. And even if they don't, the publisher's sales reps do, which makes our jobs easier. Sometimes, we get interviewed, or we connect with booksellers from other stores – it helps build relationships."

"That's it?" Nobumitsu scoffed. "You guys put in all that extra work – reading advance copies, making promotional displays – and all you get is . . . what? A thank-you?"

Aki found herself bristling at his tone of voice. He was practically calling her a soft touch.

"Well," she countered, "if a book takes off, that means higher sales for the store. That benefits us, in turn."

Agachi and Miwa watched on with amusement, like they were enjoying this couple's argument.

"Sure. Maybe," Nobumitsu conceded.

"*Your* big publishing house has an advertising budget, but a lot of smaller publishers don't. In fact, *most* don't. And sometimes, those small publishers put out amazing books. When their reps work hard, we want to support them."

"You really are a bookseller through and through, Aki," Nobumitsu said with a half-smirk. "So earnest."

"So what?" Aki shot back. "It's my job. *Our* job. We discover great books, and we introduce them to readers. *Of course* we want to support the ones we love. What's wrong with that?"

"No, no, nothing *wrong* with it. I just think you should be careful. Some people see booksellers as free advertising. You read their proofs, write reviews, and they get to use your thoughts for promotion – for free. Even if your comments get printed on the book, you don't get paid for them, do you?"

"Well, sometimes they send us vouchers or little thank-you gifts. But honestly, I wouldn't *want* to be paid for my reviews. If money was involved, I'd feel obligated to only give positive remarks."

"Yeah, but you realise ad agencies pay copywriters a fortune for that kind of thing, right? Meanwhile, publishers get booksellers to do it for free. And on top of that, if a bookseller loves a book, they'll give it prime shelf space. From a publisher's perspective, that's a win-win." Nobumitsu spoke as if he had no stake in this, despite being in the publishing industry himself.

"Maybe," Aki answered. "But we enjoy it. There are so

many books out there, and most get lost in the crowd. So, when we find something really special, we want to push it. We want to create a movement around it. Yes, sometimes we collaborate with publishers, but it's not for them – it's so we can sell good books."

With online bookstores taking over and physical bookstore sales declining with each passing year, they couldn't afford to sit back and do nothing. Creating excitement in a store was contagious. Customers picked up on it. And that, in turn, gave people a reason to keep coming back.

"Besides," Aki added, "a bookstore is like a showroom for books. Our job is to make them look as appealing as possible."

"Well said," Agachi beamed, reaching out for a handshake.

Aki shook his hand. *Manga artists really are a different breed,* she thought.

Miwa, meanwhile, clapped in appreciation.

"We promote books because we love them. And when they sell, that makes us happy. Customers trust our recommendations because we're not in it for personal gain."

"True," Nobumitsu muttered. "That's the irony, though. Your hard work benefits publishers and authors – but not you personally. And yet, because of that, customers trust your opinions."

"That's fine," Aki shrugged. "It's not just about money. We want to enjoy our jobs."

Seeing the direct impact of their efforts – seeing the response, connecting with customers, booksellers, publishers and authors – that kind of fulfilment was priceless.

"Damn, Aki," Agachi grinned. "You're the ultimate bookseller. I think I'm a fan. If you ever need anything, just ask. You're on Twitter, right?"

"Yeah, sort of."

Many booksellers were on social media, sharing recommendations and keeping up with the latest trends. Some books had even taken off purely because booksellers had hyped them online – like *Scholé No. 4* by Natsu Miyashita.

"Can I get your handle? I'll follow you."

"Wait, I thought you just used your pen name?"

"I do, but that's my public account. My personal one's private."

"Hey, can you give it to me too?" Nobumitsu jumped in.

"Same here," Konno added.

"Nope. I don't share my private account with editors," Agachi smirked. "I might write things I don't want you guys reading."

"Come on! I'm not even your editor anymore!" Nobumitsu protested.

"Yeah, but you still work in manga, same as Konno. So, no."

Nobumitsu pouted like a disappointed child.

Agachi didn't seem to care. "Alright, Aki, *you* can follow me – but don't show your husband my tweets, okay?"

"Of course."

Aki swelled up with pride. Yes, she met Agachi through her husband, but he had taken an interest in her as her own person.

"Here, write down your handle," he said, handing her a notepad. "I'll follow you when I get home."

"Man, am I jealous," Nobumitsu sulked.

He sounded less like an editor and more like a drunk at a bar.

10

"Hey, did you see this? Nishioka's in this month's *Vintage* – with a full-on photo!"

"Whoa, you're right! She's got an entire page!"

Mami and Anna were huddled over a magazine, buzzing with excitement. Curious, Aki leaned over behind them for a peek.

The article in question was a six-page feature titled "Booksellers Create Bestsellers: The Latest Trends in Hit Books". And right there on the first page – front and centre – was a photo of Riko.

When was this taken? There she was, Riko Nishioka, standing in front of the third-floor register, holding a paperback and wearing a bright smile. The caption read: "Star Bookseller Riko Nishioka, keeping an eye out for the next big hit. Photographed at Pegasus Books, Kichijoji".

The article itself began by exploring the connection between booksellers and recent bestsellers, covered the influence of in-store recommendation displays, recent trends relating to the Booksellers' Award, and then—

An upcoming release, Until Your Voice Reaches Me, *is a prime example of this phenomenon. Originally published by Natsugumo Press, a small publisher specialising in children's literature, the book sold a respectable 20,000 copies – a strong run for the genre. Yet, it remained a hidden gem, not the kind of book that typically gets a mass-market reprint. But thanks to a certain bookseller's recommendation, this magazine's parent company decided to add it to their paperback line-up.*

From there, the article gave a brief introduction to Riko Nishioka, Pegasus Books, and the supposed backstory behind the book's publication. But at its core, it was little more than a thinly disguised promotional piece for the publisher's new release.

"Wait a second – this is *our* book! The one *we* were talking about!" Mami exclaimed.

She was right. *Until Your Voice Reaches Me* had been a favourite among Mami, Makihara and the other BL-loving girls for more than six months now. Mami had even produced a fanzine about it. When Nishioka caught wind of everyone's excitement, she moved the book from the fifth-floor children's section to the third-floor literary fiction display, and sales took off. But *they* were the ones who discovered it first. And now, the article was acting like it was all Riko Nishioka's doing.

In fact, it was basically singing her praises. Page after page, it hammered home her skills as a bookseller, how much her customers adored her, how she had a sharp eye for identifying the next big thing. It was nothing more than a puff piece.

"She's always going on about how booksellers shouldn't try to steal the spotlight. Now look at her."

"Guess she just wants all the credit for herself."

"Apparently, she has a newspaper interview tomorrow, too."

"You've got to be kidding me."

"I swear, it makes you wonder why we even bother."

"What a snake."

It wasn't long before Mami and Anna's venting spilled over into insults. Aki didn't feel like stopping them.

The article in *Vintage* caused a huge stir, as was to be expected from a magazine with a circulation of 500,000 copies. With a photo that big, there was no way Riko wouldn't be affected. Customers recognised her and struck up conversations, friends called her, and publishers' sales reps brought it up. Even the old lady next door commented, "Riko, you're amazing!"

Only her father remained unfazed. When she showed him the article, he just gave a muted "Hmph", barely glancing at it. While his indifference was a little deflating, it did come as something of a relief. She would have felt even more overwhelmed if even her dad had started making a fuss about it.

The worst part was that, whether because of the article or due to some prodding from Hitotsuboshi Press, newspapers and TV stations had started reaching out to her for interviews.

"I think this is being blown out of proportion. I absolutely *don't* want to go on TV."

But her opinion didn't matter. Headquarters had given a clear directive – "Use this opportunity to promote the store. Go all out."

When she did the interview with *Vintage*, she had been honest. "This isn't my achievement. The publisher asked me about a book the younger staff were excited about, so I recommended it. That's all."

But in the final article, her words had been twisted into something entirely different. Out of the hour she had spent talking, they only printed two sentences – "Some books have an aura about them, and when you work in a bookstore and see new releases every day, you start to develop a sixth sense. I had a gut feeling this was going to be a big one."

Sure, she *had* said something about books having an aura. But that last sentence was pure invention.

It left a bad taste in her mouth. Was the whole point of that interview just to cherry-pick quotes that fit the writer's narrative?

She couldn't help but wonder what Nojima and Hatakeda thought about all this. Being the only one getting media attention felt awkward. Lately, she couldn't shake the feeling that there was a subtle sting in their words when they spoke to her. Tsujii, the fourth-floor supervisor, had started making comments like, "Nishioka really knows how to work the system," which felt more like a jab than a compliment. Was he jealous that she was the one getting noticed? Even Nojima seemed slightly more distant than before. Just yesterday, he and Hatakeda had gone out drinking, without inviting her. That had never happened before.

"I saw the magazine, Nishioka!" sounded a voice behind her.

It was Kurihara, a regular customer. She was probably in her sixties, and she stopped by a few times a month, always buying a small stack of books. Wealthy, well-read, with a taste for world literature, she was a perfect example of the clientele in this upscale neighbourhood. She preferred classics and books with established literary value over bestsellers.

Customers like her were the majority on weekdays, so books sold off the shelves more than from the display tables. Weekends, however, were a different story. Young visitors drawn to Kichijoji's lively atmosphere came in droves, and bestsellers and trendy books on display would fly off the tables.

The sharp contrast in customer base made shelving decisions tricky.

Personally, Riko valued the weekday regulars more. Weekend shoppers were often one-time visitors, but locals came back repeatedly and spent more overall. That was why she wasn't keen on overloading the store with flashy promotional signs – they felt out of place in a bookstore catering to serious readers.

Most of those customers were true book lovers, with well-defined tastes. Too many promotional signs pushing the staff's opinions might feel like an intrusion, limiting their freedom of choice. And so, instead of plastering the store with eye-catching tags, Riko preferred a more subtle approach – curating the selection so people could naturally gravitate towards what interested them.

Besides, putting up a sign meant drawing attention to one book at the expense of another. Was it really a bookseller's job to decide which books deserved the spotlight?

She wasn't a literary critic. She didn't read systematically or in large volumes – ten books a month was her best. And even then, she read them at her own pace, skimming when she felt like it. There was no way she could compete with professionals. Academics, critics and translators often visited the store – what would they think of a clumsy, self-important recommendation tag?

"My husband subscribes to *Vintage*, and he knows I shop here, so he showed me the article. And then I saw you! I had no idea you were so well known."

Here we go again. Riko suppressed a sigh.

She was getting tired of these conversations. But Kurihara was a valued customer, so she flashed her a polite smile.

"Oh, not at all. The journalist exaggerated things."

"Still, they wouldn't print anything untrue, would they? I'm so thrilled for you! You've always been so helpful. I even bragged to my husband about knowing you!"

She spoke with the refined, gentle manner of a housewife hailing from a good family, and her innocent smile only made Riko feel more awkward.

"It's embarrassing. I was just doing my job. But they made such a big deal out of it."

She meant that. Finding and recommending good books was simply what a bookseller did. There was no need for all this fanfare.

Then again, the reality was that a bookseller's efforts were only noticed when a publisher picked them up and used them for marketing. Sales reps, too. "Look, this store featured the book prominently, and now it's selling like crazy!" They loved to include that sort of thing in their pitches. Yes, it was their job, and Riko had grown used to it. It just irked her that people equated recognition with good work, as if a job well done only mattered if it was publicised.

"Well, it was a nice article. Do you have the book in stock?"

"It's actually coming out next week."

"I can't wait. Save me a copy, will you?"

"Of course. Though, to be honest, it might not be your style . . ."

Riko hesitated. She knew her customers' tastes, and Kurihara was on the conservative side, leaning more towards classic female authors like Austen and Dinesen.

"It was originally a children's book, so it might be more suited for casual readers. But I do have something I think you'd really enjoy . . ."

She led Kurihara towards the world literature section.

The truth was, *Until Your Voice Reaches Me* wasn't something Riko would typically read. Yes, it had an engaging plot and appealing characters, and it would definitely attract a devoted fan base. From a marketing standpoint, it certainly had potential. That was why she had given it prominent placement. But if she were honest, she found the themes shallow and the writing unremarkable. It wasn't her kind of book.

Still, personal taste didn't matter. A bookseller's job was to recognise what would sell and promote it accordingly. That was the difference between a bookseller and a critic. Critics had to stand by their opinions, while booksellers didn't sign their recommendation displays and could remain anonymous. They didn't need to justify their choices. Some stores put up recommendation signs for books the staff hadn't even read.

It was all about sales. If one book didn't take off, they would push another. That flexibility was what made bookselling unique.

But now, with all this media attention, people would assume this title reflected her personal taste.

She didn't want her regular customers to think that.

I knew I should have turned it down, she thought with a sinking feeling.

Too late now.

11

"Hey, did you hear? Nishioka's going to be the new manager."

"Wait, seriously? What about Nojima?"

"They're saying he's being promoted to headquarters."

"Makes sense. He's related to the president, after all. Guess it was only a matter of time."

Listening to the part-timers gossiping in the locker room, Aki felt a wave of unease fall over her. Yesterday, the full-time employees had been called into the office, where Nojima had broken the news. It wasn't official yet, but he would be stepping down by the end of the month, and Nishioka would be taking over. He had asked everyone to support her as she led the store forward.

Pegasus Books had close to twenty locations in the Tokyo area, but this would be the first time a woman was made store manager. Maybe it had something to do with the success of *Until Your Voice Reaches Me* – the book Nishioka endorsed had just come out in paperback and quickly became a massive hit. If that was the reason for her promotion, though, it felt pretty unfair. After all, it was Mami and the other part-timers who had first noticed the book's potential, and they were still stuck making hourly wages.

And then there was the issue of what would happen to *her* once Nishioka was in charge. The only reason she had managed to keep her job for as long as she had was because Nojima had her back. But with him gone, there would be no-one left to protect her.

"I'm heading out."

After changing out of her uniform, Aki left the locker room, took the service lift down to the ground floor and stepped outside. It was mid-September, but summer heat still filled the air. The moment she left the building, a wave of humidity wrapped itself around her.

She was on the early shift today, so it wasn't even five o'clock yet. What now? She had no plans for the evening. Going straight home didn't appeal to her either – Nobumitsu wouldn't be back until late. Lately, he had been coming home at two or three in the morning. There was no point making dinner just for herself. Maybe she could grab a takeaway bento from the station?

Their apartment was one stop from Kichijoji on the JR line, in Nishi-Ogikubo. Unlike the bustling commercial hub around the bookstore, it was a quiet residential area. The small roundabout in front of the station was lined with banks, cafés and real estate offices. Narrow shopping streets stretched out from there, packed with old-fashioned stores, along with the occasional trendy café or vintage shop catering to local students. Surrounding it all was a neighbourhood of stately homes – some charmingly aged wooden houses, others sleek, modern designs by famous architects. It was the kind of place you could wander through for hours, just admiring the buildings.

Back when Nobumitsu had more free time, they would take long walks together, pointing out houses they liked. The area was great for shopping, too. They had both fallen in love with the neighbourhood.

Now that she thought about it, maybe Nobumitsu had bought the apartment *because* she told him she liked the area. One day, out of the blue, he had asked her to come look at a place with him. He hadn't told her where they were going – just picked her up and drove her there.

She loved it the moment she set eyes on it. And that was when he turned to her and said, "Why don't we live here together?"

That was his proposal.

They had only been dating for three months.

Rumours flew all about when Aki first started dating Nobumitsu. Everyone assumed she was the one who pursued him, but that wasn't true. From the very beginning, he had been the one setting the pace.

"I'd love to exchange industry insights with someone from a bookstore. Let's grab drinks sometime." That was how he made his move at the book signing where they first met.

Getting to know someone in publishing wasn't a bad idea – especially an editor. She figured it couldn't hurt. At first, they went out in a group – a few people from Nobumitsu's editorial team plus Mami and Mita. She had invited Mita as a buffer, hoping to keep things strictly professional. But after that first outing, he never joined again.

She wondered why. Maybe it was because Nobumitsu was obviously interested in her, and the fact that he and the other editors were around the same age she was, too. They all worked in the same field, so the conversation naturally revolved around comics – something Mita, being the oldest and with no interest in manga comics, might have felt left out of.

At first, she only met Nobumitsu in group settings. But he soon started inviting just her out – suggesting movies, concerts, any excuse to spend time alone. It was clear he had feelings for her. He was easy-going and always had a smile on his face, which made it hard for things to feel overtly romantic, but he was fun to be around, like an old school friend.

Still, at that point, Aki liked Mita more. So, she brushed off Nobumitsu's advances, keeping things friendly and hinting at her feelings for Mita whenever possible.

Then one day, after dealing with a particularly awful customer complaint that left her utterly exhausted, Nobumitsu called, and she found herself venting.

"I'm just so tired. I need a change of scenery."

"How about a drive to the coast?" he offered lightly.

It was already nine in the evening, and she still had another hour left on her shift, so she declined. But when she got off work at ten, there he was, with his car. Before she knew it, they were headed to Odaiba.

They stopped by Umihotaru, had dinner at a restaurant, and then he drove her home. By the time she got back, it was three in the morning. But he never tried anything, never pressured her – just smiled and said, "See you," before driving off.

That night, she was simply happy – grateful for his kindness, for how effortlessly he had lifted her spirits.

It wasn't until later she found out, through one of his co-workers, that Nobumitsu had been pulling an all-nighter the day before, and barely slept before heading straight into work the next morning. On top of that, his place was in Nishi-Kasai, near Chiba, while she lived in Kunitachi – meaning he had driven more than an hour out of his way just to take her home.

When she heard that, her stomach twisted.

She realised she might be falling for him.

So, she went to Mita.

"What should I do?" she asked. "Obata keeps asking me out. He's a great guy, and if this keeps up, I think I might end up with him."

She had wanted Mita to tell her not to. If he had just said, *Don't do it,* she would have stopped seeing Nobumitsu then and there.

But Mita said nothing.

Worse, he started avoiding her altogether.

She had no idea why. As far as she could tell, he had lost interest. Meanwhile, Nobumitsu only grew bolder, and Aki stopped pushing him away.

Deep down, she kept hoping Mita would say *something*. But he never did.

That was around the time people at the bookstore started whispering she was two-timing him. Mita never confronted her about it, and she kept seeing Nobumitsu. Then, one day, he asked her to go on a trip with him.

She knew what he meant. He wanted their relationship to move past friendship.

That was when she made up her mind – she had to talk to Mita.

She could still remember it like it was yesterday. She had invited him out to a café they used to frequent, a place called Kugutsuso. It was Mita's favourite spot – quiet, old-fashioned, and one of the few cafés that still allowed smoking. He often went there to read after work.

He showed up twenty minutes late, looking pale and tense. He slumped into the seat across from her with an exhausted sigh.

"Sorry I'm late."

Without looking at her, he muttered a curt order to the waitress, "A strong blend."

Aki had spent the whole day rehearsing what to say. But seeing Mita's face, she decided to be direct.

"Nobumitsu asked me to go on a trip with him. What do you think?"

She watched as Mita lit a cigarette, moving as if he had already anticipated this conversation. He took a slow drag, then exhaled a stream of smoke, his brow furrowing slightly.

The girls at work always gushed about how good he looked smoking, and for the first time, she understood why. Something about the way he held the cigarette between his long fingers, the quiet, brooding way he carried himself – it only made him seem more unreachable.

The waitress brought his coffee, but he didn't touch it. He just sat there, half-hidden in the dim light, blending into the moody atmosphere of the café.

Aki broke the silence.

"What should I do?"

Mita didn't so much as glance at her. "Do whatever you want."

She frowned. "Come on, you *know* what he means by that. Are you really okay with this?"

Her voice cracked slightly.

"I thought we were together," she said. "Are you really fine with me being with someone else?"

"What about you?" he asked. "Do *you* want to go?"

She hesitated. "I mean . . ."

She didn't want to say it outright. But if he told her not to go, she wouldn't.

Mita saw right through her.

"Do you want me to stop you?" he asked, his voice cold.

She did. She really did.

But the way he said it – so distant, so indifferent – made it impossible for her to admit.

So, she said nothing.

"Come on, admit it. You *want* to go. You just can't say it because of how you feel about me."

"That's not true!" she blurted, her voice louder than she expected.

But *was* it untrue? She couldn't say for certain. Maybe Mita was right. Her voice must have carried all through the quiet café, as she noticed a couple of university students at a nearby table glancing in their direction.

"What *do* you want? Do you want me to fight Obata for you? Do you want me to physically keep him away?"

"No," she said firmly.

That wasn't what she wanted – she knew that much. She just wanted to know how Mita really felt about her.

They had been dating for three years, and not once had he ever told her he loved her. She had tried teasing it out of him before – laughing, playfully demanding he say it when they were in bed together – but even then, he never did. And after all this time, that uncertainty had never gone away. She still didn't know if he truly loved her, or if he was just going along with their relationship out of habit.

"You're being unfair, Aki," Mita said. "You want me to decide for you. But this is *your* problem."

"My problem?"

"Are you staying with me, or are you leaving me for Obata? That's your call, not mine."

"But what about *your* feelings?" she asked desperately. "Don't you care about me? Why won't you stop me?"

"My feelings? They don't matter, do they? If you really wanted to be with me, you wouldn't even be considering Obata. You wouldn't be weighing your options like this. The fact that you're torn means you already have feelings for him. And you feel guilty about it, don't you? You're the one who wanted to be with me in the first place, but now you're thinking about walking away."

His words cut deep. He was right – she had used Obata to test Mita's feelings. But she had only done that because she loved him. Because she truly, deeply loved him.

"I love you. But I don't understand you. I never have. And that's what scares me. What do I mean to you? Why did you want to be with me in the first place?"

She had wanted to ask him that for so long, but she had been too afraid of the answer. Her hands trembled slightly as she picked up her coffee cup.

"Does it even matter anymore?" Mita let out a frustrated sigh.

"Yes, it does! I've been anxious about this for years."

This was how it always was with him. The closer she tried to get, the further he pulled away, like a skittish cat slipping just out of reach. No matter how much she wanted to understand him, he never let her in.

"So that's why you're drawn to Obata?" he said flatly.

She froze. She wanted to argue, to deny it, but no words came out. Maybe he was right. But that wasn't what she wanted to hear from him.

"Forget about me," she said, mustering her energy. "Tell me what *you* feel. That's what I want to know."

"It doesn't matter how I feel. Your feelings have already changed. There's nothing left to do."

His detached tone crushed her.

He felt so far away. He was sitting right in front of her, and yet he felt utterly out of reach.

To him, she already belonged to the past.

A solitary tear slid down her cheek.

For the first time, Mita looked surprised.

"Why are you crying?" he asked. "*You're* the one who wants to be with someone else. *I'm* the one getting left behind. There's nothing for you to feel sad about. You get to be with the man you want."

"Are you angry at me?"

If only he would yell, if only he would curse at her, or hit her, even. Anything would be better than this cold indifference.

"No," he said simply. "I just hate that we're having this conversation *here*."

His voice was eerily calm.

"There's no point talking about it anymore."

Without another word, he picked up the bill and walked to the register.

Aki could only sit there, frozen.

The apartment building was easy to spot with its warm terracotta-tiled exterior. A black wrought-iron fence with an antique design enclosed the property. Inside, the entrance hall had orange walls, and a fixed stained-glass window let in a cascade of soft, colourful light. Even the lift, with its transparent doors, had a retro touch.

Their apartment was on the fourth floor, at the very end of the hallway to the right after stepping out of the lift. Aki unlocked the door and stepped inside. The air was cool and still. She made her way to the living room.

On the table, a half-finished cup of coffee sat forgotten, while the newspaper was scattered across the floor. Nobumitsu must have left in a hurry this morning. Aki picked up the pages, folded them neatly, and tucked them into the rack.

Nobumitsu had rushed into marriage because he knew his job was about to get that much more demanding.

"We're finally getting serious, Aki. I can't stop worrying you might leave me if we stop seeing each other so much."

He had a colleague at work who barely saw his wife during the chaotic launch of a new magazine, and when he finally went home after weeks of non-stop activity, she was gone – along with all her stuff. "That kind of thing happens a lot in this industry," Nobumitsu had joked. But deep down, Aki suspected he was more afraid of her ending up back with Mita if he got too busy. He must have thought marriage would offer some insurance against that possibility.

Aki appreciated his honesty, so she said yes. After her painful break-up with Mita, there was something comforting about Nobumitsu's more straightforward approach. He wasn't mysterious or distant – he made an effort, always trying to hold her attention. It was sort of cute, like a puppy wagging its tail. With him, she could imagine a bright, happy life. Mita, on the other hand ... She admired him so much, but half the time, she couldn't even figure out what he was thinking.

That uncertainty had been part of the thrill, though.

With Nobumitsu, they laughed at the same things, and

they got annoyed at the same things, too. Being with him felt as natural as hanging out with an old university friend. For a lifelong partner, maybe that was the better choice.

But Nobumitsu's work schedule turned out to be even worse than she expected. He had insisted he wouldn't be like his co-worker – that no matter how late he finished, he would always come home. And technically, he did. Plenty of his colleagues slept at the office, so even if he dragged himself home at dawn, he was still making an effort. But his schedule didn't line up with hers one little bit.

At first, Aki tried to stay up and wait for him. Or she would go to bed but make sure to wake up and keep him company when he got home. They were newlyweds, after all – if they didn't make time to talk now, when would they? But then Nobumitsu told her it was stressful knowing she was staying up for him. He didn't want to have to keep checking the clock at work, and he didn't want her to put her health at risk just to match his hours.

In truth, she felt the strain of trying to stay up for him, too. So, she stopped.

Now, she went to bed alone, and in the mornings, she left for work while he was still asleep. They might be able to exchange a few words when she worked late shifts, but otherwise, they were ships passing in the night. Even on weekends, he rarely had a full day off, and when he did, he spent most of it sleeping. Their conversations had dwindled to almost nothing.

This wasn't what marriage was supposed to be. It felt like they were mere room-mates.

She had told herself it didn't matter that they had only been together a short time before getting married, that they could take their time building a deeper connection. But if anything, they were seeing each other less now than before the wedding. Nobumitsu kept insisting his work situation would settle down once the launch was over – but would it really?

Aki sank into the couch.

Was this okay? Could they still call themselves a married couple if they never saw each other?

Maybe she wouldn't be feeling this way if her own work was going well, but that wasn't the case, either. No matter what she did, something was always going wrong. The harassment hadn't stopped, and now that Nishioka was about to become manager, her situation was only going to get worse.

Maybe she should just transfer to another bookstore?

But she had secured this job through a connection, so quitting wasn't an option without a solid reason.

Ugh. What a hassle. It feels like I'm going nowhere.

The more she thought about it, the worse she felt. Heaving a long, tired sigh, she let herself fall sideways on the couch, burying her face in the cushions.

12

Riko received her official promotion notice in the first week of September. That morning, Nojima called her into the conference room to read it aloud.

"Starting October first, you'll be Pegasus Books' first female store manager. Good luck!" he said in his usual calm tone.

"Thank you."

She had worked five years as a part-timer and fifteen as a full-time employee. It wasn't like she had been desperately chasing after advancement, but this promotion served as recognition of all her hard work – and more practically, it meant a higher salary. And of course, after spending her entire career as a bookseller, she had always wanted to try running a store. She was curious to see how far she could go.

She had finally made it. A new step forward.

The frustration that had been weighing on her mind suddenly lifted. A fresh challenge, a new perspective – this was what she needed.

"I'll announce it to everyone at this morning's staff meeting," Nojima said.

"Thank you," Riko replied, bowing slightly.

Nojima, meanwhile, was being reassigned to the company's systems department. Riko had spent her entire career in this store, watching managers come and go. Some were great. Some were terrible. Nojima had been one of the better ones.

Would *she* be a good manager? Would her team respect her? This was where the real challenge began.

"Congratulations!"

Shiho Ozaki was the first to speak. A moment later, the others tapped their glasses together with a sharp clink.

A few days had passed since Riko's promotion was announced, and tonight, she was celebrating with five close colleagues at their go-to izakaya bar, Momokichi. In a place like Kichijoji, full of trendy bars and restaurants, this spot stood out for being cheap, serving great food and staying open until midnight – perfect for stopping by after work. Practical rather than stylish, it was the kind of place Riko and her team liked most.

"Thanks."

"We're ready to order!" someone called out.

The table quickly filled with requests – garlic-spiced grilled chicken thighs, fried chicken cartilage, minced meat cutlets, a green salad, and cucumbers with pickled ginger and plum. Bookselling was a physically demanding job, and this group knew how to eat and drink.

"You're the first female store manager in company history, Nishioka. You're our guiding star!" Ozaki said with a grin.

"The store's only going to get better with you leading it. Pegasus Books wouldn't be what it is without you," chimed in Shoko Yamane.

Riko knew they were just flattering her, but she couldn't help but feel good about it.

"So, now that you're manager, who's going to take over the third floor?" Ozaki asked, a little more seriously.

"Yeah, it can't be you, Ozaki," Yamane teased. "Don't they need a full-time employee? In that case . . . maybe Obata?"

Besides Riko, there were only three other full-time employees – Tsujii, the fourth-floor supervisor, Hatakeda, who oversaw the fifth, and Aki Obata. Riko had been in charge of the third floor up until now, but managing the whole store and supervising a floor at the same time wasn't realistic. Normally, Aki would be the obvious choice.

"She's not quite ready to take that on," Riko answered. "We'll either have to transfer in another full-time employee or have Hatakeda take over."

Ozaki's face immediately relaxed. Riko understood why. Ozaki *hated* Aki. The last thing she wanted was for Aki to end up supervising the floor she worked on. And to be honest, Riko wasn't inclined to hand her the section she had worked so hard to improve, either.

Just then, the food arrived, bringing a temporary end to the conversation as plates and chopsticks were passed around. Once everyone had served themselves, Yamane dived back in.

"Who's going to be the new assistant manager? I didn't see anything about that in the announcement."

"That's true. I wonder what their plans are . . ."

Riko was a bit worried on that score. Typically, an assistant manager would be appointed at the same time as the store manager, but so far, only her promotion – and Nojima's transfer – had been made official.

"Actually," she said, "I was thinking about pushing for some of the contract employees to be promoted to full-time."

Ozaki's face immediately flushed, and Riko doubted it was

from the alcohol. They all knew that if anyone was getting promoted next, it would be either her or Takahiko Mita. However, the company hadn't promoted a contract employee in years. Now that Nojima was leaving, reducing the number of full-timers, Riko wanted to push for both of them to be promoted.

"Has headquarters said anything about that?" Yamane asked, leaning in with interest.

"Not yet," Riko admitted. "I'll have to discuss it with them soon."

She had already started transition meetings with Nojima, but whenever she brought up the new store structure, he brushed her off. "Sort it out with HQ once you're officially manager," he kept saying.

That didn't sit right with her.

Nojima had been dropping by headquarters on an almost daily basis, and she had a feeling he knew something he wasn't telling her.

"Well, Yamada should be dropping by from headquarters tomorrow, so I'm sure we'll have a chance to talk about it then," he said, brushing her off.

Nojima had seemed oddly distant ever since the transfer was decided. And it wasn't just him – Tsujii and Hatakeda were acting strangely as well, holding secretive discussions and keeping her out of the loop. They hadn't invited her out for drinks in ages.

It used to be a tradition – once or twice a month, the four of them would go out for what they jokingly called Floor Supervisor Meetings. They were part strategy session, part casual venting, a chance to exchange ideas and keep up morale. But all of a sudden, she was no longer included.

Why? She was about to become store manager. She needed their support.

Even tonight, Ozaki had invited them, but they both turned her down, claiming they were too busy. That only made Riko more uneasy.

"Hey, Nishioka, need a refill?" Ozaki asked, noticing her empty glass.

"Thanks."

Ozaki waved over the waiter to order another beer.

"Hope that promotion works out for you, as well," Yamane said, giving Ozaki a nudge.

Riko hadn't said who she planned to recommend for a full-time promotion, but everyone seemed to assume it would be Ozaki.

"Stop it." Ozaki swatted at Yamane's arm, but she looked pleased.

"Seriously," Riko added, smiling.

She didn't mind whether it was Ozaki or Mita. What mattered was getting someone she could trust in the role – someone who would have her back.

Riko scooped some instant coffee into a mug and waited for the water to boil. She figured she would grab a CalorieMate energy bar from the station kiosk on the way. She had overslept, and there was no time for a proper breakfast. Last night's little pre-celebration had got out of hand, and she was still reeling from the effects.

Today, however, was her first day as store manager. She couldn't afford to be late. On top of that, an executive from headquarters was coming at eleven. She had a lot to discuss – who would replace her as assistant manager, whether they could finally promote some of the contract employees, and more. She needed to get her act together.

Normally, her father would check in on her if she slept in. Today, however, he seemed to have overslept himself. He had gone out with an old co-worker yesterday – hiking, apparently. Takao or Ome, maybe? It was great to see him getting out of the house, but he looked exhausted when he got home. He had been saying his blood pressure was high lately, so she hoped he hadn't pushed himself too hard.

She wished she could have prepared dinner before heading out, but there was no time for that. Instead, she threw on a scarf, finished her coffee without bothering to add milk and called up the stairs, "I'm going! I've got the early shift, so I'll be back by evening!"

And then—

A strange noise, something between a groan and a garbled murmur, sounded from the second floor.

Riko froze. Was that her father?

"Dad?"

She bolted up the stairs.

"Dad!"

She threw open his bedroom door – and gasped.

He was lying collapsed on the futon, face-down, his head turned slightly towards the door. He must have been in the middle of getting dressed, as his pyjama top was half off.

"R-R-Riko . . ."

His voice was slurred, strangled.

"Dad!"

She rushed to his side, grabbing him.

"What's wrong?! Are you okay?!"

"I . . . I . . . I . . ."

He was trying to talk, but his body wouldn't cooperate.

"What is it? What are you trying to say?"

She took his hand and squeezed it hard – but he didn't squeeze back. His fingers were limp.

"I . . . I can't move . . ."

The words came out in a strained whisper.

"What do you need? Hey. What should I do?"

Riko's mind went blank.

What was she supposed to do? What was happening to him?

". . . Ta . . . Taka . . ." he groaned.

"Taka?"

". . . Takami . . ."

"Ah, Takami Clinic! You mean Dr Takami!"

Her dad didn't answer, but there was a flicker of relief on his face.

Takami Clinic was his go-to doctor's practice. He had been a loyal patient there for more than thirty years. Even for problems that should have been handled by an internalist – colds, stomach aches, and the like – he always went to Dr Takami. In fact, he had gone there just the other day to pick up his blood pressure medication.

"I'll call him!"

Riko flew down the stairs, grabbed the phone, and started flipping through the address book. Her dad was meticulous about keeping his contacts organised. There it was – *Takami Clinic*. There was even a listing for Dr Takami's home number.

Fortunately, the doctor picked up right away.

Riko rushed to explain what was happening.

"Call an ambulance. Now," he said immediately. "It sounds like something with the blood vessels in his brain."

"Huh?"

Something was wrong with his brain . . .?

Her mind raced through a list of terrifying words – brain haemorrhage, stroke, aneurysm, cerebral infarction.

All of them were life-threatening.

Even if he survived, there could be paralysis, or memory loss – permanent damage. If something like that happened to him . . .

"His blood pressure was over one hundred and sixty when he came in the other day," Dr Takami continued. "I warned him to be careful, but—"

The doctor's voice dragged her back to her senses.

"I – I understand. I'll call an ambulance right away."

Her voice was shaking.

"Riko. Do you know the emergency number?" Dr Takami asked gently. "Say it out loud for me."

"I, uh, um . . ."

For a split second, she was offended. *Of course* she knew it. Didn't she? It was 110. No . . . Wasn't that the police?

"It's 119," the doctor said. "Take a deep breath. Now, hang up and call them."

He could tell, just from her voice, how panicked she was.

"Thank you," she managed before slamming the phone down, her hands fumbling again for the dial pad.

The paramedics gave her father an injection as soon as they got him into the ambulance. He was sweating profusely and complaining of nausea, and since he hadn't eaten anything that morning, he ended up dry heaving, bringing up yellowish stomach bile.

When they arrived at the hospital, they wheeled him

straight to a room and hooked him up to an IV drip, while a doctor gave Riko a brief rundown of the situation and told her to wait while they prepared for a CT scan.

"Dad? Are you okay?"

He didn't answer, but he did manage to shift his body slightly and stretch his legs a little.

Riko let out a small breath of relief – at least he could move.

"I just need to call work for a minute," she told the attending nurse before stepping out of the room.

She had been in such a rush that she left her phone at home. Not that it really mattered – she wouldn't be able to use it inside the hospital, in any event. She made her way to the public phone near the nurses' station and called the store.

It was already past 9:30. The early shift should be in by now. After a few rings, someone picked up.

"*Pegasus Books, how can I help you?*"

She recognised the voice at once – Aki Obata. *Definitely* not the person she wanted to deal with right now.

"It's Nishioka. Is Tsujii or Hatakeda around?"

"*Hatakeda is on the sales floor. Do you want me to get him?*"

"Please."

After a short wait, Hatakeda answered.

"Sorry for calling so late, Hatakeda. My dad collapsed this morning, and we had to call an ambulance. I'm still at the hospital."

"*Oh . . . That sounds serious. Do they know what's wrong?*" he asked in his usual flat monotone.

"Not yet. They suspect a stroke, but he can move, so it might not be too bad. They're saying we should know more within the next twenty-four hours."

"*That's rough. So, you won't be coming in today?*"

"No . . . I feel terrible, especially since it's my first day as manager."

"Well, it's an emergency. Nothing you can do about it."

"They're still running tests, so I don't know how long I'll be here . . ."

"Right. Someone from HQ is supposed to be coming in at eleven. What should we do about that?"

"Sorry about this, but could you call Yamada and ask him to reschedule? I don't have his number with me, and I left my phone at home."

"What if he's already on his way?"

"Then just apologise and try to get as much information from him as you can."

"I'll see what I can do."

"I'll call again later today."

With that, she hung up. At least work was taken care of for now.

She had wanted to give a speech at the morning meeting to introduce herself properly as the new manager. But that could wait.

Right now, all she cared about was her father.

Praying he would be okay, she headed back to his hospital room.

"Hey, Aki? I just heard something crazy!"

Aki was busy shelving the latest shipment of magazines when Mami came rushing over, looking far too excited for this time of day.

"Hmm? What happened?"

She kept her hands moving as they talked. It was always a

challenge to fit the endless stream of new magazines into the limited display space.

"You know Shibata from Hitotsuboshi Press? The guy who recently had a shotgun wedding with that woman who works under him?"

"Of course. He's helped us out a lot over the years . . ."

Shibata was the deputy sales manager at her husband's company. Even before Aki and Nobumitsu got married, he had always been on good terms with both of them.

"What about him? Did something happen?"

As she spoke, Aki was trying to decide which to keep on display – a scandalous tell-all about in-law drama or a women's comic based on fairy tales. Both were about the same thickness.

"Apparently, before he got married . . . he was dating Nishioka!"

"Wait – Nishioka? You mean *our* Nishioka?"

"Yep! Can you believe it?"

"No way."

Aki's hands froze mid-task. Shibata and Nishioka? That was a combination she hadn't remotely considered before. They had never shown anything to so much as suggest it – not even once.

"Seems like they were keeping it a secret. But in the end, he dumped her," Anna, who had been listening in, added with a grin.

"Where did you hear this?" Aki asked casually, fighting to keep her hands busy.

Mami and Anna continued stacking the magazines alongside her.

"There's a publishing industry chatroom online. It's a hot

topic right now. I mean, she *has* been getting a lot of media attention lately."

"But this was a while ago, right?"

"Not really. Turns out Shibata was two-timing her. When the shotgun wedding was announced, Nishioka totally lost it. Word is, she even started borderline stalking him."

"Stalking him?"

Riko? She was as composed as they came. That didn't sound at all like her.

"This all happened around the time of your wedding, Aki. That's probably why she was acting so weird about it. She must have been lashing out because her own relationship had just crashed and burned."

"Oh yeah, she was really on edge back then. So that's what it was – she got dumped!" Anna giggled.

Aki, however, felt downcast. It was a brutal story. For someone like Nishioka, who carried herself with so much confidence and pride, getting tossed aside for a younger woman had to be humiliating. Of course she wouldn't want anyone to know.

And yet, that was what made it such prime gossip material. People loved to savour others' misfortunes.

"You two should keep this to yourselves," Aki said, lowering her voice. "You got it from the internet, so who knows if it's true? And if she finds out you've been spreading rumours about her, she's going to be furious."

"Oh . . . Yeah, you're right."

Mami suddenly looked like a naughty kid caught in the act. She had clearly expected Aki to find the story just as amusing as she did.

But Aki didn't feel like laughing along. It was a nasty

piece of gossip, and no matter how she felt about Nishioka as a boss, dragging someone's love life through the mud felt like crossing a line. She knew first-hand how awful it was to have people speculate about her own relationship with Mita. She didn't want to do the same thing to someone else. Even if that someone was Riko Nishioka.

Just then, the store's speakers crackled to life to signal opening time.

"Oh, wow, is it that late already?"

"Just in time."

Aki shoved the last magazine into place.

"I'll go and put the cart away," Mami said, hurrying off to stash it in the back.

"Welcome!"

Anna greeted their first customer of the day – a young man in wire-rimmed glasses, wearing a plain Uniqlo T-shirt and jeans. Aki recognised him immediately.

Oh. Him again.

He was a regular, coming in once or twice a week. He wasn't interested in comics – his passion was light novels. He would show up first thing in the morning and stay until evening, standing and reading the whole time.

"I'll take the register," Anna said, walking off.

Aki sighed.

What a lousy way to start the day.

Still unsettled by the conversation, she slowly made her way to the counter.

13

"Where the hell is Nishioka?" barked Takayuki Watanabe, the executive director of General Affairs from headquarters, his chin jutting out arrogantly.

"Where is she?" Nobuo Yamada, the head of Human Resources, stood beside him, mirroring his bad mood with his own protruding chin.

The two of them had shown up right on schedule, only to find that Riko was nowhere to be seen. Their indignation was immediate.

"It seems she's called in absent today," Hatakeda answered, apologetic.

Since headquarters was sending someone over, he, Tsujii and Aki – being the only full-time employees – had come out to meet them.

"Why?" Watanabe snapped. "This is her first day as store manager. Why the hell would she be absent *today* of all days? She knew I was coming, didn't she? And she didn't even leave a message?"

His tone was pure frustration, the kind that would make a weaker subordinate shrink back on the spot. Watanabe was one of those bosses who grovelled to his own superiors but treated everyone below him like dirt.

"Well?" Yamada pressed – but unlike Watanabe, his voice was high and grating, taking away some of the intimidation factor.

"I haven't heard anything. Have you, Tsujii?"

"I'm not sure. Did she say anything to you, Obata?"

Aki shook her head. Not surprising – Nishioka had been avoiding any contact with her, so there was no way she would have left a message with her.

"What's going on with her? Is this a frequent occurrence?"

"Not ... exactly," Hatakeda said vaguely, as if trying to imply it *had* happened before.

"Maybe she's just running late? They had a little pre-celebration for her promotion last night, after all."

Tsujii's comment was hard to read – was he defending her, or trying to insinuate something?

"Hmph. So, she had too much to drink? What a cushy life." Watanabe practically spat out the words. "This is why women shouldn't be store managers. They're pushy, arrogant, and have zero sense of responsibility."

"Honestly." Yamada nodded in sync like a bobblehead. He was Watanabe's little lapdog, always sticking close to him.

Tsujii and Hatakeda didn't say anything, but Aki couldn't fail to notice the faint smirks on their faces. They were clearly pleased to see Nishioka taking the heat.

"Actually," Aki spoke up, "she did call in this morning. I answered and passed it to Hatakeda. Didn't she tell you anything?"

She wasn't about to let that sexist remark slide, and Hatakeda's smug expression was pissing her off no end.

Hatakeda visibly flinched, caught off guard. "Uh . . . Oh, right. Yeah, she did call. Said she wouldn't be coming in today. She seemed flustered, hung up quickly, didn't really give a reason . . ."

The way he acted, like he had only just now remembered, added yet more fuel to Aki's suspicions. If that were true, then wasn't this just his own lapse in communication? But, of course, no-one pointed that out.

"Probably a hangover, then," Watanabe sneered.

"That would make the most sense," Yamada agreed, eager to pin the blame on Riko.

"But if that's the case," Aki said, keeping her tone even, "wouldn't she have just said so? It's her first day as store manager – there has to be a real reason she couldn't come in. If she was so panicked she didn't have time to explain herself, then maybe something serious happened. Why don't I try calling her mobile?"

She herself couldn't say why she was sticking up for Nishioka. Maybe she just wanted to push back against Watanabe's smug, sexist attitude.

Hatakeda, playing it cool again, nodded. "That's a good idea."

Before Watanabe could say anything else, Aki pulled out her phone and dialled Nishioka's number. The call rang several times before going to voicemail. She was about to try again when Watanabe cut her off.

"Forget it. If she can't take the time to explain herself, she's not fit to be store manager. Tell her that."

With that, he stood up, clearly done with the conversation.

"Make sure she gets the message," Yamada echoed shrilly before scurrying after him.

*

"Don't you think it was awful, the way they treated her?" Aki asked Nobumitsu, who had come home early for once. "I mean, her father collapsed. He was in critical condition – and Hatakeda had the nerve to pull that kind of stunt. What the hell is wrong with him? How would *he* feel if someone treated him like that when one of his parents was in hospital?"

She was furious. They had finally got a call from Nishioka in the evening, explaining why she hadn't come in. Everyone at work knew she lived alone with her father, and given the circumstances, the women were all sympathetic. Most of them were single too, so the thought of dealing with a sick parent hit close to home.

But even after hearing what happened, Hatakeda and Tsujii acted like they simply didn't care. Aki was certain now – they had known the whole time and deliberately kept quiet.

"There's no way Hatakeda just forgot. The second I called him out, he panicked."

"Hmm," Nobumitsu murmured absentmindedly.

"And that guy, Watanabe, from headquarters? What a piece of work. Who does he think he is? The more incompetent a man is, the more he likes to throw his weight around. And saying crap like women aren't fit to be managers – what century does he think we're living in?"

Aki kept talking, but Nobumitsu just sipped his beer, looking bored. As she was busy in the kitchen, however, she remained oblivious to his expression.

"Yeah, well, people like that are everywhere," he said, poking at his cucumber salad with his chopsticks. "Idiots who think getting promoted makes them superior to everyone else. And the suck-ups who cling to them – they're no better."

"Well, yeah, I can see that."

"At the end of the day, they just don't like the idea of Nishioka becoming manager. Simple as that."

"You think so?"

"Of course. They can't stand the thought of a woman being in charge," Nobumitsu said, like it was the most obvious thing in the world.

"I guess that's it ... But still, Watanabe's an old man. Hatakeda's only in his thirties. You'd think *he'd* be more progressive."

She handed Nobumitsu a plate of grilled shishamo.

"Age has nothing to do with it. Most men just don't like being outranked by a woman. If she were way older than them, maybe they'd accept it. But it's a different story when it's someone their own age."

"Really?" Aki was surprised. "Do *you* feel that way?"

"I wouldn't say I'm against having a female boss ... But if I had one, I think it'd be a little awkward. I mean, I've never worked under one before."

He started eating his fish. Shishamo was one of his favourites.

"Even if she was really competent? Even if she had a great personality?"

"That's not the issue ... Women think differently, you know? And you have to be careful about what you say around them. It's a hassle. Plus, it's not like it's common. No-one really knows how to deal with it," he said casually, biting into a fish head.

Aki wasn't convinced. "I don't know about that. Isn't work supposed to be about skill?"

"Sure, they go on about meritocracy and gender equality, but that's all just for show. Take my company – there was this woman who was about to become editor-in-chief of a women's magazine, but out of nowhere, they reassigned her. No real reason for it. People say she got sabotaged just because she was a woman. The jealousy can get intense when a woman starts climbing the ladder. Guys can get really petty about that. Some will even make up rumours just to take her down. I don't think *I'd* go that far."

That reminded Aki of the gossip surrounding Riko and Shibata. Could the rumours floating around online be part of some kind of smear campaign?

"That's awful."

"Yeah, well, the company's struggling. There's even talk of lay-offs. So, the backstabbing is worse than usual."

"I've never been harassed by men too much. If anything, it's the women at work who don't like me."

As she spoke, she placed some chilled tofu in a bowl and started chopping the spring onions and ginger for garnish.

"Well, yeah," Nobumitsu said. "The guys don't see you as competition yet. You're still young."

His offhanded remark made Aki freeze for a second.

So . . . was she just invisible to them? Was she only getting by unscathed because she didn't matter yet?

"So, if I really put in the work, if I became a real threat to the guys at my job . . . you're saying they'll try to take me down?"

Like they were doing to Nishioka.

"Probably. When a woman climbs the ranks, even guys who normally hate each other decide to team up. Male jealousy is an ugly thing."

Nobumitsu stretched his arms and let out a yawn.

Aki, meanwhile, felt like she had been hit in the gut.

In the end, she was just like Nishioka. What had happened today could just as easily happen to her, too. For the first time, she saw herself in Riko.

"Are men really that obsessed with getting ahead?"

"Of course. Men are always competing with each other. Some of them will do anything to win, even if it means playing dirty."

As Aki placed the dish of cold tofu in front of him, Nobumitsu reached out to grab her wrist, pulling her close. Barely managing to set the dish on the table, she ended up losing her balance, falling into him as he wrapped his arms around her from behind.

"Come on, none of this affects you, does it? Forget about it. Let's skip dinner and go to bed," he whispered before pressing a kiss to the nape of her neck. His breath reeked of fish.

"You're gross." Aki grimaced. "I'm not in the mood."

She wriggled out of his grasp and went back to the kitchen.

Nobumitsu sighed. "Here we go again."

That night, Riko stayed at the hospital. After all, the doctor had told her the next twenty-four hours would be critical.

"If there weren't any clear warning signs before this, it's likely a transient ischemic attack rather than a full-blown stroke. But we can't say for certain yet. We need to monitor him closely for the next twenty-four hours. His life isn't in immediate danger, but if he has another attack or develops paralysis within that time, it could mean a long recovery."

The hospital had round-the-clock nursing care, so there was no need for her to stay. But after hearing that, she couldn't bring herself to go home. And so, she was brought a cot to sleep in her father's room, settling in for the night.

Even lying down, she couldn't sleep.

What's going to happen now?

She had heard the term *elder care*, of course, but she never could have imagined it would become her reality this soon. Her father was only sixty-eight. He was still strong, still independent. She had assumed he had plenty of time.

No – she *wanted* to believe he had plenty of time. She didn't want to think about him collapsing, about him getting sick. She wanted to believe he would always be okay.

But what if he wasn't? What if he ended up paralysed? Could she take care of him while working full-time? She was an only child, meaning it would all be on her. Would she have to put him into a home? And even if she did, weren't those places impossible to get into?

Stories of people struggling to care for their ageing parents – things she had heard from friends or read in the news – flashed through her mind.

Had this happened because she wasn't paying enough attention? And on the very day she became store manager . . .

Maybe this was karma. She had been so focused on work, neglecting her father. And now, here they were.

Should she have tried harder to get married after all? If she had someone to rely on, someone to talk to, maybe this wouldn't feel so overwhelming.

Her thoughts kept spinning around her head, making it impossible to sleep. It was only as dawn approached that exhaustion finally started to creep in. And then, what felt like moments later—

Clattering sounds echoed in the hallway.

"Good morning!" A cheerful young nurse opened the door, her bright voice filling the room.

"Morning," Riko mumbled, sitting up quickly. She wasn't in pyjamas, just a sweatshirt and sweatpants, so at least she didn't look completely unkempt, but she was still embarrassed to have been caught half-asleep.

"How are you feeling?" the nurse asked, peering at her father.

"Good morning," he replied, his voice clear and steady.

"Oh, you're looking much better! Your colour's good, too. I think you'll be just fine."

Riko hurried to his bedside. "Dad! How do you feel?"

"I'm fine."

His response was curt, but his eyes were sharp, and while his movements were a little stiff, he could still move his body.

Later that morning, the doctor came by on his rounds. "Looks like it was just a transient episode. He's not in any immediate danger. As long as there's no paralysis, he should be able to go home in about a week."

"When will we know for sure if there's any lasting damage?" Riko asked.

"We'll run some tests later, but from what I'm seeing, he's moving well. I think he'll be okay."

Hearing that from the doctor, the tension drained from Riko's body.

He was okay.

For now, at least, nothing had to change.

Her heart filled with something part gratitude, part relief. Before she knew it, she was breathing a long, deep sigh.

14

Riko headed to work that afternoon. She had already taken the day off on what was supposed to be her first day as store manager, so she figured she should at least make an appearance. She slipped out of the hospital at around three in the afternoon and made her way to the store.

Awaiting her was a report from Tsujii saying that Watanabe had come by the day before, got angry and stormed off.

She was annoyed to learn that Hatakeda hadn't handled things properly – but of course, today was *his* day off, so there was nothing she could do about that now. First and foremost, she needed to call headquarters and apologise.

"I'm very sorry about yesterday."

But before she could say anything more, Watanabe cut in. *"You think a phone call is enough? If you want to apologise, come and do it in person."*

Then – *click*. He hung up.

Typical Watanabe, she thought with a sigh. Among the executives at headquarters, he had a reputation for being short-tempered, nitpicky and impossible to please. And now she had managed to get on his bad side.

Still, couldn't he cut her some slack? Her father was in hospital, for crying out loud.

Trying to shake off her irritation, she turned to Tsujii at the desk in front of hers.

"Watanabe's in a bad mood for some reason. Do you mind if I step out for a bit?"

"It's business as usual today, so we should be okay."

"Good. Then I'll head over to HQ and apologise in person. I had better go smooth things over before it gets any worse."

"Maybe he just woke up on the wrong side of the bed. You know how he is."

"I hope so. Either way, I had better go now."

With that, she started getting ready to leave.

Riko pushed open the door to the General Affairs Department. Inside, close to a dozen people were working in silence, heads down and focused on their tasks. The room was always intimidatingly quiet.

At the very end, in the best spot for surveying the whole office, sat Watanabe, leaning back in his chair and barking into the phone.

"This is Watanabe. Who the hell are you?"

His voice cut through the silence of the shared office space.

"Huh? *Where* are you from? You seriously don't know who I am? I'm the managing director of Pegasus Books."

It sounded like he was calling someone outside the company.

"*Now* you get it. Good. Is Kamiya there? What? He's out? On a business trip? Fine. Tell him to call me when he gets back. Yeah, yeah. That's all."

With that, he slammed the receiver down.

Riko flinched. She couldn't help it – she had spent years

drilling into her team the importance of handling calls politely. Even when hanging up, they were expected to be courteous. And yet, here at headquarters, it was a different world.

"Hmph. So, you actually showed up," Watanabe snorted.

"I'm very sorry about yesterday," Riko said, trying to keep her voice steady. "The truth is my father collapsed and—"

"Spare me the excuses. Come with me."

He got up and strode towards the exit. Then, as if suddenly remembering something, he turned back.

"Yamada," he called, jerking his chin towards the man sitting closest to him.

Yamada, clearly expecting this, rose to his feet and fell in line behind him. Riko had no choice but to follow.

"Calling in sick with a hangover on your first day as manager? That's a hell of a way to start."

The moment Riko stepped into the conference room, Watanabe came at her without warning.

"With all due respect, I wasn't hung-over," she said, keeping her voice even. "My father collapsed at home yesterday morning. He had to be taken to the hospital by ambulance. It's just the two of us, so I had to stay with him and—"

Watanabe waved a dismissive hand, cutting her off. "Enough. That's your personal business. The issue is you didn't show up to work and you didn't bother to inform anyone."

"What? But I *did* call, from the hospital. I explained the situation to Hatakeda and asked him to contact headquarters to reschedule—"

"Nobody told *me* anything."

"Are you *sure* you called?" Yamada interjected, his tone sceptical.

"Yes. I left a message. It would have been around nine-thirty in the morning."

"Hatakeda, you say?"

Watanabe and Yamada exchanged glances.

"If there was a miscommunication, then Hatakeda must have forgotten to pass it on," Riko insisted. She hated throwing a colleague under the bus, but facts were facts.

"So, you're saying Hatakeda forgot to relay your message?"

"Yes."

"Well, that's strange," Yamada said, tilting his head. "Because Hatakeda claims you only told him you wouldn't be coming in. He never heard anything about your father."

"That's impossible. I called from the hospital – I was *very* clear about the reason." Riko could feel her blood beginning to boil. "Why would I hide something like that? It doesn't make any sense."

Watanabe smirked. "Then it's not just a communication issue. It's a leadership issue."

"Excuse me?"

"If your staff aren't passing along your messages, it means they don't respect you enough to follow your instructions. You've got a management problem."

"Exactly," Yamada added smoothly. "You don't seem very well-liked, do you?"

"That's—" Riko faltered. "I've only just been promoted, and as for my popularity . . ."

She was caught off guard by this unexpected turn of events. Only now did she realise she hadn't been called here to apologise for what had happened yesterday.

But before she could gather her thoughts, Watanabe leaned

in, lowering his voice to make it sound more menacing. "You know, we've been keeping an eye on you for a while."

"What do you mean?"

"You stand out too much. We approved those interviews, sure. But that wasn't so you could boost your own profile – it was for Pegasus Books. And yet, here we are. Now people are calling you a 'star bookseller', and it's made you too full of yourself."

Yamada tossed a magazine onto the table. A large photo of herself beamed up at her, next to one of the author of *Until Your Voice Reaches Me*.

"This wasn't my doing," Riko said quickly. "Hitotsuboshi Press arranged that without consulting me, and—"

Yamada ignored her. "We've also received multiple complaints about you."

"What?"

"Too strict. Self-righteous. Emotional. Unfair treatment of employees you don't like." He listed them off like he was reading from a report.

"Who said that?" Riko demanded, her voice unsteady. "Don't tell me Aki Obata . . .?"

Aki's name popped into her head at once.

"No," Yamada replied. "But apparently, you've been highly emotional when it comes to her. We even heard you got into a physical altercation with her."

"That's not—"

"But Obata herself hasn't said a word. Speaks to her breeding, doesn't it? Being the granddaughter of Chairman Kitamura and all. It was another employee who came forward. Said they couldn't stand watching you bully her."

"Besides," Watanabe added, "you've got a reputation. Talented, but inflexible. Attention-seeking."

The blood drained from Riko's face.

"You don't give your staff enough praise. You take credit for their accomplishments." Yamada kept going, oblivious to – or perhaps enjoying – her discomfort.

"Then why did you promote me?" Riko snapped, unable to hold back any longer. "If I'm such a problem, why make me store manager at all?"

She could feel the sting of tears threatening, a mix of shock, anger and humiliation.

"Well," Watanabe said, almost regretfully, "if it were up to us, we wouldn't have."

"The president saw that magazine article," Yamada added. "He thought having a female store manager would be *progressive*."

"Hey." Watanabe shot him a sharp warning glare.

Yamada flinched, shrinking back.

Riko sat frozen as the realisation sank in. She hadn't earned this promotion. It had been a whim – a decision made on impulse by the company president.

"Anyway," Watanabe continued, "there were plenty of objections, but in the end, the president insisted on letting you hold your position. For now."

"For now? What does *that* mean?"

Watanabe jerked his chin towards Yamada, signalling for him to take over.

Yamada cleared his throat dramatically. "Well, the company's been evaluating some internal restructuring due to declining performance. One option on the table is store closures and consolidation. And the Kichijoji branch is at the top of the list."

*

Riko was in a daze. Everything she had heard at headquarters was swirling around in her head.

In six months, the store would be closed. Until then, she was just a temporary manager, a placeholder.

That alone came as a shock. But what hit even harder was the fact that, before she had even started, headquarters had already decided she was unfit for the job. And worse, this wasn't just their own judgement. Someone – or more likely, several someones – from within the store had gone behind her back and reported her.

Who would do that? Did the staff really hate her that much? It *couldn't* have been just one person. But Yamada wouldn't give any names, which only made her more paranoid. Who was against her? Hatakeda, who had deliberately *forgotten* to relay her message? That much was obvious. But who else? Was Tsujii, Hatakeda's close friend, involved? Yamada had denied it, but Aki Obata still wasn't immune from suspicion.

Was *everyone* against her?

Before she realised it, she was back at the bookstore. She had intended to go to the hospital, but her feet had carried her to work purely by instinct.

"Are you okay, Nishioka? You look pale," Ozaki said, looking concerned as they passed each other. "You must be exhausted from taking care of your father."

"Thanks. Maybe I am." She smiled faintly in response, but right now, she didn't feel like talking. Not when she was questioning everyone around her. Was Ozaki truly on her side?

She went up to the fifth floor and stepped into the office. Inside, Takahiko Mita was sitting alone, searching for something on his computer. Riko went to her desk in the far corner. Mita kept working, not paying her any attention.

Suddenly, she had the urge to ask him.

Mita was serious and dedicated to his job. He only cared about books. He wasn't the type to gossip or scheme against his co-workers. There was no way he would have conspired with Hatakeda and Tsujii to push her out. If he knew something, he wouldn't lie about it.

Mita must have finished his search, as he stood up and headed for the door.

"Mita," she called after him in a raspy voice.

"What is it?" He turned towards her.

"Um . . . Can I ask you something?"

He gave her a puzzled look, prompting her to hesitate.

"Mita . . . Has anyone ever said anything about me? Like, that my attitude is a problem?"

"Why do you ask?"

Seeing how calm he was, Riko decided to lay it all out.

"Keep this between us, but someone went to HR and reported me. Apparently, they don't think I'm fit to be manager. HR wouldn't tell me who, but it seems to be more than one person . . . I can't get it out of my head."

"So, are they going to punish you or something?"

Mita sat in the chair beside her and looked her straight in the eye.

"No, not exactly . . ." She trailed off.

In a way, this temporary manager role did feel like a punishment.

"They just gave me a warning. But I never expected to be told something like that."

She trusted Mita, so she spoke honestly with him. She had taught him all about the job. She had looked out for him. She knew he wouldn't spread rumours or use this information against her.

"If you know anything, please tell me."

Mita thought for a moment.

"Now that you mention it . . . About a month ago, Nojima asked me something. He wanted to know if I thought you would make a good manager. And not just me – he asked a few others, as well."

Riko's stomach tightened.

"And? What did you say?"

Mita hesitated.

"Do I have to tell you?"

"Yes. Please."

"I said . . . that you're very competent at your job. But I also said that you can be emotional at times. That bringing personal likes and dislikes into work isn't appropriate."

His voice was steady, each word deliberate.

Riko felt like the air had been knocked out of her. She never imagined Mita of all people would see her that way.

"Why . . . ?"

"I'm sorry. But I've been wondering about the way everyone treats Aki – Obata, I mean. And it seemed like you were the one taking the lead on that."

He was calm and collected – like he had been wanting to say this for a while now.

"But she's so superficial, so unprofessional . . . And after everything with you—"

She stopped herself. She had assumed Mita still resented Aki for what had happened between them. That he would be the last person to defend her.

"That doesn't matter," he cut in sharply. "What happened

between Aki and me is our business. No-one else's. We both do our jobs. No-one has any right to criticise our private lives at work."

"But her attitude was disrupting the workplace . . ."

Riko tried to argue, but Mita cut her off.

"Disrupting the workplace?" His lips curled into something that wasn't quite a smile. "If anything, *you* were the one causing the disruption. It was obvious you had a personal grudge against her. This wasn't about me at all, was it? You just didn't like her. And you weren't the only one. *Everyone* was jealous of her. Because she's young. Because she's beautiful. Because she has everything."

He practically spat the words out. She had never seen Mita like this before. He was always calm, always composed – never angry.

"I hated it. The constant judgement, the gossip. People acting like they knew what was best. Saying Aki wasn't good enough for me. The truth is, *I* wasn't good enough for *her*. I'm just some guy with a shitty personality and a dead-end job."

It wasn't just what he said – it was the look in his eyes as he said it. That deep, almost suffocating darkness.

She remembered their first meeting – seven years ago, when he had walked into the store looking for a job. His eyes had been the same back then. Dark. Withdrawn. He told her he had dropped out of university. That he had spent months holed up in his room, reading books, not seeing anyone. That his parents were finally forcing him to get a job. He figured that if he had to work, a bookstore was the one place he might fit in.

To be honest, Riko hadn't wanted to hire him. But the economy had been doing better back then, and nobody wanted a low-paying bookstore job. They were short-staffed, so she had little choice but to give him a chance.

Fortunately, he turned out to be a great fit. He was tasked with the difficult and often-overlooked specialist books section, and he quickly transformed it. Since Tsujii, the floor supervisor at the time, was next to useless, Mita had plenty of opportunities to showcase his talents. His achievements were recognised, his confidence grew, and slowly, he came out of his shell, all but blossoming before their very eyes,

"I hate it," he said now, his voice low but seething. "People prying into things they don't understand, acting like they know everything. I wish they'd all just disappear."

Mita hadn't changed. Not really.

That darkness, that intensity – it was still there, buried beneath the surface. And it was all for Aki.

Riko said nothing. She felt like she had crossed a line, like she had stumbled into something she was never meant to see.

"Sorry," he muttered after a pause, lowering his head. "I went too far."

Knowing him, Riko suspected he wasn't apologising for what he had said – only for losing control.

Without another word, he stood up and walked out. He didn't even look back.

Riko watched him go, her eyes following his retreating figure.

15

"Sounds like Nishioka's had a rough start as manager. It must have been tough, her dad collapsing like that."

"Well, he was up and about today, apparently, so I don't think it's anything too serious. Oh – can I get another beer?" Mami waved her empty glass at a waiter.

Aki, meanwhile, quietly poked at her food with her chopsticks.

Tonight's drinks party was the follow-up to an event hosted by Kitchi-Yomu, a group made up of bookstore employees from Kichijoji. The event itself had been a forum titled "From the Frontlines of Sales", in which Shunsuke Shibata, a senior sales manager at Hitotsuboshi Press, addressed several well-known local booksellers. The party was both a way to celebrate the hard work that went into organising the event and to congratulate Shibata on the birth of his child. In short, this was Shibata's night.

Aki was a semi-regular at these Kitchi-Yomu get-togethers and was also close to Shibata, which was why she had been invited. Since there were so few women in the group, she had brought Mami along with her. The venue was a long-standing yakitori joint near Inokashira Park, a place called Iseya, famous for its cheap prices and old-fashioned charm. The thick wooden pillars and floorboards were stained dark from years of cooking smoke.

"But still, Nishioka's an only child, right? Taking care of your dad on your own must be hard work," Shibata said, loosening his tie. His face was already flushed from drinking.

The upstairs tatami-floored room was packed with more than thirty people. Only five or six were Kichijoji booksellers – the rest were either from other bookstores or publishing houses, with a noticeable contingent from Hitotsuboshi Press.

"You sure know your stuff, Shibata," one of his subordinates teased.

Aki tried to recall the man's name – Sekiguchi, maybe? She had been introduced to so many people at once that her head was spinning.

"Oh, by the way, I heard you and Nishioka used to date," Mami blurted out, completely unfiltered.

Aki winced – too late. Mami was already half-drunk, and so were most of the others.

"Yeah, I remember hearing that rumour," another sales rep jumped in. "What's the deal, Shibata?"

Riko had become something of an industry name lately. Everyone here knew who she was.

"That was a long time ago. I'm married now, with a kid," Shibata said, taking off his glasses and wiping his face with a towel.

Aki wondered if he was simply trying to hide his embarrassment.

"So, the rumours were true after all."

"Wow, you and Nishioka? I can kinda see it. You two probably made a good match."

The comment had an edge to it – half playful, half taking a dig at Shibata for marrying a much younger woman. He wasn't particularly short, so it wouldn't be too noticeable, but he had a bit of a paunch, and his neatly parted hair was starting to thin. The unspoken question hung in the air – how did a guy like him land such a young wife?

"When was this, exactly?" someone pressed.

"Oh, before I met my wife," Shibata said, looking around for an escape route.

The group wasn't about to let him off the hook that easily.

"You sure about that? Maybe you were two-timing?" Sekiguchi said with a smirk. He appeared to be enjoying this chance to poke fun at his boss.

"Hey, hey, don't even joke about that," Shibata protested, flustered.

"Aha, so it *was* like that!"

"Wait, so you went after a younger co-worker while you were dating Nishioka? Man, that's rough."

Laughter rippled through the group as they egged him on.

"No, no, it wasn't like that! *She* was the one who asked *me* out!" Shibata protested.

"Come on, you expect us to believe that?"

"I swear! I wouldn't go after my own subordinate like that!"

Shibata was getting worked up. He was drunk, and with everyone teasing him, his tongue was starting to loosen. Three empty sake bottles sat in front of him.

"Man, must be nice," Sekiguchi said with a shake of his head. "Even at your age, you still managed to marry a twenty-seven-year-old. Talk about living the dream."

Sekiguchi himself had just turned thirty and was still single.

"Yeah. And on top of that, you're saying she approached you first? You're one lucky bastard, Shibata."

"Good thing she never found out you were playing the field."

"Damn. If I'd known, I would've spilled the beans before you tied the knot."

The guys were letting loose, half out of jealousy. Aki and Mami kept to themselves, silently picking at the food on their plates.

"Hold on – my wife already knew I was seeing someone when she came after me," Shibata claimed. His already flushed face was turning redder by the minute.

"That just pisses me off even more."

"So, what, she knew she had competition and that just fired her up? Women are scary creatures, huh?"

"That explains the shotgun wedding. You got played, Shibata."

"Lucky bastard. Wouldn't bother me at all if a twenty-seven-year-old wanted to snare me."

"Pfft, say whatever you want," Shibata deflected, but he couldn't hide his crooked grin.

Aki found herself smouldering. Did men really brag about this sort of thing?

"Wasn't it rough on Nishioka, then? I bet the break-up wasn't exactly smooth."

"Nah, we were both adults about it. But after that . . ." Shibata smirked, dragging out his words.

"Yeah? What happened?"

"Three months later, I was getting off the subway on my way home – and there she was."

"No way. Nishioka?"

"I was halfway up the stairs, looked up, and there she was at the top, just staring down at me. Like, fixated. It was almost midnight, right before the last train. Creepy as hell."

"That's seriously freaky."

"What did you do?"

"Well . . . I panicked. Honestly, I just pushed past her and bolted."

The men roared with laughter.

"Wow, seriously?"

"Cowardly move, Shibata."

"Serves you right for trying to juggle two women."

"Come on, put yourself in his shoes. Getting stalked by your ex? That's terrifying."

"Well, it's on you, Shibata. You should be grateful she didn't stab you."

Aki could feel her blood pressure rising. Was this really something to joke about? Why would he even bring it up? Men always wanted to be the centre of attention at these kinds of gatherings. They would exaggerate, spill secrets – whatever it took to get a reaction. Was Shibata really turning a messy break-up into a funny story just for a quick laugh?

"Come on, Shibata, you're always exaggerating," Aki interjected, cutting in before the conversation could take an even more unpleasant turn.

The group's attention shifted to her.

"I actually heard about this from Nishioka. She told me she happened to run into you at the subway station, and you ran off, looking terrified. She laughed about it – said it wasn't like she was going to eat you alive. Maybe you were just feeling guilty and read too much into it?" she said lightly.

Others immediately chimed in.

"So, it was just Shibata's imagination?"

"More like wishful thinking, maybe? Hoping she'd chase after him?"

"Uh . . . Well . . ."

"Yeah, no way someone like Nishioka is still hung up on a middle-aged guy like you."

The conversation quickly shifted, as was the norm at drinking parties. Or maybe everyone was tired of indulging Shibata's boasting.

"It just proves how kind-hearted you are, Shibata," Aki said smoothly, throwing him a bone. "You probably still feel bad about how things ended, right?"

"Uh, yeah . . . I guess . . ." He gave an awkward laugh, but his smile was strained.

"Excuse me – could you pass me the fried chicken?" Aki asked casually, reaching for a plate of tatsutaage.

"Wait a sec – I thought you and Nishioka didn't get along?" Sekiguchi piped up.

"Yeah, I heard you two had a fight on the sales floor."

"No, that wasn't what happened," Aki said brightly, though she felt her stomach tighten. "Who's been saying that?"

"You know how the publishing industry is with rumours. Everyone says Nishioka's been giving you a hard time."

The group was practically leaning in now, intrigued. The gossip must have spread further than she realised. Yet Aki played it off like it didn't bother her.

"Gossip is the worst. Do I *look* like the kind of person to just sit there and take it? Sure, we've butted heads at work – because we both take our jobs so seriously. But that's all there is to it."

"Really? I heard some pretty specific stuff. Like how she didn't even give you a wedding gift."

"Oh? What do you mean?"

Inside, Aki froze for a second, but she forced a puzzled look. She could feel everyone's eyes focused on her.

"Uh . . . Well . . ."

"You guys just love your gossip, huh?" Aki pouted a little, feigning annoyance. "It was just a disagreement over rearranging the fifth-floor sales area. Yes, we both got heated, but it was purely about work. We're both too busy to hold grudges over something like that. Seriously, who keeps making up these ridiculous stories?"

"Now that you mention it, it would be weird for someone like Nishioka to hold a grudge."

"So, it was all just talk, huh?"

"Are you disappointed?" Aki teased again. "Would you rather we actually hated each other?"

She pretended to frown in protest, knowing exactly how these little gestures shaped the way men saw her. As a woman, it was next to impossible to survive long in a male-dominated industry if you couldn't do that.

"Nah. But it would've been interesting," someone chuckled.

"Well, too bad. I'm not here to fuel your entertainment. Speaking of which, did you hear about Ando from K Press? I heard he was hospitalised."

With that, she steered the conversation to another topic.

As soon as the gathering wrapped up, Aki turned down the invitation to the after-party and set off towards the main street. Behind her, Mami hurried to catch up.

"Aki? Where are you going? Aren't you heading home?"

"I'm just stopping by the store. I forgot something. Sorry, but can you head home without me?"

Aki's expression was intense. Mami looked at her, worried.

"But..."

Before Mami could say anything else, Aki took off at an almost alarming speed.

"We've gone over the closing checklist for the third and fourth floors. And the fifth. Are you ready to close?"

"Thanks. I'll take care of the rest," Riko said, waving goodnight at the last of the late-shift employees.

"Alright, I'll be off then."

"Good work today."

Through the frosted glass of the office door, she watched the lights on the sales floor go out. It looked like everyone had left. Aside from the low hum of the air conditioning, there wasn't a sound to be heard.

Riko remained at her desk. Ever since returning from headquarters, she hadn't been able to move.

Her father had collapsed. That alone was a shock. But now, there was also this mess at work. And on top of it all, Mita's words still cut deep.

If anything, you were the one causing the disruption.

She had nothing to say to that.

She still couldn't believe he thought of her that way.

But he wasn't wrong. She *didn't* like Aki. She had just used Mita as an excuse to justify herself.

Still, did she really deserve this much criticism? No explanation, no chance to defend herself – just thrown to the wolves?

What have I been doing here all this time? What was the point of everything I've put into this place?

A tear slipped down her cheek.

At that moment, the office door swung open.

"Ah. I thought you'd still be here."

Riko hastily wiped her face and turned to the door. Who on earth would come barging in at this hour?

Standing there was Aki Obata, her face slightly flushed.

"You. Have you been drinking?"

Of all the people Riko didn't want to see right now, Aki was at the top of the list. Her carefree attitude, her complete lack of awareness – they really got under her skin.

"Yeah, I've been drinking," Aki answered. "Which is exactly why I need to ask you something."

Her eyes sparkled, and her cheeks were tinged with a rosy glow. Whether it was the alcohol or just Aki being Aki, she seemed more alive than usual. Riko was struck by her vitality.

That's it, she thought. *That's what draws men to her. That energy she has. That life.*

"I don't feel like dealing with a drunk right now," Riko said coldly.

Mita was right. She envied Aki – her youth, her beauty, the ease with which the world seemed to favour her. This wasn't just about Mita. *Everyone* was jealous of her.

"You need to hear this," Aki insisted. "Rumours about our spat at work are spreading all over the industry. Any idea why?"

"Rumours?" Riko scoffed. "What, you mean the one about me only being a temporary manager?"

Aki frowned. "Temporary? What do you mean?"

Screw it, Riko thought.

"Exactly what it sounds like," she all but spat. "This store is shutting down soon. I'm just here to keep things running until then."

"What? No . . ."

Aki was stunned. That, at least, caught Riko off guard.

"Oh, come on. It's good news for you, isn't it? You won't have to work under a manager you hate. I'm sure they'll find a place for you at one of the other branches. Plenty of people in HR think I'm unfit for this job. I'm sure you led the charge, didn't you?"

"What am I, some stupid kid? I'd never do something like that!" Aki snapped.

Riko sighed. She was right.

Aki was a lot of things, but underhanded wasn't one of them. If she didn't like something, she would say it straight to your face. She wasn't the kind of person to snitch to HR with her complaints.

"You're right . . . Only a child would do something like that," Riko muttered.

But that didn't change the fact that she was getting pushed out.

"More importantly – what's going on with the store? It's closing down?"

For Aki, that was the bigger issue. Naturally. She worked here too, so if the store closed, she'd likely be transferred to another location.

"The building's getting torn down next March," Riko said flatly. "And the company decided it's not worth reopening afterwards."

"But . . . this is Pegasus Books' first store. The flagship. Why would they shut it down?"

"Because it's a money pit," Riko said, her smile bitter.

"That's not true! The financial reports never—"

"Because our rent is practically free," Riko cut in.

"What?"

"This building's owner is related to our company's founder. That's why we've been paying next to nothing in rent. Didn't you know that?"

"No . . ."

"Well, you do now. That's the only reason we've managed to stay in the black. But after the rebuild, they're going to start charging market rates."

Riko rambled on about everything she had just heard earlier in the day. She didn't see any reason to keep it a secret. Even if someone had told her to, she wasn't in the mood to listen.

"So, that's how it is . . ."

"It used to be fine back in the day. We were the only bookstore around with this much space. But now, Kichijoji is flooded with bookstores. There's one in the station building, another in the fashion mall nearby, a few more in the shopping district, even a huge one *under* the station. Every time a new one pops up, our sales take a hit. There's nothing left to turn things around."

"Who told you that? The Evil Magistrate Duo?"

Riko blinked in surprise. Aki had a habit of saying the most random things.

"Evil Magistrate? Who?"

"Watanabe from HQ and Yamada from HR. You know, they're like those villains in old samurai dramas – the corrupt magistrate and his sneaky sidekick. One goes, *Oh, you're quite the scoundrel,* and then the other is like, *Oh no, my lord, you're the true villain.* That kind of thing. Don't you think those two fit the part perfectly?"

"I suppose they do," Riko chuckled.

They really did look like bad guys. If this were a TV drama, they would definitely be cast as villains.

"But why did they make you the manager, then? If they already knew the store was closing, why bother?"

"I didn't ask, but they probably didn't want to stain Nojima's career. He's related to the owner, after all. Closing a store is a messy job, and they probably didn't want to make him the scapegoat."

So, they picked me instead. The one with the bad reputation. And Nojima, looking out only for himself, probably threw in a few comments to make sure I got the job.

Am I the villain here? Or am I just a disposable extra who disappears halfway through the story?

"So, they figured you were the best choice?" Aki asked.

"Exactly. HQ doesn't like me, my team doesn't trust me, and my industry reputation is in the gutter. Might as well give the dirty work to someone already covered in mud."

Who's the protagonist of this story? If all we have are villains and side characters, where's the hero?

"I don't like it," Aki muttered, irritation clear in her voice.

"Don't like what?"

"All of it. Nojima not wanting to do the job, so they dump it on you. The way all these rumours are flying around. And most of all, why everyone's acting like the store's doomed from the start? Why isn't anyone even trying to save it?"

"Do you know how much the rent is going up? A million yen a month."

Riko's voice was tight with frustration. To cover that, they would have to increase sales by nearly five million yen. She couldn't see how that was remotely possible.

"Well, we don't have a choice, do we?" Aki said, like it was the simplest thing in the world.

"Excuse me?"

"If the only other option is shutting down, then we *have* to boost sales. When exactly is the building getting rebuilt?"

"Next March."

"Then we have six months. That's plenty of time to figure something out."

"That's easy for you to say. We've already tried everything, and sales still haven't gone—"

But before Riko could finish, Aki cut her off.

"Then quit."

". . . What?"

"Stop whining. If you don't have the will to fight, don't wait another six months – just quit now. No-one wants to work under a manager who's already given up."

It was dramatic, almost theatrical. Saying it was easy. Actually doing it was another story. Was she just playing the part of the passionate saviour here?

Riko looked at her with scepticism. "Easy for you to say."

"This isn't just *your* problem. If the store shuts down, it affects all of us. You're not the only one who's going to suffer."

"Well . . ."

She had a point. Ozaki, Yamane and everyone else who believed in her – it would impact them just as much as it did her. But hearing it from Aki still grated.

"Or do you have some other brilliant idea? Some magic way to keep the store open?" Aki pressed.

"Well . . . I don't see how we can suddenly make an extra five million yen a month."

"You don't know unless you try. If we all work together, we should be able to figure something out."

"Work together? You're serious?"

Riko stared at her. That was one suggestion she would never personally come out with. Especially not to someone like Aki.

"Of course."

"Why? I thought you'd be happy to see me crash and burn."

"We don't have time for that. Let's call a truce."

"A truce?"

That was so like Aki. Always the naive, straight-shooting idealist. Young, earnest, unwilling to play games.

"We can't afford to waste energy fighting each other right now. And besides, you're the first female store manager we've ever had. You need to succeed to prove women can handle this job. If you fail, the guys will say, *See? Women can't do it.* You have a responsibility."

Aki was dead serious. There was no hesitation in her voice, no doubt in her eyes.

Maybe that's what I hate most about her.

"That's . . ."

And yet, it was also the one thing she couldn't compete with.

"Honestly, seeing you roll over and accept this – it isn't like you at all. Where's your confidence gone? Your pride? Doesn't it piss you off to just sit back and lose?"

Maybe Aki was the real protagonist here. That blind, unwavering determination – that was what a hero needed.

"If you really think it's impossible, then walk away now. We don't need a weak-willed manager. What we need is someone who will stand with us and fight. If you're just going to sit back and watch the store go under, then leave."

Aki's voice was firm, without so much as a trace of doubt.

She didn't play games. No tricks, no ulterior motives. If she believed something was right, she went for it. Even if it meant reaching out to someone she had considered an enemy just the day before.

But could Riko take that hand? What did she actually *want* to do? What role did she want to play?

"... I don't know. Let me think about it."

16

Riko got on the Nishinokubo Loop bus from Musashi-Koganei Station. It wasn't her usual route, but she wasn't in a hurry to go home to an empty house.

After around ten minutes, she got off at the stop in front of the supermarket. It was past 10:00 p.m., so the store had already closed, and the streets were deserted. Relying on the dim glow of the streetlights, she walked along the edge of the narrow road, heading south. In less than two minutes, she reached her destination – her neighbourhood bookstore, Isshindo.

Whenever she was feeling down, whenever something hard happened, she always ended up here.

Her thoughts took her back to a long time ago, when her mother collapsed from illness and the doctors said she didn't have much time left – she had come here then, too. That morning, her father had sat her down and explained the situation for the first time. Her mother would be starting treatment, but it was less about getting better and more about prolonging the inevitable. The battle wasn't about survival – it was about how to make her remaining time as painless as possible.

That news alone was devastating enough. But then her father hit her with something else.

"Your mother's treatment is going to cost a lot. I want to do everything I can for her. So, I'm sorry, but we can't afford to send you to a private university. You'll have to go to a public school, or maybe a junior college."

It was Christmas, right before her entrance exams.

She had a dream school – an elite private university known for its English programme. She had worked so hard for it, poured everything she had into getting in. Switching to a public university at the last minute simply wasn't an option. She hadn't registered for the standardised tests required for public school applications.

That left her with only one path.

So, now I have to go to a junior college? What was the point of all this? Why did I push myself so hard?

Of course, she was heartbroken about her mother's illness. Of course, she wanted her to get the best treatment possible. That was never in question.

But why did that have to mean giving up her own future? She couldn't accept it.

And she hated herself for thinking that way.

Carrying all that frustration, she had wandered into the bookstore. Not for any particular reason – just out of habit. She always came here when she had time to kill.

That day, Shimizu greeted her with his usual gentle smile. But this time, he did something he never had before. He recommended a book.

"This one's really good. You should give it a try."

It was *Kitchen* by Banana Yoshimoto – a bestseller at the time. She wouldn't normally have picked it up. The cover seemed too cutesy, and the fact that it was so popular put her off. She had something of a rebellious streak back then – if a book was a bestseller, it meant people who didn't usually read were buying it, which, to her, meant it probably wasn't real literature.

But that day, she bought it anyway.

Maybe because she still had an unused five-thousand-yen book voucher her aunt had given her for her birthday.

Maybe because, in that moment, nothing really mattered anymore.

Maybe just because the old man had suggested it.

She went home and read it. And she cried.

The grief of losing family. The loneliness. The hollow emptiness that never really goes away. The despair. And the will to move forward.

It felt like a made-up story, with a kind of dreamy, girls' manga feel to it. But she cried anyway, unabashedly, through the entire night. She couldn't help but feel the story was about to happen to her.

She hadn't cried when her father told her about her mother's illness. She had been too shocked, too numb to process it. But a novel – *that*, she could cry for. And somehow, after crying her heart out, she felt lighter. Like she could finally breathe.

Losing someone you loved was unavoidable. It happened to everyone, sooner or later. The sadness, the loneliness – they were a fact of life. But maybe, just maybe, there was something on the other side of that grief. Something you could only gain by going through it. A kind of connection that wouldn't exist otherwise.

That book gave her the strength to keep going.

For the protagonist in *Kitchen*, her comfort was a bowl of

katsudon. For Riko, it was this book. It gave her the resolve to face her mother's illness head-on, to stay by her side in the time they had left. And to make the most of her university years, even if they weren't what she had planned.

Later, when she told Shimizu, "I'm glad I read it. It really helped me," he simply nodded and said, "That's good. You looked like you were going through a tough time, so I thought a book like that might be what you needed."

He had seen right through her.

It meant the world to her that someone had cared enough to notice.

That was why, years later, whenever work got too overwhelming, whenever life felt too heavy, she found herself coming back here. Not because she expected anything to happen. Just because being here, in this quiet, familiar space, made her feel at peace.

More than that – this place was the reason she had become a bookseller.

Discovering *Kitchen* was what saved her. She wanted to do the same for someone else. To be the kind of bookseller who could place the right book into the right hands at the right time.

By now, the store was probably closed. But just standing outside and looking at it might give her the courage she needed. That was why she had taken this detour tonight.

But when she got there, the lights were still on – at least halfway. Shimizu was inside, talking to someone.

She stopped in her tracks, observing from a distance.

Then, she watched as he stepped out – with a customer in tow.

"I'll bring the documents again tomorrow."

"Sorry for making you come all this way again. I appreciate it."

Shimizu bowed slightly as he saw the customer off. When he straightened up, he noticed Riko standing nearby.

"Oh, Riko! On your way home? You're working late."

"Yes. But what about you, Uncle? I didn't think you kept the store open this late."

"Oh, no, I wasn't actually open. I was meeting an estate agent. I asked them to come after hours, and we ended up talking longer than I expected."

"An estate agent?"

"Oh . . . I haven't told you yet, have I? The truth is the store's closing at the end of the month."

"What? Really?"

"I want to thank you, Riko. You've always been such a great customer."

"That's not fair!" The words flew out before she could stop them.

He had promised. He had said he would keep the shop going for as long as he could.

Isshindo was closing down? She couldn't accept it. She didn't want to.

"This is the only bookstore around here. The station's so far away, and there are kids and elderly people who rely on you. Where are they supposed to buy their books?"

When she was a child, her whole world was only as big as the places she could walk to. And this shop, sitting right at the edge of that world, had been her gateway to so many others. She was sure it was the same for the children growing up here now.

"I know, I know," the old man sighed. "Believe me, it's hard for me too. There are customers who've been coming here forever. If it weren't for my back, I would've kept going . . ."

"Your back?"

"A herniated disc. I've been pushing through it for years, but it's getting worse. To tell you the truth, I've reached my limit."

". . . Is it really that bad?"

Riko's heart sank. He had mentioned back pain before, but he had always brushed it off with a smile like it was nothing. She had assumed it was just an occupational hazard.

"My doctor told me if I don't take it seriously, I might not be able to walk anymore. What with my age, it's time for me to call it quits," Shimizu said with a gentle smile.

She couldn't help but notice how much smaller his shoulders seemed. His hair was stark white, as well. She had always thought of him as the same as ever, but somewhere along the way, he had got older. He really was at the age where the term "old man" was no exaggeration.

"That's . . . unfortunate."

A deep, aching sadness welled up inside her. She had so many memories tied to this place. She would come here every Saturday when she was in elementary school to flip through her favourite weekly girls' manga magazine, reading every page. Once, when she couldn't afford to buy anything, she stood there and read an entire children's mystery novel from cover to cover. Shimizu never scolded her for it – he simply smiled and let it slide. It was here that she discovered so many writers, so many books, so many worlds, all of them waiting for her on these shelves.

Isshindo wasn't just a place she loved – it had shaped the person she was now.

"You're not the only one who feels that way," Shimizu said. "A lot of people have begged me not to close. Some regulars have gone so far as to say they won't buy books anywhere else. It really hits me now, just how much this shop has been supported by its customers. I can't tell you how much I'll miss it."

Of course he would. This store was special. Not just to Riko, but to so many others.

"At least the delivery service will continue," he added. "Kagome Books over by the station agreed to take it over. That's some relief..."

"But... it's so sad. You're the reason I started working at a bookstore – because I wanted to be like you. There's still so much I wanted to learn from you."

"What are you talking about? You're already a better bookseller than I ever was. Oh, that reminds me – congratulations on becoming store manager."

"Where did you hear about that?"

"Your dad told me. Ever since you started working there, he's been stopping by here from time to time, telling me all about you. He even showed me the magazine articles you've been featured in. He couldn't have been prouder of you."

"That's impossible." Riko frowned. "My dad doesn't care about my job."

When she was featured in the magazine, when she was promoted, all he ever said was, "Oh." That was it. It was almost disconcertingly underwhelming.

Shimizu chuckled. "No, no, he's just embarrassed to say it to your face. He even brought me a scrapbook filled with clippings of all the articles you're mentioned in."

A scrapbook? She had no idea.

"Do you know what he said? *She doesn't take after me, but*

she's got a real knack for business. I never got anywhere at my company, but she's something special."

"That's not true. My store could go under any day now. No-one else wanted to be manager, so the job just landed on me."

"Well, then, this is your moment to prove yourself."

"Huh?"

"The store's future depends on you, doesn't it?" he asked with a knowing smile.

"Well . . . I suppose."

But was it really her responsibility? The store's financial struggles weren't her fault – they were the result of years of decisions made by past managers and the executives at head-quarters.

"I'm in no position to talk," Shimizu said, "but when a store closes, the biggest loss is for the customers. Your store is one of the oldest in Kichijoji, so I'll bet you have a great many loyal customers. If you close, they're the ones who'll be hit the hardest."

Faces flashed through her mind. The customers who always came to her for recommendations. The ones who said they wouldn't shop anywhere else. The people who congratulated her when she was featured in the magazine, as happy as if it were their own success.

She remembered one woman in particular.

"I'm so thrilled for you! You've always been so helpful."

Thinking of her, Riko's chest tightened.

If the store closed, where would that customer go? She once told her that no other bookstore in Kichijoji carried the kind of books she liked.

Riko wouldn't be the only one in trouble if the store went under. If she allowed it to close, she would be taking something important from her customers, too. A place where they felt at home. A place where they could always find the books they loved. She knew exactly how that loss would feel. Because she was feeling it now.

She didn't want to do that to them.

"You're right," she said, straightening her shoulders. "I have to do everything I can."

No matter how tough things got, she was the manager. *She was responsible for the store, its employees and its customers.*

"That's the spirit." Shimizu nodded. "I believe in you. If anyone can do it, Riko, you can."

He wasn't flattering her – his voice was calm, confident, like he was stating a simple fact.

That certainty settled deep into her heart.

When Riko finally made it home, she dashed upstairs without removing her shoes and flung open the door to her father's room to look around.

He always cleaned it himself, so she rarely had any reason to go in. She had no idea where anything was, but she spotted what she was looking for right away – a scrapbook tucked neatly onto the bookshelf.

She grabbed it and started flipping through the pages, letting out a startled gasp.

Every single page was about her.

The first clipping was from over a decade ago – an old company newsletter announcing her promotion from part-time worker to full-time staff. Then, there was an article about her being recognised as an outstanding employee, and another about her ten-year work anniversary. There were flyers from the publisher's recommendation display contest she had taken part in, clippings from magazines and newspapers that had interviewed her or published her comments. Everything was carefully dated, documented and preserved.

And of course, there was the big feature article from *Vintage*.

"When did he put this together?" she murmured.

Riko never kept things like this. Even when she was interviewed, she would skim through the magazine once and then throw it away. But her father had quietly saved every item, collecting them piece by piece, to keep a record of her career.

Your dad couldn't have been prouder of you. Shimizu's words earlier came rushing back.

She doesn't take after me, but she's got a real knack for business. I never got anywhere at my company, but she's something special.

He had never once let it show. Not so much as a hint. Saving all of this, keeping it so carefully – was her work really that important to him? Did he really believe in her that much?

A teardrop landed on the scrapbook.

Panicked, Riko wiped at it with her sleeve.

She wasn't anything special. She was the kind of boss her subordinates badmouthed behind her back, the kind who got reported to headquarters.

She was the kind of daughter who, when her father collapsed, worried more about how *she* would handle it than about him.

"Dad," she choked out.

The floodgates burst open. All the tension from the day unravelled at once, and she sank to the floor, clutching the scrapbook to her chest.

17

Two days later, Pegasus Books' monthly store managers' meeting, where the executives and the managers of the various branches gathered to discuss company policies and share updates, and exchange information, was held at headquarters.

It was Riko's first time attending.

As soon as she walked into the conference room, two managers – one from the Okubo store and the other from Iidabashi – called out to her. She had mentored them both years ago, back when they were new hires, but they had climbed the ranks faster than she had, getting promoted to store manager years before her.

"Glad to see you finally caught up, Nishioka," one of them said with a grin.

"Took you long enough," the other added.

Riko couldn't tell if they really meant it, but it was still nice to hear.

As they chatted, another familiar face walked in – Nojima, her former boss. He had transferred to the systems department at headquarters, so he was here representing that division.

The moment their eyes met, he quickly looked away.

Riko excused herself from the conversation and walked over to him.

"Hi, Nojima."

"Oh, uh . . . Hey."

"This is my first time at these meetings. I don't really know how things work yet, so I'd appreciate your help if I look lost." She looked up at him, feigning nervousness.

Nojima wasn't the kind of person to turn someone away when they asked for help.

"Oh, sure. Right. If you need anything, just ask."

"Thank you." Riko gave a polite bow.

Nojima blinked, clearly caught off guard.

He's trying to figure out what I'm up to. He must have heard about what happened with HR.

Riko knew Nojima wasn't on her side. But openly showing hostility would only make things worse for her.

"Oh! Eto. Hey," she called out after she spotted the manager from the Ogikubo.

"Ah, Nishioka! Congrats on your promotion."

Eto managed the chain's largest store, though rumour had it he got the job through connections rather than merit. His face was puffy and red, likely from years of drinking, and his body had a bloated, misshapen look. She often saw him at company parties, but never once at a book launch or training seminar.

"Thank you," Riko said. "But I only got the position because of Nojima's transfer. I didn't do anything special."

"Come on, don't be modest. You're the company's star bookseller."

"Oh, please," Riko chuckled. "That was just because Nojima encouraged me to do it to promote the store. I'm certainly no 'star bookseller', especially not compared to someone as accomplished as you."

Eto threw his head back, roaring with laughter.

Men like him were easy to flatter.

"I'm probably not cut out to be a manager, so I'll be relying on your guidance," Riko added, bowing slightly.

"Sure, sure! Anytime." Still grinning, Eto strolled off.

Nojima was staring at her, eyes wide in disbelief.

Yeah, you weren't expecting that from me, were you?

"You should take your seat, Nojima. The meeting's about to start," she pointed out.

"Oh, right." He hurried towards his spot at the back of the room.

At that moment, Watanabe and Yamada – the Evil Magistrate Duo – walked in. Riko took a seat in the furthest row. Finally, the president entered through the back door. As soon as he sat down, the meeting chair announced, "Let's begin."

The president was in his fifties – the second son of the company's late founder. When their father passed away ten years ago, the ambitious older brother took over the restaurant division, while the younger one inherited the bookstore chain.

Riko didn't dislike him. With his round, smiling face, he had the air of a cheerful Ebisu statue. Rumour had it he wasn't particularly involved in the nitty-gritty of business matters, leaving most major decisions to the executives.

Frankly, Riko thought that was probably for the best. No-one wanted corporate micromanaging store operations.

"Alright. Let's start with this month's sales reports."

The first half of the meeting was a dull recitation of numbers from each store.

"The Akabane store's total sales for September were

19,827,655 yen. Cost of goods sold, 15,465,570 yen. Gross profit, 4,362,085 yen. Operating profit . . ."

An accounting representative read through the figures, but Riko tuned it all out. This could all have been handled with written reports, but the company's founder had insisted on verbal sales reports to foster team spirit.

Riko kept her head down, pretending to listen attentively while discreetly scanning the room.

Some managers were doodling on their papers, while others were sneakily checking their phones. It was like a scene straight out of a university lecture.

". . . Non-operating revenue, 175,008 yen. Non-operating expenses, 10,100 yen . . ."

The droning voice combined with the post-lunch hour had people nodding off left and right. It was two in the afternoon, and most in the room were stifling yawns. Eto, for one, was practically sound asleep. Only Watanabe and Yamada were managing to stay awake, shooting daggers at Eto for dozing off. The president looked like he was listening, nodding every now and then with his eyes closed. But then, suddenly, his head jerked forward. The movement woke him up, and he quickly straightened his posture, flustered. In that moment, his eyes met Riko's, and he gave her a sheepish grin.

At that moment, she was sure. *Just as I thought – the president's the one to do it in front of.*

The meeting dragged on with announcements from the different sections and divisions, followed by an explanation of the new accounting system. It was slightly better than a wall of numbers, but still – did they really need to gather everyone just for this?

Finally, after all the tedious reports were over, the chair

said, "To wrap things up, I'd like to invite Nishioka, the new manager of the Kichijoji branch, to say a few words."

Riko straightened up. *Finally, my turn.* She had already been told by HR that she would be expected to give a closing statement. Smiling warmly, she rose to her feet.

"I'm Riko Nishioka, the new manager of the Kichijoji store. I'm deeply honoured to be Pegasus Books' first female store manager. It fills me with a great sense of responsibility. I'm determined to do my best to live up to your expectations – especially the president, who has been actively pushing for greater opportunities for women in the workplace."

Watanabe and Yamada's faces twisted in discomfort. The president, meanwhile, looked visibly amused.

"That said," Riko continued, "as you all know, our Kichijoji store has been in a long-term slump for the past few years. While this is partly due to the overall decline in the industry, there are also specific local factors at play. Redevelopment around Kichijoji Station has led to increased competition in recent years, with a large competitor opening inside the station mall, along with three other new bookstores and two second-hand ones within a hundred-metre radius. Though I'm sure our previous manager is much more familiar with the situation than I am."

At that, all eyes turned to Nojima. He blinked rapidly in response, looking at Riko as if to say, *What on earth are you doing?*

"As reported earlier, our current operating profit sits at around three per cent of revenue – not a great figure. But the bigger problem is that, as of next March, our lease with the building's management company will expire. Since opening, we've been paying significantly below market rent thanks to a longstanding relationship with the management company. However, with the building set to be rebuilt due to ageing infrastructure, they've informed us that the rent will increase. We don't have exact numbers yet, but it looks like it will be around one million yen per month."

Riko spoke clearly, projecting her memorised lines throughout the room. She had always been told she had a low but strong voice, and this was the perfect time to make use of it.

"Alright, that's enough," Watanabe snapped, trying to shut her down.

The president, however, casually raised a hand, signalling her to continue. Riko took the cue.

"This is no small number," she continued. "To cover an additional one million yen in rent purely through profit, we would need to increase revenue by approximately five million yen per month. Of course, cutting costs might offset some of it, but still . . ."

She paused, glancing at Nojima, whose eyes darted away.

"At our current sales levels, we're heading straight into the red. Upper management is already considering shutting down the store. In fact, I wasn't made aware of this until after I took on the role of manager."

A murmur spread through the room. She had just publicly exposed internal company affairs. Even those who worked at the Kichijoji store had no idea, so there was no way the other store managers did.

Watanabe's face turned bright red, but the president's hand was still raised in front of him. The president, for his part, was watching Riko closely, intrigued.

"I was stunned when I first learned about this situation.

I seriously considered turning down the position. I thought maybe it would be better if Nojima stayed on as manager until the end."

Nojima kept his head down. The other store managers were now looking at him, their eyes all but saying, *If the store is set to close in six months, why didn't he just see it out?*

"But regardless of the circumstances, I accepted this role. I decided that if I'm going to do it, I'm going to give it my all. I would like to believe that being promoted under these conditions is a sign that management sees potential in me."

Watanabe and Yamada both pressed their lips into identical thin lines. Riko slowly scanned the room, making eye contact with each person, drawing out the moment.

Now, for the final blow.

"I promise that by next March, we will increase revenue enough to cover the rent hike and keep the store open."

With that, she sat down.

Silence.

Everyone was staring at her.

Riko could feel it – the attention, the weight of the moment.

I won't just play a minor role and fade into the background. Even if I have to leave the stage eventually, I'll play the lead until the last moment.

"You – this isn't the place to—" Watanabe spluttered, struggling to form words.

"This isn't something to discuss here," Yamada said, stepping in.

And then –

Applause.

The president was clapping.

"Ha-ha! Just as they said – you've got guts, Nishioka!"

"President . . .!"

Watanabe and Yamada stared at him in disbelief.

"You're saying that despite these circumstances, you still want to fight for the store?"

"Of course," Riko answered, meeting the president's gaze. "As manager, it's my responsibility to do everything in my power to keep it running. I hope that everyone here can support me in that effort."

She wasn't naive. The decision to close might already be final. If that was the case, then even if she miraculously boosted sales, it would all be pointless. She had to know – was there any chance of saving the store?

"I see," the president said. "So, what you're really asking is, if you manage to turn things around, will we let the store stay open? You want my word on that."

He was sharp, as expected. He still wore his Ebisu-like smile, but his eyes weren't laughing.

"Alright. If you're that determined, I'll give you the chance. Let's see what you can do."

"President!" the Evil Magistrate Duo blurted out in unison.

"Thank you." Riko bowed deeply.

The conference room was abuzz – most of those present had no idea what had just happened.

"That concludes today's meeting," the chair announced. "The next meeting will be scheduled for . . ."

I did it, Dad, Riko whispered to herself.

There was no turning back now.

I'll do this. For myself. And for our customers. Because this store isn't just ours – it belongs to them, too.

From across the room, Nojima watched her like he was witnessing some terrifying spectacle.

18

"Hey, Nishioka. Got a minute?"

Shortly after closing, the day after the meeting, Riko received a call in her office from Eto, the manager of the Ogikubo store. Eto, it seemed, had found her bold declaration in front of the president amusing, and he had invited her out for drinks after the meeting. And so, assuming the call was about that, she answered cheerfully.

"Eto! Of course, I always have time for a call from you."

"Well, you see ... This whole situation is actually great for us in Ogikubo, but I was wondering – are you guys going to be okay?"

"Huh? What do you mean?"

"I had a visit from Tsujii and Hatakeda this morning. They seemed to think they'd be working for me from next month."

"Tsujii and Hatakeda? Wait, what?"

"Whoa, so you really didn't know? Seriously?" Eto sounded genuinely surprised.

"What are you talking about?" she asked. "From next month ...?"

"Well ..."

After some hesitation, he finally told her. Apparently, Tsujii and Hatakeda were being reassigned to the Ogikubo store.

"You've got to be kidding me . . . No-one told *me* anything."

"Yeah. I mean, we just opened. We're still trying to get this place running smoothly since, so having experienced staff transferred over is great for us. But I had no idea you weren't being kept in the loop . . ."

Eto sounded uncomfortable. And frankly, it *was* difficult to believe – what kind of manager wasn't informed when their staff were being transferred?

"We haven't even replaced Nojima, and we're already struggling to get by."

"Yeah, I figured. Every store is in the same boat."

"This is all news to me. I'll have to check with HR. Thank you for letting me know."

Riko hung up. Then, hands shaking slightly, she dialled the number for General Affairs. To her surprise, Nobuo Yamada, the head of Human Resources, picked up directly. It was already past eight in the evening, and Yamada was the type to leave the office the second the workday ended.

"Oh, yes. That's what happened," Yamada said in his usual high-pitched, indifferent tone when Riko confronted him.

"When was this decided? No-one informed me."

"Huh? Really? That's weird. Must've been a miscommunication. I talked to Nojima about it before he left. He didn't mention anything during the handover?"

"No . . ."

Since Nojima's time? What was going on here?

"Are we getting any replacements? With Nojima gone, that makes it three full-time employees we're down."

"Yeah, well, it all happened pretty fast."

"This is ridiculous! Are you saying you want me to shut the store down here and now?" The words slipped out before Riko could stop them.

Only then did it hit her – this was pressure from General Affairs. They had always wanted to shut the store down, but now that Riko had gone directly to the president to make her case, they couldn't do it outright. This was their way of retaliating.

"Come on, now. Didn't you say you would turn the store around in six months? We're all counting on you," Yamada said in a sickly sweet, condescending voice that sent a chill down her spine. "But just so you know, Hatakeda and Tsujii had their own reasons for transferring. HR has to stay neutral, after all."

"Their own reasons? What do you mean?"

"I can't go into detail. Let's just say they weren't happy working under you."

Riko clenched the receiver tighter, at a loss for words.

"You know how it is these days – workplace harassment is a big deal. We can't just ignore it. There were openings at Ogikubo, so we thought it best to move them over there."

"Are you saying the Ogikubo branch matters, but my store doesn't?!"

"Look, this wasn't easy for us, either. But if someone files a complaint about workplace harassment, what do you expect us to do?"

Workplace harassment? Riko could feel a headache coming on. Had Hatakeda and Tsujii really told HR that?

"Sort it out yourself, Nishioka. You're supposed to be a 'star bookseller', aren't you?" Yamada spat, slamming the phone down.

Riko dropped her head onto her desk.

Unbelievable. Just when she was trying to stay positive

and push through this. Did Hatakeda and Tsujii really hate her that much? Did General Affairs want to kill the store that badly?

"Nishioka."

She looked up to find Shiho Ozaki standing there. And not just her – most of the late-shift staff had gathered around, too.

Right. The store had closed.

"Um. Hatakeda mentioned something at the end of our shift today . . . Is it true the store's shutting down?" Ozaki asked hesitantly.

"What?! Hatakeda said that?"

"I heard it from Tsujii," a part-timer working in the textbook section added. "And he also said he's been reassigned to Ogikubo. Is it true?"

"Their transfers aside, the store is *not* shutting down," Riko said firmly, forcing herself to stay composed.

The staff were already rattled – she couldn't afford to let them see her panicking.

"But Tsujii said we're closing at the end of March."

"If that's true, we need to start looking for other jobs . . ."

"We have bills to pay. What are we supposed to do if the store closes without warning?"

Everyone started talking over each other.

"Listen, everyone. Please, calm down."

The room fell silent. All eyes were on Riko. The pressure made it hard to speak.

"The thing in March isn't about closing. The building is scheduled for renovations then," she said, fighting to keep her tone even.

"Renovations?"

"Yes. This building is getting old – there isn't even an

escalator. They've been talking about rebuilding it for a while, and now it's finally happening."

"So, we're *not* actually closing? But Tsujii and Hatakeda said we were."

"They must have misunderstood. What's uncertain is whether we'll be able to return here after the renovations. Our rent will go up, after all."

Everyone held their breath, waiting for her next words. If she didn't handle this right, the store might make it as far as March – employees could start quitting *tomorrow*.

"That's why we need to increase sales. It won't be easy, but it's certainly not impossible. If we hit our targets, we can stay open. The president himself told me so."

That seemed to settle the staff down a little.

"This is Pegasus Books' flagship store. You all know that. They wouldn't shut it down so easily."

Her words rang hollow in the quiet room. No-one looked convinced.

"Then how much do we have to increase sales by?" one of the contract employees asked.

"There's no exact number as of now. Building management hasn't decided the new rent yet."

Riko forced a smile. In truth, she didn't want to say the number out loud. The moment people heard it, they might panic. And yet –

"I heard you promised the president five million yen per month," a voice said from the doorway.

It was Tsujii. Hatakeda stood beside him, smirking.

Damn it. Riko hadn't expected them to show up now.

"I *did* say that," she admitted, maintaining a cheerful

demeanour. "But that was just a target. A goal I set *because* I believe we can reach it. It's not set in stone."

She kept her cool, but inside, she was falling apart. She knew exactly what was happening – Tsujii and Hatakeda were trying to humiliate her in front of everyone.

"Either way, it's impossible," Tsujii scoffed. "Watanabe from headquarters already said the store is finished."

"If it wasn't, we wouldn't be getting transferred, would we?" Hatakeda added.

The room filled with uneasy murmurs. A five-million-yen sales increase – hearing it spelled out like that sent a shockwave through everyone.

"You don't know if it's impossible until we try," Riko shot back.

"Oh yeah? Then what's your plan, exactly?" Tsujii snorted. "Let's hear it."

"Right. Tell us, *boss*," Hatakeda pushed further.

Riko felt sweat gathering under her arms. Everyone was waiting, holding their breath, expecting her to say something. This was it – she had to take control. The hopeful, expectant looks from Ozaki and Yamane were almost painful.

How do I get out of this? How do I outsmart Tsujii and Hatakeda and get everyone on my side?

The more she fretted, the more her mind went blank.

Help me, she wanted to scream out loud.

"Enough already!"

A voice rang out from the corner of the room. Everyone turned at once.

Aki stood behind Tsujii and Hatakeda, her face pale with anger. She looked furious – even more than she had at the wedding when she had thrown Riko's gift envelope back in her face.

"What the hell is wrong with you two?"

"Obata, you—"

Before Hatakeda could say anything else, Aki strode forward and slapped him. Hard. The crisp sound echoed through the room.

Then, without missing a beat, she turned to Tsujii. He was taller than her, so she had to go up on her toes, but she wound up and hit him just as hard, making him stumble back.

"I can't believe you two," she said, rubbing her palm.

Hatakeda and Tsujii stood there, stunned. The whole room stared at Aki in shock.

I can hardly believe her, pulling a stunt like that, Riko thought wryly.

"Do you guys hate Nishioka that much?" Aki demanded.

"Wh-what? No, I . . ." Hatakeda stammered, visibly shaken.

"Really? Then why are you going out of your way to screw her over? You lied to Watanabe the other day. You said she was skipping work when she wasn't."

"I – that was—"

"You told him she wasn't fit to run the store. You even spread rumours about me and her. Why? Are you trying to take her job? Or do you just have a problem with her because she's a woman?"

"V-violence isn't the answer, Obata," Tsujii said weakly.

"Well, you know Watanabe . . ." Hatakeda added.

"Oh, please." Aki rolled her eyes. "And enough with the *headquarters this, headquarters that* performance. You act like they're gods or something. They want this store to fail. But Nishioka is actually trying to do something about it. She got a promise from the president himself – she's fighting to keep this place open. And all you two do is try to tear her down. So, tell me – do you *want* to see this store close?"

She was practically spitting fire now. Tsujii and Hatakeda shrank under her glare.

"N-no, that's not—"

"If you actually gave a damn, you'd be helping us instead of pulling this crap! The store's in trouble, and instead of stepping up, you're just thinking about yourselves!"

Hatakeda and Tsujii opened their mouths like fish gasping for air, too dumbstruck to respond. The other employees were starting to get a sense of what was going on – and they weren't looking at either of them kindly.

"But, Obata . . . I thought *you* hated her," Tsujii muttered.

"Are you seriously still on about that?" Aki grabbed him by the collar.

"Alright, alright, that's enough," Mita finally stepped in, placing a hand on Aki's shoulder. "Let's all take a breath."

"But—"

"I don't think yelling at them will fix the store's problems."

Scowling, Aki let go of Tsujii's shirt. She was still breathing hard, her fists clenched.

"We had no idea things were this bad," one of the contract employees said from the back.

The others, who had been watching in stunned silence, started nodding. They all turned to Riko. But unlike before, their gazes weren't just expectant – they were softer, almost sympathetic. She probably had Aki to thank for that.

Encouraged, Riko took a deep breath and spoke. "The truth is, I only had that conversation with the president yesterday.

I'm still processing the situation myself. I didn't know how to tell you all without causing a panic."

She paused, then let out a slow breath.

"I'm sorry you all had to find out this way."

With that, she turned her gaze towards Tsujii and Hatakeda. Everyone else followed suit. The two of them, looking thoroughly humiliated, quietly slunk out of the room.

"I understand your position," Ozaki began hesitantly. "But the bottom line is we need to increase sales by five million yen a month by March, or the store is done?"

"Yes. But so long as there's the slightest chance we can pull it off, I refuse to give up," Riko answered firmly.

"That's all well and good, but—"

"What about overtime?"

"Are we even going to get paid properly?"

Worried whispers spread through the staff.

"You don't need to worry about that," Riko reassured them. "The store isn't in the red. We have the budget for wages. And until the building renovation starts next March, we're staying open."

A wave of relief rippled through the room. Their jobs weren't in any immediate danger.

"And don't forget – we're Pegasus Books. A major book chain. Even if this store shuts down, your wages are guaranteed."

Someone hesitated, then spoke up. "But do you actually have a plan . . .? I mean, do we actually have a chance at increasing sales that much?"

Riko turned to face the worried voice. "We're a bookstore. There's no miracle solution. But we can cut waste, improve our stock, improve the store layout and focus on customer service. Those things work."

"So basically, just do what we've been doing? That doesn't sound like it'll be enough . . ." sounded a disappointed part-timer.

"There are plenty of stores making it work. I thought it would be impossible, too, at first. But when you stop to think about it, other stores survive under much harsher conditions than ours. Not every Pegasus store is lucky enough to be in a company-owned building like we are. If anything, we've had it easy up until now."

"I guess that's true . . ."

"I've started reviewing our operations, and honestly, our returns rate is far too high compared to other stores. Our turnover is poor, as well. There are many areas we can improve in. We're not being efficient with our resources. And we haven't tried things like special promotions or book signings – those could bring in more customers. We could expand into selling other products, as well. There are plenty of things we can do. I don't want to give up before we've even tried turning things around."

Someone let out a long sigh.

"I know it's going to be tough, but I'm asking you all to stay on and work together. I truly believe we can do this, so long as we put in the effort. And if we can't – if the store ends up shutting down . . ." Riko hesitated for a moment, then took a deep breath and declared, "In that case, I'll resign too."

19

Riko had feared the worst, but fortunately, there weren't a great many resignations. Tsujii and Hatakeda transferred to the Ogikubo store the next day, and a couple of their close friends also said they wanted to leave, but aside from them, most of the staff seemed willing to stay – at least for now.

Still, that didn't mean things were running smoothly. The atmosphere in the store felt stagnant. Riko could tell people were watching her, sizing her up. She was still being tested. In the end, action was the only way she was going to prove herself.

But first, she had to fill the staffing gaps. She put up job advertisements in magazines, on the store's front window, and reached out to nearby universities and vocational schools to post listings in their student centres. On top of that, she contacted former employees who might be ready to come back and tried convincing them to return.

At the same time, she had to reassess expenses and inventory while rejigging the management roles to cover for Tsujii and Hatakeda's departure. On the fifth floor, she promoted the full-time Aki to floor supervisor, which solved that problem. But the third and fourth floors had to be left to contract employees. She convinced Shiho Ozaki to take over the third floor with the promise that, once the store was stable, she would push headquarters to make her a full-time employee. But the fourth floor was still up in the air.

Ideally, Takahiko Mita would take it on – he had the skills and the respect of his co-workers – but he had turned her down. "I can't take on that level of responsibility as a contract worker," he said. He was polite, but his tone left no room for negotiation. And he wasn't wrong. Riko couldn't force him.

Of course, she knew the real reason – Mita simply didn't want to support her. He had been avoiding her ever since she pushed him to open up about his feelings. It was clear he didn't recognise her as the real boss. Ultimately, there was no-one else cut out for the job, so for the time being, she would have to manage the fourth floor herself.

And that was just one of many things on her plate. Alongside all the other work, she had started holding one-on-one meetings with each member of the staff. HR's criticism about being *self-righteous* still stung, and Mita's accusation that she was *too emotional* had hit her harder than she cared to admit. She set aside thirty minutes to an hour for each conversation, asking each employee to be completely open about their frustrations, what needed improvement, what they wanted to try, and any expectations they had for her as manager.

It was exhausting, juggling all of it. But in the end, she was glad she did it. Some of the feedback was difficult to accept – there was a lot of blunt criticism about her rocky relationship with Aki, and many voiced concerns about the store's future. But there were also plenty of constructive ideas, and, most importantly, people appreciated that she was genuinely listening. She made a point to turn the best suggestions into real changes.

First, she cut unnecessary expenses by stopping the practice of issuing uniforms to new part-time hires – an apron alone would do. She also relaxed the strict dress code requiring leather shoes, allowing sneakers in neutral colours like black or brown. The younger male staff, in particular, loved that change.

On top of that, she adjusted the shift system. In addition to the usual early and late shifts, she introduced a four-hour midday slot – mainly to make it easier for former employees, especially mothers, to come back to work. Another change was pushing the store's opening time back by thirty minutes. Staff hours stayed the same, but the extra time before opening was now dedicated to unpacking shipments, managing inventory and restocking shelves. This addressed one of the biggest complaints – that they were so busy during the day that they barely had time to focus on customer service or proper inventory management. Riko figured the new system would ultimately boost efficiency.

Within a month, people were saying, "Nishioka has really changed."

The irony wasn't lost on her. The perception shift wasn't just because of the policy changes – it also had a lot to do with her relationship with Aki. They still clashed, and each still stood their ground when they disagreed. They didn't sugarcoat their opinions, and they certainly didn't shower each other with praise. But they no longer dismissed each other outright, and they had stopped talking behind each other's backs. And that small improvement hadn't gone unnoticed.

"Nishioka's mellowed out," she overheard one part-timer say.

Then, one day, Ozaki casually remarked, "You and Obata are kind of alike, you know?"

That one caught Riko off guard.

*

And then, one day, a hiccup.

"Nishioka, we've got a problem! There's, um . . . a customer, and . . ."

Mami Hagiwara from the comics section burst into the office, her face pale. It had been raining all day, and business had been slow. But now it was past seven in the evening, the time when the store should be filling up with commuters on their way home. Something serious must have happened for Mami to leave the floor to come and get her.

"What's wrong?" Riko asked.

A customer had placed an order for a manga comic, Mami quickly explained. When asked how long it would take to arrive, Anna Nakamura, the part-timer who had helped him, replied, "About two weeks." Today, he came to pick it up – except the book hadn't arrived yet. When Anna told him, he completely lost it, yelling at the top of his lungs.

"You said two weeks! That's why I came all the way here! What the hell is going on?!"

Anna apologised, and Aki, the floor supervisor, had bowed to him as well, but he wasn't having it. Now, he was demanding to see the manager.

"Alright. Let's go."

Difficult customers were nothing new. Some just wanted to make a scene and take out their frustrations, while others were hoping to squeeze some kind of compensation out of the store. Which one was it this time?

Anna had made a mistake by saying two weeks so definitively. She should have stuck to the script – "It usually takes about two weeks. We'll call you when it arrives." But even so, was that really worth screaming at someone over?

When Riko reached the third floor, she noticed a small

crowd gathered near the registers. In the centre, Anna and Aki were bowing repeatedly. The customer was a man in his late twenties or early thirties, glasses, skinny, navy suit – your average office worker on his way home. His face was red with anger, and he was shouting at the top of his lungs.

"We found a copy at our Ogikubo store," Aki was saying, trying to keep her voice calm. "If you don't mind waiting, we can send someone to pick it up right away."

Anna stood frozen next to her, too terrified to speak.

"You want me to wait even longer?!" The man slammed his umbrella against the ground, swinging it around wildly. "I just got off work! I'm exhausted! And I still made the trip here in the rain, expecting it to be here! Now, you're telling me to wait *again*?!"

Drops of rainwater flew off his umbrella, landing on the nearby books.

Riko clenched her teeth.

The other customers kept their distance, watching, but not wanting to get involved. Some pretended to browse the shelves, sneaking furtive glances at all the commotion. Others saw what was happening and quietly left the store.

"Sir," Aki said carefully, "why don't we step into the back office and discuss this privately?"

"Oh, I see how it is," the man snapped. "Trying to brush me off, huh?!"

His voice grew even louder.

"You think you can get rid of me that easily? You expect me to accept some half-assed apology from a couple of kids? Get me someone in charge!"

Here it comes, Riko thought. *My turn.*

She stepped forward.

"I sincerely apologise for the trouble, sir. This was entirely our mistake."

The man turned, eyes narrowing.

"Who the hell are you?"

"My name is Riko Nishioka. I'm the store manager." She bowed.

"You've got to be kidding me. A woman? Get me someone who actually knows what they're doing."

"I'm the highest authority in this store," Riko said smoothly, handing him her business card. "If you have any complaints, I'll handle them personally."

The man snatched the card, glanced at it, then scoffed. "A woman manager? What a joke." Then, his lips curled into a vulgar smirk. "Alright then, Miss Manager. How are you going to make this right?" He jerked his chin towards Anna. "This girl told me my book would be here today. I made a special trip to pick it up, and now it's not here. So, what are you going to do about it?"

Anna shrank back, looking like she wanted to disappear. She was still new, and this was probably her first time dealing with a customer like this.

"I sincerely apologise," Riko said, bowing again. "We'll arrange to have the book delivered to your home as soon as possible."

The man snorted. "Oh, sure, the book's coming. But what about me? I wasted my time coming all the way here. And I wanted to read it tonight!"

Riko glanced at the order slip on the counter. It was for a manga comic that had been popular a few months ago. Hardly anything urgent.

"Again, I'm terribly sorry."

"Sorry isn't enough!" The man's smirk widened. "If you really mean it . . ." He paused for effect, then pointed at the floor. "Get down on your knees and apologise."

Anna and Aki gasped.

The spot he was pointing to was wet and muddy from the rain.

"A-apologies, sir," Aki stammered, stepping forward. "We're deeply sorry, but that's a bit—"

"Oh? Then why don't *you* do it instead?"

The man grinned, his eyes flicking between them. He was enjoying this.

"Actually—" Aki began, when Riko held up a hand to stop her.

"Understood."

"Nishioka!"

Riko stepped forward to shield Aki and stood on the dirty floor where the customer had pointed. She could feel everyone's eyes on her. She caught a glimpse of Anna and Aki's tearful expressions, and she noticed the other employees holding their breath from a distance.

She couldn't afford to make a fool of herself here.

Slowly, she bent her knees and lowered herself to the ground. She felt the damp, grimy floor against her legs, but she didn't flinch. Keeping her back straight, she took a deep breath, placed both hands in front of her, and bowed deeply until her forehead touched the floor.

"I sincerely apologise," she said, forcing the words from deep within her gut. She held the position for a few seconds before raising her head.

Then, looking the man straight in the eye, she asked in a calm, steady voice, "Will this be enough for you?"

She felt mud on her forehead, but she maintained a quiet smile.

The entire store fell silent. The man stared at her, caught off guard, as if the words had been knocked right out of him. The surrounding customers glanced between him and Riko, their accusing gazes clearly saying, *Did you really have to make her go that far?* The other employees looked ready to pounce. The man must have sensed it too, because his expression shifted into one of uncertainty.

"Maybe it's time to let this go," a voice suddenly called out.

A man stepped forward from the crowd – tall, broad-shouldered, built like he might have played rugby in his younger years. He looked like an ordinary businessman in his brown suit, but there was an undeniable presence about him.

"She's already gone this far. You must feel better now, right?" he said, coming to a stop right in front of the complaining customer. His imposing frame made the man seem even smaller in comparison. With a sharp glare, he told him in no uncertain terms to back off.

The man hesitated, then took half a step back.

"Fine. I'll let it go. This time," he muttered before turning on his heel and all but fleeing the store.

No-one said a word as they watched him go. Once he was out of sight, Anna rushed over to Riko, clinging to her.

"I'm so sorry, Nishioka."

Her voice wavered, on the verge of tears.

Riko stood up, clapped the dirt off her skirt with brisk slaps, and whispered with a small smile, "It's fine. It's over now."

Then, she turned to the other customers, straightened her posture, and said in a clear, steady voice, "I apologise for the disturbance. Please, enjoy the rest of your evening."

With a graceful smile, she folded her hands in front of her and gave a polite bow.

Seeing this, the other employees scrambled to follow suit, bowing and echoing her words. The tension in the air finally lifted, and the customers began to disperse.

"Thank you, Nishioka," Aki said.

The other employees gathered around as well, murmuring their thanks. Anna, still teary-eyed, desperately tried to brush the remaining grime off Riko's skirt, as if that could somehow make up for what had happened.

Riko gently stopped her hand. "Don't worry about it. A store manager is essentially a professional complaint handler," she said lightly, flashing her a reassuring smile.

A moment later, the tall man from earlier approached them.

"Thank you for stepping in back there," Riko said, bowing her head. Aki and Anna quickly followed suit.

"It was nothing," the man replied.

"No, really. That customer was really digging in. He might have been here all day if you hadn't spoken up. Your timing was perfect."

"Well, guys like him love throwing their weight around when they think they've got the upper hand. But the moment the tables turn, they tuck tail and run. He just needed a little push."

"Indeed."

The man gave Riko an appraising look. "Still . . . You didn't even hesitate to bow like that. I think that's what threw him off."

"If bowing is all it takes to resolve a conflict, I'll do it as often as it takes," Riko replied with a smile. "That's part of the job."

The man studied her for a moment, then nodded, impressed. Under his steady gaze, Riko found herself glancing down, embarrassed.

That evening, Riko returned to her office after the end-of-day meeting to wrestle with the sales figures, when –

"Nishioka."

She looked up to see Mita standing there with a serious look on his face. It had been about a month since he last initiated a conversation with her.

"What is it?" she responded, keeping her surprise under wraps.

"About that thing we talked about the other day . . ." He hesitated.

"The other day?"

For a moment, Riko wasn't sure what he meant.

"The fourth-floor supervisor position," he clarified.

Oh, that.

He had turned it down when she first suggested it to him. At the time, she had assumed he didn't trust her because of the situation with Aki.

"If you still want me to do it . . . I'd like to take the position after all."

"Wait – really?" Riko blinked in surprise, then broke into a smile. "Of course! Everyone will be thrilled, and honestly, it will be a huge help for me."

Right now, she was covering the position herself, and it added a lot to her plate. Mita was more than capable, and she had hoped he would take on extra responsibilities.

"I understand. Then I'll start tomorrow," Mita said, bowing slightly. "I'm looking forward to working with you."

"Thank you. I really appreciate it."

Without thinking, Riko reached out and took his hand. Mita's eyes widened in surprise, but after a brief pause, he squeezed her hand firmly in return.

Riko felt a wave of relief.

For the first time in a long while, it felt like things were moving forward.

20

Inspired by recent efforts on the third and fourth floors, Aki was keen to come up with an exciting new initiative of her own.

On the third floor, Ozaki – who had recently taken over as supervisor – had launched a campaign called Discovering the Heart of Japan. Thanks to its creative decorations and bold book selection, sales had picked up by a surprising amount. While the core line-up featured essays by well-known female authors, Ozaki had also included unexpected choices, like Hiroko Endo's *The Girl Who Loved Math*, as well as old bestsellers like Ruth Benedict's *The Chrysanthemum and the Sword*.

However, by far the biggest change Ozaki had made since taking over was the way the literary fiction section was displayed on weekdays versus weekends.

During the week, the displays were subdued – minimal pop-up signs, fewer bestsellers and a calmer, more sophisticated atmosphere overall, tailored to their regular customers. But on weekends, eye-catching signs went up, and the hottest bestsellers were placed front and centre, making the store more inviting for casual shoppers. It took a lot of effort to switch things up twice a week, and Aki was impressed by Ozaki's dedication.

Meanwhile, over in the textbook section, there had been another standout success. When a well-known history professor was appointed president of a nearby university, Mita wasted no time setting up a special corner featuring the professor's books. Then, by pure luck, the professor himself stopped by the store. Mita seized the opportunity and asked him to recommend several history books – especially ones that more casual readers would enjoy.

Mita ordered the suggested books and displayed them alongside the professor's own works, complete with handwritten recommendation cards featuring the professor's comments. The response was incredible. With so many students from the university visiting the store, the section became a major draw – the university newspaper even came to do a feature on it. Sales skyrocketed, making it one of the most successful promotions in the history of the store's textbook section.

Aki had been trying out new ideas on the fifth floor, as well. The biggest change so far was how comics were displayed. Before, books were lined up so only their spines were visible. Now, at least one book per shelf was placed face-out, showcasing its cover. With covers on display throughout the section, the space looked livelier and more appealing.

To take things further, every displayed book had a recommendation card. Instead of the usual large pop-ups, they used elegant, business-card-sized notes in a soft, pale green with carefully chosen lettering for a refined look. To maintain consistency, the most artistically skilled member of the staff wrote all the cards by hand.

Aki had also worked with the team to strengthen anti-theft measures. Ever since a second-hand bookstore opened nearby, shoplifting had been on the rise – especially in the comics section. With theft eating into profits, they had to take action. They added more mirrors, moved high-value books closer to the registers, and reorganised the layout to eliminate blind spots. They also developed a clear protocol for handling shoplifters throughout the entire store and trained the staff on how to respond.

All these improvements were good, but they weren't directly boosting sales. And that was Aki's real goal – she had to show results by March.

She wanted to do something big. Something that would grab people's attention. Something that would bring in more customers.

She had brainstormed a few ideas, but so far, nothing had clicked.

It was tough to pull off a major promotion in the comics section, where the average retail price was so low.

So what could she do?

"Does it have to be *today*?" Aki asked Nobumitsu, unable to hide the disappointment in her voice.

"Yeah . . . The author's insisting on it."

"But it's my birthday. We've made plans."

Since Nobumitsu had said he wouldn't have time to pick out a present in advance, they had decided to go shopping together in Shibuya so she could choose something she liked from a department store. After that, they had planned to have dinner at her favourite French restaurant in Azabu. It had been a while since they last had a whole day to themselves, and Aki had been looking forward to it.

That morning, she had let herself sleep in, then sat down for a relaxed brunch – until Nobumitsu's phone rang. From the way he reacted, she could tell it was a work call. She stayed quiet and kept eating. He was on the phone for a solid thirty minutes, and as soon as he hung up, he turned to her and said, "I have to go to work."

"Which author?" she asked.

Nobumitsu named a female manga artist.

"Of course. That woman has no boundaries. Calling her editor on his day off?"

The artist was a cult favourite. Nobumitsu had always said, "She's going to be huge someday," and had personally taken charge of her work. They were planning to feature her on the magazine's inaugural cover. But she was also high maintenance. If she got stuck on her storyboards or started feeling overwhelmed, she would call her editor and rattle on with her complaints. Sometimes, she would even summon him to her home, irrespective of the hour.

"That's just how it is with female manga artists," Nobumitsu said, like it was some universal truth. "They test their editors to see how much we care about them."

Aki felt a twinge of indignation.

"But it's work, isn't it? That's kind of weird."

It wasn't like they were in a relationship. Why would she be *testing* him?

"That's just how they are," he said dismissively.

"So? You have to keep *her* happy?"

Aki meant it as a jab, but Nobumitsu just nodded in all seriousness.

"Exactly. Any publisher would kill to feature her work. She didn't debut with us, but she still chooses to publish here. We've got to treat her well, or she'll take her work elsewhere."

"Must be nice, being a manga artist."

"Only if you're successful. It's the ones who sell who get to be demanding. That's just how it works."

"I suppose."

Seeing Aki's sulky expression, Nobumitsu chuckled and flicked her forehead with his finger.

"If I leave now, I'll be back in time for dinner. It's only eleven. Let's meet in Shibuya at six. That way, we'll have time to shop and still make it to the restaurant by eight."

With that, he left.

But Aki was far from satisfied. She wanted to spend the whole day with him, not just squeeze in a quick shopping trip before dinner. She had imagined them taking a leisurely stroll, maybe checking out the new shopping mall in Omotesando. Was it really that hard for him to take just one day off for her birthday? She knew work was important, but was this the best he could do?

If it had been a male author, maybe she wouldn't have felt so uneasy. But it wasn't. It was a young woman. And if that woman had feelings for Nobumitsu – what then?

Aki recalled the magazine article where she had first seen the manga artist's face. She was barely in her twenties, fresh-faced, with delicate features. The article had even called her beautiful. She came across as quiet but strong-willed – not the type who seemed helpless without her editor.

I hate this.

She hated how eagerly Nobumitsu had left. And she hated that she couldn't just brush it off and tell herself it was nothing.

Sitting around without anything to do was only making her more anxious, so she got up and turned on her laptop. She figured she might as well get some work done. It would keep her from dwelling on toxic thoughts, and maybe she could come up with an idea for a new event. Work like this was hard to focus on at the office, in any event. At least this was more productive than sulking.

She browsed the websites of several major bookstores. These days, Pegasus' competitors weren't just hosting book signings – they were organising full-fledged events. A big bookstore in Aoyama had an event space that could fit nearly a hundred people, which they used for things like author talks and panel discussions.

Pegasus Books, however, didn't have that kind of space. She needed to host something smaller. Something that could work in the comics section.

Then, something caught her eye on a major bookstore's website. An upcoming event with a famous critic. The concept was simple – the critic had selected a hundred books that had influenced him, which the store was showcasing prominently.

Seeing that, an idea sparked to life.

That's it. What if we did this, but with a manga artist instead?

It wouldn't just be about showcasing the featured guest's own works – they could highlight different manga comics, and host signings and exhibits. If the right artist was involved, it would be sure to generate buzz and bring in a crowd.

But the artist would have to be willing to collaborate. On top of that, it couldn't be someone tied to an exclusive contract with any one publisher. Some publishers were so strict, they wouldn't even share an artist's contact information.

Which meant . . . there was only one option.

She needed someone popular, someone cooperative, and – most importantly – someone she had access to.

She clicked over to Twitter and searched for the username Rainbow Prism – Nao Agachi's private handle. The two of them had started following each other after they had hit it off at her home party.

Agachi would be perfect. A big name. And the second season of his work's anime adaptation was starting in January. The first season had been a hit, so now, after a six-month break, it was making a comeback. The publisher was already planning a major marketing push to promote it. If the timing lined up right, it could be huge. It was November now, so two months would be plenty of time to prepare.

I should run this by Nobumitsu first.

If Pegasus Books wanted to host an event with Agachi, they would need to go through the publisher's sales department, who would then get in touch with the editorial team. Either way, Nobumitsu would find out eventually. Since he had been Agachi's editor before, and of course, they had only met through him in the first place, it was better to let him know upfront.

Aki clicked on Agachi's Twitter profile. There was a new post. Since his account was set to private, his tweets were full of unfiltered thoughts and insider gossip about the industry. Things like *"Had a deadline, but snuck out to a concert anyway,"* or *"My editor rejected my storyboard. So frustrating."* Aki figured any editor reading these would have a hard time staying calm. No wonder Agachi didn't want his seeing them.

Today's post was another work rant.

"Had a fight with my editor at Hitotsuboshi today. I don't think he understands my work. Honestly, I wish I could have my old editor back."

That could only mean Konno – Nobumitsu's junior colleague, who had come to the party where Aki had met Agachi. He had come across as a nervous, uptight kind of guy. The old editor was obviously Nobumitsu.

Aki felt a little smug – so Nobumitsu really *was* the better editor.

But the next line wiped that feeling away.

"Not that it matters. My old editor is too busy doting on some hotshot female artist these days."

Aki froze.

Was that the same woman Nobumitsu had ditched her birthday plans for today? Was this such common knowledge that people were gossiping about it online?

She was still furrowing her brow at that disquieting thought when her phone buzzed. A text message. From Nobumitsu.

"Sorry. I won't be done in time for dinner. We'll have to cancel. I'll make it up to you, I promise."

Aki threw her phone onto the couch.

She knew this would happen. He really had been held up by that artist.

Why was he so willing to bend over backwards for that woman? Aki was always putting up with him being busy all the time, but how much more did she have to tolerate?

And for Agachi to say something like that ... Was Nobumitsu's obsession with this artist really strictly professional? Or was he just using work as an excuse to spend time with her? What was so important that it absolutely had to take priority over his wife's birthday?

In the end, her husband only cared about what *he* wanted.

He endlessly obsessed over his own job, but when it came to *her* work, he never showed the slightest hint of interest.

Fine. If *he* could do whatever he wanted, then so could she.

Fuming, Aki turned back to her laptop and clicked the message icon under the handle Rainbow Prism. She was going to reach out to Nao Agachi directly.

21

The customer research meeting was held on the first Saturday in November.

"Publishers invite us booksellers to hear our opinions – so why don't we do the same? Let's bring in some customers and get their direct feedback on the store," one of the staff had suggested, and so they were doing just that.

They had already set up a suggestion box and a feedback page on the store's website, but most of the responses they got were complaints, and it was proving difficult to capture other kinds of feedback. Riko had some reservations about the idea. Wouldn't this kind of meeting feel like giving special treatment to a select group of customers? A professional bookseller should be able to anticipate customer needs without having to be told. Still, Aki and the younger staff pushed for it, so in the end, Riko gave in.

Would they get any useful input? It was hard to say. But the general consensus was to give it a shot, so maybe this was the right approach.

"We don't want to upset important customers," she had warned. "What if someone posts something bad about us online afterwards?"

"If that happens, we'll deal with it then," Aki fired back, her cheeks flushed with excitement. "If we do nothing out of fear of taking risks, we'll never achieve anything."

At least *she* seemed to be enjoying herself, Riko thought. Aki made it sound like a grand, well-thought-out idea, but wasn't she just excited about doing something new?

Deep down, Riko was equally curious about what customers really thought of the store. It didn't belong solely to the staff, after all. A bookstore existed for its clientele.

"Look! I made a poster." Aki held up something she had designed on her laptop.

First Annual Supporters' Meeting – Your Voice Can Change Our Store! it read in bold letters.

"*Supporters' Meeting?*" Riko raised an eyebrow.

Aki grinned, as if she had been waiting for her to ask just this question. "Well, *Research Meeting* sounds stiff and uninviting. *Supporters' Meeting* feels more casual – like something people would drop by to out of curiosity."

Riko wasn't so sure, but since there was no precedent for this sort of event, she had no solid argument against it. She let the name stand. They put up posters, posted announcements on the website, and Riko started encouraging regular customers to attend. After all, the whole affair would be pointless if no-one showed up.

"If turnout is low, we can make an announcement over the PA system," suggested Ozaki, who was just as nervous as Riko.

Five people had signed up by the day before. Hopefully, that would be enough. The meeting was scheduled for Saturday at three in the afternoon – not ideal, since the store would be busy, but they had chosen that time to make it easier for customers to take part.

When the day arrived, five people showed up – just about. One had cancelled at the last minute, but when they put out an in-store announcement, another man volunteered to take the spot. So, they were back to five.

The meeting was held in the part-timers' break room. It only had space for five or six people, so the set-up was simple – the five customers sat, Riko as store manager joined them, and the three floor supervisors stood nearby, listening in.

The group consisted of four men and one woman. Most of them were regulars. Among them was an older man who came to the literary fiction section every day, and another who spent hours reading light novels in the aisles each week. Riko was surprised to see one man in particular – the one who had stepped in the day she had been forced to bow in apology to the customer with the umbrella. He introduced himself as Saburo Hoshino.

They served tea and brought out slices of cake on paper plates. The customers started out a bit stiff at first, but as they settled in, the conversation began to flow more naturally.

"I wish the staff had more time to actually talk to us," one customer said. "I have questions sometimes, but everyone always looks so busy. I feel bad interrupting them."

"Honestly, some of the younger part-timers just don't know enough," another added. "The other day, I asked about Yutaka Haniya, and the clerk asked me, *What genre is that?* That's unacceptable. The staff need to be more informed."

"Also, why do you guys have so much BL stuff?" another man complained. "As soon as I walk into the comics section, I'm hit with a huge display of BL manga. It makes it awkward for male customers. And the light novel section is totally neglected. Like, why are you still stocking *Galactic Frontline*

Crisis? That came out five years ago – no-one reads it today. The *Yayoi-chan* series is blowing up now, and you only have the latest volume of it. That series should be stocked in full!"

"The bathrooms are terrible. Too small, too dark, and they smell weird," someone else grumbled.

"Yeah. And squat toilets? Seriously? It's time to upgrade to Western-style ones."

"Forget that – can you put in an escalator? Climbing the stairs every time is a pain."

"Also," said their female participant hesitantly, "I like *BeBe* magazine, but you only ever have one copy in stock. Half the time, it's already gone when I come in. And the magazine section is too cluttered – it's difficult to find anything."

As soon as they started talking, the complaints started rolling in. Some of the issues were valid, but others – like toilet renovations – were out of their control, as they depended on the building's management. The conversation was getting out of hand, and Riko wasn't sure how to steer it back on track.

Then, she caught Hoshino's eye. As if reading her thoughts, he spoke up. "But you know, I really like how the literary fiction section is arranged. It looks great."

The light novel fan jumped in. "Yeah, and the Top Ten Comics display is nice, but . . . it feels kind of incomplete."

"Incomplete?" Riko asked.

"Like, wouldn't it be cool if the whole store got involved? Not just one section, but all three floors at once?"

"All three floors at once?"

"Like when department stores do those full-store bazaar events. Something like that," the lone female participant added.

"Exactly. It would make the store feel more alive. Like how Book On does it – with loud music playing and the staff all greeting you. This place is kind of dull. It could use more excitement."

Book On was a fast-growing used bookstore chain, and it had recently opened a branch in the building next door.

"I hate that style," grumbled a middle-aged man. "Too loud. You can't focus on browsing."

Riko, however, felt a spark of inspiration.

"Loud music aside, a full-store event could be a great idea," she mused. "Next month, perhaps. Maybe each floor could have its own Christmas-themed displays."

"Sounds great! Maybe put up a tree," the woman suggested.

"Some stores had staff dress up for the *Harry Potter* book release. Why not have everyone wear Santa outfits?"

"That could be fun," Riko answered, mentally filing the idea away. A store-wide theme and a festive atmosphere – that could work.

She shifted gears. "Since we're talking about Book On, what do you all think of their customer service approach? They're big on direct engagement, while we try to give customers a bit of space. Which do you prefer?"

The conversation was starting to resemble an actual research meeting. Aki, watching from the back, sighed in relief.

At that moment, her phone buzzed in her pocket. It was on silent mode, so it didn't make a sound. She glanced at the caller ID. Nobumitsu.

What could he want, calling her during work hours?

Slipping out of the room as quietly as possible, she picked up.

"What's up? You know I'm at work, right?"

"This isn't a *what's up* situation, Aki. We've got a serious problem with Agachi."

"What?" She blinked, caught off guard.

"You reached out to him directly about holding some event, didn't you? Well, that's caused a huge mess for the editorial team over here."

"But I thought all you did was check in with him? The formal request went through Hitotsuboshi Press's sales department. You followed the proper procedure, so what's the problem?" Riko asked Aki the next day as they discussed the Nao Agachi Fair.

Somehow, their plans seemed to have taken a turn for the worse.

"I mean, I *thought* I did everything by the book . . ." Aki muttered.

When Aki had reached out to Agachi over Twitter, he had loved the idea. He was so into it, in fact, that he kept coming up with suggestions of his own.

With the author on board, Aki put together the proposal, got approval from within the company, and passed it to Iwata, their sales rep at Hitotsuboshi Publishing, which published Agachi's major works. Iwata had said they would seriously consider it, so Aki had assumed it would all work out.

Clearly, she had been wrong.

"Apparently, Agachi and his editor aren't on great terms."

According to Nobumitsu, Agachi and Satoru Konno had been butting heads from the start. Their meetings always seemed to turn into arguments, and ever since Konno took over, Agachi's serialised manga had repeatedly been forced to cut pages because he wasn't producing enough content to fill them.

But the real problem was that Hitotsuboshi Press were

already planning their own Nao Agachi Fair in January to coincide with the TV adaptation of his manga. The centrepiece was supposed to be a brand-new collected volume of his ongoing series – but thanks to all the reduced page counts, there wasn't enough material.

With their big release delayed, Konno panicked. Desperate to have something new for their fair, he unilaterally decided to re-release an old Agachi short story collection, originally published by a small press when Agachi was a rookie. The book had done surprisingly well for its original publisher – selling 50,000 copies despite its high price and large A5 format. But Konno figured that if Hitotsuboshi repackaged it as a cheaper, standard B6-sized edition, they could sell even more.

"Besides, it's Agachi's own fault we don't have a new book," he reportedly said.

Agachi, however, had a strong sense of loyalty to the small press that first took a chance on him. He saw Konno's move as a power play, and he was having none of it. The two of them got into a fight, during which Konno made the fatal mistake of saying, "Let's not forget – it was our company that turned you from a nobody into a star."

That was it. Agachi completely lost it. His pride as a creator had been trampled over.

The whole thing escalated beyond just editor and artist, reaching the higher-ups in the publishing house. In the end, Hitotsuboshi's executive editor had to step in to smooth things over. They agreed to re-release the short story collection in January *and* remove Konno as Agachi's editor.

But that wasn't enough for Agachi. Furious, he flat-out refused to participate in any of the publisher's planned book signings in Tokyo and Osaka.

"And then, just as all this was blowing up, we reached out to him with our proposal. And to make matters worse, Agachi agreed to do a signing and an event *for us*. So now, Hitotsuboshi Press is furious."

"That was bad timing," Riko remarked. "But at the end of the day, this is between Agachi and Hitotsuboshi. It has nothing to do with us. Yes, it would be a problem if their sales department wanted to shut our fair down, but they haven't said anything yet, have they?"

"Not yet, no . . ."

"Then let's wait for their official response before we panic. Whatever dramas are going on in their editorial department, it's their sales team we're dealing with."

With that, Riko gave Aki a reassuring pat on the shoulder.

"Right," Aki replied – but she still couldn't shake her unease.

What she hadn't told Riko was that she and Nobumitsu had got into a heated argument about this just the night before.

"You've really screwed this up for me. Sales are furious."

Nobumitsu had come home unusually early, but instead of unwinding, he immediately launched into an attack.

It turned out that Hitotsuboshi Press had planned a book signing at a *major* Shinjuku bookstore – one that almost never hosted manga signings. That alone showed how seriously they were taking their fair. And then, just like that, the whole thing was scrapped at the whim of the author.

To make matters worse, Pegasus Books, a mid-sized chain out in the suburbs, had reached out about holding their own event and signing session – which Agachi had already agreed to. It was a slap in the face to Hitotsuboshi's sales team, who now looked like they had no control over their own author. Their anger, of course, was aimed straight at editorial. Nobumitsu had got an earful from Iwata, who was in charge of organising the Shinjuku signing.

"You've really backed me into a corner here," Nobumitsu groaned. "I was Agachi's original editor, and now it looks like my wife went behind my back and convinced him to undermine our work."

"This has *nothing* to do with your position," Aki shot back. "Yes, I ran the idea by Agachi first, but I followed the proper procedure and went through our sales rep."

"Yeah, but *I* was the one who introduced you to him. Everyone knows that. If it weren't for me, you wouldn't have been able to contact him directly."

Nobumitsu's voice was getting higher – a clear indicator of just how incensed he was.

"Fine," Aki snapped. "If you don't like it, why don't you just shut it down on your end?"

"We can't do that. Agachi's already on board. If we cancel now and he thinks it's because of us, it'll just make him even angrier," Nobumitsu groaned, bouncing his leg in agitation.

"You *have* to be kidding me . . ."

"He agreed to your fair as a way to get back at our editorial team. He's pissed that we pushed him into publishing that reissue, so now he's using you to get back at us. He's a calculating son of a bitch, you know."

Aki was taken aback by those harsh words. Nobumitsu and Agachi had seemed like close friends at their house party, but maybe that was just for show. The relationship between editor and creator was evidently much more complicated than she had realised.

"Listen," Nobumitsu said, his tone shifting. "Could you please just cancel the fair on your end? The last thing we need is to piss Agachi off even more. He's one of our biggest money-makers. But we can't have your store going ahead with a solo event, either. It's putting us in a really bad spot." He looked at Aki, practically begging her.

"That's *your* problem," Aki said firmly. "We're trying to do whatever we can to boost sales. If your sales department decides to shut us down, fine. But I'm not going to cancel it from our side."

She broke into a frown. She wanted to support her husband, but this wasn't just about him or her – everyone at the store was counting on this fair.

"There are *plenty* of other authors out there," Nobumitsu argued. "It doesn't have to be Agachi."

"I can't think of any other big-name authors who would make this event work . . . I know it puts you in an awkward position, and I'm sorry about that, but—"

"Then at least push it back a few months," he pressed. "This is *really* bad timing."

"We don't *have* a few months. We need results by March. You know that."

"If your store is on the verge of collapsing over one fair, then it's already doomed," Nobumitsu muttered. "No point in working there anyway."

That did it.

"Excuse me?" Aki snapped. "*That's* what you have to say? My job matters just as much as yours does! Or don't you take my work seriously?"

Nobumitsu opened his mouth, then shut it again. She had hit a nerve.

"All you ever talk about is your authors – how important they are, how everything revolves around them. You even ditched me on my *birthday* to run off to that eye-candy manga artist's place," she added, not bothering to hide her resentment.

"Oh, come on! That was work! It doesn't matter if she's pretty or not – it's my job to look after authors," Nobumitsu shot back.

"Well, *my* job is running promotions and boosting sales for the store. You're not the only one with responsibilities, you know? Can't you see how desperate we are? The store's hanging on by a thread! If your magazine was about to go under, you'd do whatever it takes to save it, wouldn't you?"

"Well . . ." Nobumitsu hesitated.

"Please," Aki pleaded. "We're fighting for survival here."

"Ugh," he huffed. "Do whatever you want."

With that, he stormed out the room.

22

Riko opened the front door. It was already past midnight, but she could hear the TV playing in the living room.

"I'm home," she called out, kicking off her boots.

"Welcome back," came her father's voice as he peeked out into the hall. "Happy New Year."

"Oh – Happy New Year," Riko replied.

Right, it was officially New Year's Day now. On the TV, the hosts were wishing everyone a happy new year.

"You're home late."

"There was a lot to wrap up now the holiday break has started."

She finally managed to peel off her boots, practically yanking them off her swollen feet, then stood up with a sigh.

"You had a rough year. You should take it easy," her dad said.

"I know . . . But I haven't done anything to prepare for the New Year. I didn't even write any cards."

"Then write them now. Anyway, I made some year-end soba noodles. Want some?"

"Thanks. Let me just go and change."

After changing into her loungewear and washing her hands, Riko sat down at the table. A bowl of soba was waiting for her. It was plain soba, but the broth looked light. Making sure her father's back was turned, she discreetly sprinkled some table salt into the soup. She was glad to see he had started cooking, but everything he made was low-sodium, and for Riko, that meant bland. She didn't want to discourage him, though, so she secretly adjusted the seasoning on her own.

"Here's the garnish," her father said, placing a small dish of chopped spring onions in front of her. The pieces were thicker than if she had cut them herself, and he probably hadn't soaked them in water beforehand.

"Thanks."

"I've got shichimi spice blend too. Want some?"

"Please," she said, then suddenly found herself smiling.

"What?" her dad asked.

"It's just ... it feels like we've switched roles. I never imagined you'd be taking care of me like this."

"Well, you're the one out there working now. I can't be dragging you down. Got to stay strong while I can."

Her father had become much more disciplined since his health scare. He had quit smoking, something she never thought he would do, and he went for a walk every morning, without fail. He even joined a local radio calisthenics group, where he had made some new friends. And now he was cooking his own low-sodium meals.

He had been lucky this time, but the doctor had made it clear – if he didn't change his habits, a real stroke was inevitable. That warning had hit home.

"Thank you," Riko said with a warm smile. "That means a lot to me."

Her father, embarrassed, changed the subject. "So, how's work? Everything okay?"

He sat down across from her, placing two cups of tea on the table. Ever since she had found out about his secret scrapbook filled with clippings about her work, he had started talking to her about her job more often.

"Yes. We've been busy through December with the Christmas Fair, but we managed to increase sales by fifteen per cent over last year."

"That's great!" He sounded as proud as if it had been his own achievement.

The Christmas Fair had turned out to be hit. It was the first time they had coordinated a store-wide event, and it had only come about because of their Supporters' Meeting. The building was old, the walls and ceilings were stained, and the bookshelves were worn, meaning they had been forced to get creative with the decorations.

Each floor had a large Christmas tree, with themed book displays set up beside them. They featured seasonal new releases along with Christmas classics, beautifully illustrated photo collections and pop-up books that made for great gifts. They also included Christmas cards and garlands from the stationary section. At the registers, they placed Santa and reindeer figurines, and from the ceiling, they hung holly branches dusted with artificial snow. Behind the counter on the third floor, they put up a giant Christmas tapestry that one of the employees had brought from home. "The idea is for customers to feel the Christmas spirit from the moment they walk in," the young part-timer had said excitedly.

The stairwell walls were covered with red and green craft paper, decorated with gold and silver origami stars and real wreaths. Someone had suggested displaying Christmas picture books, shrink-wrapped so customers could see the covers. Two brothers, Kaito and Takato Kurata – art school students who had taken casual jobs because they were interested in visual displays – had put it all together.

Customers had noticed. Several had commented on how nice the decorations were, including Hoshino, who had been at the Supporters' Meeting. Sales had increased, and the collaborative effort had lifted morale. The work had been exhausting, but for a while, everyone had been able to forget about the store's financial struggles.

"The younger staff loved it," Riko told her father. "They got very involved, even bringing in their own decorations. One of the girls asked if she could wear a Santa-style mini dress."

"I don't really get it, but if it makes customers happy, it has to be a good thing."

"Yes, that's what I figured. Since she works in the comics section, I allowed it. But if she had been in the literary fiction section, I would have had to say no."

"Huh. Is that how it works?" her father asked, listening on in amusement.

Riko chuckled. "Kind of. Anyway, it wasn't a big deal."

Her dad studied her for a moment. "Something else on your mind?"

"Yeah ... A few things." She let out a tired sigh.

Lately, what worried her most was the drop in new book shipments. The distributor's representative insisted nothing had changed, but she knew better. Books that had consistently arrived in quantities of ten or more were now coming in at half that or less. It was hard not to suspect foul play.

Rumours about the store's possible closure were starting

to spread through the industry. With sudden staff transfers like Tsujii and Hatakeda, it was impossible to keep everything under wraps. If those rumours hurt sales now, just when they needed them to be at their strongest, it would be devastating.

"You've got a lot on your plate as store manager," her father said. Then, as if to lighten the mood, he added, "Hey, I have some wine. Want a glass?"

Riko blinked. "Wine?"

"Yeah. Got it as a gift from the neighbour when I was released from hospital."

"Ah. That's nice. Sure, I'll have a little."

Her father got up, pulled a bottle from the cabinet, and set out the glasses. That was when Riko noticed it.

Baccarat wine glasses.

The same as the ones Shibata had given her. She had thrown hers away in a fit of anger after finding out he had given Aki Obata the same set. Had her father fished them out of the bin?

"You okay?" he asked.

"Oh. Yeah. It's nothing."

They were just glasses. It didn't matter where they came from.

Her father poured the wine, the deep red liquid glistening in the cut crystal.

"Well then, let's toast – to the new year. We made it through another one, at least."

She was grateful for that. Her father was healthy. Work was still manageable, for now. The future was uncertain, but for the moment, things were okay.

She wished this peaceful feeling could last forever.

"Hope it's a good year for you," her father said.

"You too, Dad."

They clinked their glasses together.

Aki was drifting in and out of a sleep when she was awakened by the sound of the bedroom door opening. She could hear someone moving around in the darkness, changing clothes.

"Nobumitsu? Did you just get home?"

What time was it? She had stayed up until about two waiting for him, but she must have dozed off at some point.

"Did I wake you? Sorry. Go back to sleep."

Nobumitsu finished changing and slipped into bed beside her. There was a faint scent of alcohol on him.

"Hey, do you have tomorrow off?" she asked. "When do you go back to work?"

"Mmm . . . I'm off tomorrow, but I think I have to go in the day after," he said, sounding like he couldn't be bothered.

"Oh. I was hoping we could visit our families for New Year."

Both of their parents had called, expecting them to drop by for the holiday.

"I'm too busy this year. And I'm exhausted . . . Let it go."

With that, Nobumitsu pulled the covers over his head to make it clear he didn't want to talk. He had been like this a lot lately. Come to think of it, he hadn't even wished her a happy New Year. Was this how they were going to spend the holiday?

Aki knew the reason. He was still mad about the Nao Agachi situation.

In the end, Hitotsuboshi Press's sales department had approved the fair at Pegasus. Agachi himself had sent Aki an email: *If they try to shut this down, I'll raise hell.* Maybe the publisher had been too afraid of upsetting him to object.

Had Nobumitsu been right? *Should* she have turned it down?

Her co-workers, however, were thrilled about it. Nao Agachi was the hottest manga artist right now, and several of the staff were huge fans. Agachi himself dropped by when the fair was officially confirmed, which only made everyone more excited. Keeping morale up was crucial, especially now. With the looming threat of closure hanging over them, it would have been all too easy for everyone to lose hope.

At this point, it wasn't just about her anymore.

But Nobumitsu wouldn't let it go. He barely spoke to her. Maybe one of them needed to back down, but neither was willing to compromise when it came to their work.

Still, the thought of this driving a permanent wedge between them made Aki miserable. Work was work. It had nothing to do with their marriage. Nobumitsu had always been the one to say that.

Pulling the blanket up to her face, Aki let out a quiet sigh, careful not to let him hear.

Was he already asleep, lying there with his back to her? Or just pretending?

What should have been a joyful New Year's holiday stretched out before her, long and heavy with dread.

23

As soon as the New Year holidays were over, Aki and the rest of the team in the fifth-floor comics section were thrown into a frenzy preparing for the fair.

First, they had to make sure they could get hold of all the comics Nao Agachi had picked out. He had listed fifty titles, but many were from smaller publishers, and some were out of print. Still, they wanted to track down as many as possible in physical form. Even if a book was no longer listed in a publisher's catalogue, there was always a chance a few copies were still sitting in a warehouse somewhere. They asked the sales reps to help chase them down.

Then there was everything else – the displays for the original artwork, putting together a timeline of Agachi's career, getting his friends to contribute signed illustrations to show their support. Someone suggested filming an interview with him and playing it in the store. It was a solid idea, but making it happen wasn't quite so easy. None of them had any experience of conducting an interview. And on top of that, they still had to keep up with their regular work.

It was exhausting – but also exciting. She never would have

guessed how much fun it could be to bring her own ideas to life. It felt like getting ready for a festival.

Best of all, Aki didn't have to think about the tension with her husband while she was busy with work. And so, she threw herself into it.

It wasn't long before the day of the fair rolled around. As soon as the store closed the night before, everyone sprang into action, rushing to get the decorations up. The central display table, which had been showcasing books to help with winter break homework assignments, was cleared to make way for a selection of books related to Agachi. The posters lining the staircase walls were all taken down, to be replaced by the artist's original illustrations, which were carefully arranged one by one. Meanwhile, a TV was set up in the centre of the main display, and they tested the prerecorded interview video to make sure it played smoothly. Were all the tickets for the signing event and talk show ready to hand out the next day? Where should they put up the posters announcing the signing session? How could they make Agachi's hand-drawn character sketches stand out as much as possible? There was a lot to do, and even more to think about.

A line had already formed outside the building – fans were willing to camp out overnight just to get their hands on a ticket to the Q&A session. It was rare enough for Agachi to take part in a signing event, but this would be his first time fielding questions from his fans. It was no wonder anticipation was through the roof. They needed extra staff just to manage the crowd. Every bookseller in the store, not just the team from the fifth floor, had been called in to help. At this rate, they were in for an all-nighter tomorrow.

*

"Aki! We've got a problem!" Mami Hagiwara shouted, running up the stairs in a panic.

Aki was in the middle of hanging the artworks with the Kurata brothers on the landing. It was already past ten in the evening.

"What's wrong?"

Mami was supposed to be handling the fair display. What could have thrown her into such a frenzy? Aki paused her work and turned to face her.

"Uh . . . I just checked, and Agachi's new book, *Wings of the Caucasus* – only a hundred copies came in."

"What? That can't be right."

The fair was planned with two major events – a signing session in the middle of the day and a Q&A session in the evening. *Wings of the Caucasus* was the featured book for both, and customers who bought it in-store would receive a ticket for one or other of the events. Since they had planned for around a hundred attendees at each, they needed at least two hundred copies – ideally, two hundred and fifty to three hundred, seeing as some customers would just want to buy the book without a ticket. While the fair was meant to promote Agachi's previous works and related titles, the main goal – the whole point, really – was to push the new release. It was supposed to be the star of the show, displayed front and centre.

"I should've checked the shipment as soon as it arrived, but things were so hectic, and I – I didn't realise until just now. I'm so sorry," Mami stammered, on the verge of tears.

"But I went over the numbers with Yamamoto from the distributor!"

The plan had been to get two hundred and fifty copies delivered on the first day and then restock as needed. That was the agreement. Aki felt numb. Without enough books, the fair was doomed from the start.

"What do we do? It's going to be a disaster!" Mami's voice was shaking.

"First, we need to talk to Nishioka. She's still in the back, right?"

Aki handed the illustration panel she was holding to one of the Kurata brothers and hurried to the office with Mami.

"Do we know what went wrong?" Riko asked.

"No."

"The priority right now is figuring out how to get the rest of the books delivered first thing tomorrow."

As expected, Riko remained calm.

"Right." Aki nodded. "But can we manage it in time?"

"The distributor is probably closed for the night," Mami pointed out.

"That's a problem. Yamamoto's mobile number – do you have it?" Riko asked.

"Oh! Right! Yes, here."

Aki pulled out her phone, found Yamamoto's number in her contacts, and dialled. It rang six or seven times before he finally picked up.

"Hello?"

"Hi, this is Obata from Pegasus Books. About *Wings of the Caucasus* – we only got a hundred copies. What happened? Was there some kind of mistake?"

"Uh . . . Well . . ."

Yamamoto's voice was low, hesitant. Aki could tell immediately – he knew something and was struggling to say it.

"So, it *wasn't* a mistake. You knew about this, didn't you?"

"I'm really sorry . . . but that's all we could manage this time."

"You promised us two hundred and fifty! The fair starts tomorrow, and you've sent us less than half of what we agreed!"

Aki was desperate. They had worked so hard to pull this together, and now, without the main attraction, all their efforts would go to waste.

"I really am sorry, but it was out of my hands . . ."

"You do realise we're doing a signing and a Q&A session, right? A hundred copies of *Wings of the Caucasus* isn't nearly enough!"

Aki's voice was rising. Riko, standing beside her, held her breath.

"Uh . . . yeah . . . I mean . . . what am I supposed to do here . . . ?"

Yamamoto sounded uncharacteristically flustered. He and Aki got along well, often chatting during breaks at work. He had been supportive of this event from the start – or at least, he had seemed to be.

"Just tell me the truth. Did this come from higher up?"

"Uh . . . Yeah, pretty much."

"Why? You told me yourself this was a great idea."

"I don't know the details . . . Orders from above, that's all I can say."

"Look, we need those books. *Now.* Is there any way you can make this work?"

"I'll check first thing tomorrow, but right now . . . there's nothing I can do."

"Alright. So, I need to go over your head. Got it."

With that, Aki hung up.

Riko stopped her just as she turned towards the door. "What are you doing?"

"I'm heading over to the distributor. I'll talk to them directly."

"It's eleven o'clock at night."

"So? There has to be *someone* still there, right?"

Her voice wavered. She was on the verge of tears.

"Calm down. You need to talk to the *right* person, or you'll risk making things worse."

"I don't care. I *need* this event to be a success. No matter what it takes."

Aki was desperate. If the fair flopped, then everything she had fought for – even at the cost of making Nobumitsu hate her – would have been for nothing.

"There are other options if the distributor is a dead end. Try the publisher."

At that, Aki pulled out her phone again and dialled Iwata, Hitotsuboshi's sales rep. His phone must have been switched off, however, as she couldn't get through.

"Nothing. He's not picking up. Not that he was ever all that helpful to begin with . . ."

"That trouble with Agachi is still haunting us, huh?"

"Seems like it. Iwata even hinted he didn't want to be there for the signing event."

"This *is* a problem."

"What do we do? If we don't have enough copies for the ticketed events, customers are going to lose it. We've advertised this everywhere, and we've already had tons of enquiries. I'll go and see the distributor first thing in the morning. They *have* to give us the stock."

Aki could feel herself spiralling.

"Calm down," Riko said. "Worst case scenario, we can make all of Agachi's books eligible with a ticket, not just the new release."

"Yeah . . . Yeah, I guess . . . But hardcore fans will already own all the old books. That will just rile them up big time."

Aki started pacing the office.

"That's true. But if necessary—"

"This is a disaster. If the distributor won't budge, I'll just have to hit up every comic store in town tomorrow morning and buy out their stock myself."

"Absolutely not. That's ridiculous. *I* will take care of the books," Riko said firmly.

"Can you really fix this?"

"I don't know. But I'll try. You need to focus on setting up the displays. And what about the line outside? Without you to direct them, the staff won't know what to do. We have to handle what we can here and now."

"Alright."

Aki took a deep breath and left the office.

Riko let out a long sigh.

So, the deadline was opening time – 10:30 a.m.

Looks like I'm going to have to pull a few strings.

It wasn't something she wanted to do – but at this point, there was no other choice.

She took out her phone, inhaled deeply, and dialled a number she would have preferred never to have to call again.

Ten minutes before opening time, there was already a long line of customers outside the store – easily more than a hundred. That wasn't out of the ordinary when a famous manga artist or celebrity held a book signing, but Pegasus Books rarely hosted such events. This was the first time a crowd of this size had ever gathered outside its doors.

The staff were on edge. They had called in extra help at the last minute, bringing in part-timers who weren't scheduled to work that day to help manage the crowd. They had the line form two rows along the staircase, starting from the fifth floor and stretching all the way down to the first. If it got any longer, it would start wrapping around the entire building.

"We just did a headcount – there are already more than two hundred people."

"What should we do? Should we go ahead and put up the poster saying we're expanding the list of eligible items for the ticket holders?"

Mami and Anna took turns reporting to Aki, who, along with the rest of the comics team, had pulled an all-nighter. They had already prepared a poster, just in case they couldn't source more copies of Agachi's latest book.

"Let's wait a little longer. We'll decide once Nishioka gets back."

Riko had left around two in the morning, saying, "I'll take care of the missing books first thing in the morning, so don't put the poster up until the last minute."

"But we only have ten minutes left. If she doesn't get back soon . . ."

Just as Anna was voicing her concerns, Aki's phone rang. She checked the screen – Nishioka.

"I just got to the station. I managed to get a hundred copies. I'll be there any minute."

"Thank goodness! That's enough to cover the tickets, right?" Aki practically shouted in relief.

Anna, standing next to her, looked startled. "But Nishioka, are you carrying all that by yourself? That's gotta be heavy. Should we come and help you?"

"I'm fine. It's only a five-minute walk. I'm still a bookseller, you

know – a hundred comics is nothing. More importantly, is there anyone there who can run an errand – now?"

"We can spare one or two of us," Aki answered.

"The Ogikubo store has twenty copies, Iidabashi fifteen, and Okubo ten. They're willing to let us take them. Send someone to pick them up ASAP. Just have them ask for the manager at each of them."

"Got it!" Aki answered in an almost childlike shout.

"Wow, she actually pulled it off," Anna said in amazement.

"How did she do it?" Mami added, equally impressed.

Aki breathed a sigh of relief. "I knew she'd come through."

The staff started handing out the tickets as soon as the store opened, and they were gone in less than an hour. The event was planned for two hundred people, but, anticipating no-shows, they had printed two hundred and thirty tickets. Which meant that in under an hour, they had sold two hundred and thirty copies of Agachi's new release. For a store that didn't specialise in comics, that was unprecedented.

Most of the customers who received tickets didn't just leave – they stuck around, watching the recorded interview and checking out the displays. Even with a thousand square metres of floor space, the store was packed. Regular customers were browsing other books as well, and even with double the usual number of cashiers, the registers were barely managing to keep up.

By late morning, the extra stock they had brought in from the other stores had sold out as well. But just past noon, Yamamoto from the distributor showed up with another hundred copies, helping to keep the hordes at bay.

The crowds didn't thin out until well into the evening.

After finishing on the fifth floor, customers drifted down to the third and fourth floors, making the entire store busier than it had ever been. Aki ended up staying on the sales floor right until closing time.

She had spent the entire day saying, "Thank you, thank you," until her voice was hoarse. At some point, she realised she hadn't eaten lunch. Her feet ached, her pinkie toes throbbed from standing all day, and her ankles were swollen – but that didn't lessen the thrill of watching the books fly off the shelves. It was great to see the store so full of energy, and in a way, she was savouring the exhaustion.

Riko was just preparing to leave for the day when she decided to drop into the office.

"Good work today," she said to Aki as she stepped inside.

"You too. Thank you. Honestly, there was a moment when I wasn't sure we were going to pull it off . . ."

Before Aki could finish, Riko gave a small, embarrassed wave of her hand, stopping her. "Well, it all worked out in the end. I'm burned out, though, so I'm finishing for the day. I'm looking forward to tomorrow's sales report."

She was about to walk away when Aki suddenly spoke up. "Um . . ." She reached out and lightly tugged Riko's sleeve from behind.

"What is it?" Riko turned around.

"This morning, the extra hundred copies you brought in . . . How did you get them? I've been wondering all day, but I haven't had a chance to ask."

Riko flashed her a grin. "I'd like to say it's a trade secret, but I actually just negotiated directly with the publisher."

"But how did you manage to get hold of the right person at that hour?"

"It isn't something I can pull off all the time," Riko admitted. "I went straight to their office and got them to hand over their internal review copies."

"Wait, they have copies like that? And they just gave them to you? Hitotsuboshi Press isn't exactly renowned for their flexibility . . ."

Aki trailed off – and then it hit her. Of course. She must have asked Shibata for help. As a senior manager, he would have had the pull to make it happen.

"It doesn't really matter how, does it?" Riko said, dropping her gaze slightly. "We got what we needed."

"Yeah, you're right. Thank you," Aki said, bowing her head.

With that, Riko gave a little wave over her shoulder and headed for the exit.

24

"Good work today."

"Yeah, you too."

With those words, people started breaking off into small groups, heading their separate ways. It was already midnight, the second round of drinks had wrapped up, and most people were making their way to the station to catch the last train. A handful of younger bookstore staff, along with a few writers and editors who were clearly in it for the long haul, were heading off for a third round. Though all the stores along the shopping arcade had their shutters down, the streets were still full of people, and if you ducked into one of the alleys, you could find plenty of places that stayed open all night.

"I'm not done yet! One more stop!"

Nao Agachi, still in high spirits, was putting up a fight, and his editor was doing his best to talk him down. The gathering had been a joint celebration between Hitotsuboshi Press and Pegasus Books to toast the success of the book fair. As the guest of honour, Agachi was adamant it was his duty to see the night through to the bitter end.

"Come on, Agachi, give me a break," his editor insisted.

"You barely got any work done this month because you kept sneaking off to check on the fair. Starting tonight, we're getting back on schedule. Let's go back to the office."

"Oh, lighten up! It's a celebration! And Miwa's here, too!"

His editor wasn't having it. Practically dragging Agachi by the arm, he led him out of the shopping district, flagged down a taxi, and shoved him inside before climbing in after him. Through the rear window, they could still see Agachi protesting as the vehicle pulled away.

Riko and Aki, along with a few others, watched the whole thing. Once the taxi disappeared, Shunsuke Shibata from Hitotsuboshi Press let out a relieved sigh.

"Looks like the new guy's handling Agachi pretty well."

"Indeed," Riko nodded. "They were getting along well at the drinks party."

The new editor was a veteran – and he knew how to keep Agachi's self-absorbed tendencies in check.

"Thanks again for tonight," Riko said, turning to Shibata with a small bow. "And for covering the bill . . ."

"Don't mention it. It was only right. The fair was a huge success, and we managed to patch things up with Agachi. We owe you one."

"*We* should be thanking *you*. If you hadn't got us more stock that first day, I don't know what would've happened."

"That was our mistake. We should've worked with you guys more closely from the start. Young editors can be a little . . . hot-headed sometimes. They get too caught up in their emotions. We should've been more flexible, especially considering how much you guys helped us out when we launched *Until Your Voice Reaches Me*."

As he spoke, Shibata met Riko's gaze and held it. She hesitated, then glanced away.

He had seemed surprised when she called him in a panic, though he later admitted, "I know I'm not in a position to say this, but . . . I'm happy you turned to me for help."

Even though they had broken up, it was clear he still wanted to support her. That realisation alone helped to loosen something tight inside her chest – not that she let it show, of course.

"Well, if he's that passionate, I'd say it just means he really cares about his work."

Shibata followed her gaze to Iwata, the sales rep, who was laughing and chatting with Mami, the textbook section lead. Iwata seemed to have taken a liking to her – though whether it was down to her quirky personality or her looks was anyone's guess. Despite her sweet, gentle persona, Mami knew how to charm men when she wanted to. If she played her cards right, she could wrap a guy like Iwata around her finger in no time.

Riko had asked the younger female staff to focus their attention on Iwata tonight. Keeping him happy was crucial for future business dealings – they couldn't have him holding a grudge against their store. A little flattery could work wonders to smooth things over. Judging by how things were going, her plan was a success.

Just then –

"Hey, Obata, you're late!"

"Agachi just left. You just missed him."

Turning towards the new arrival, Riko spotted Aki's husband, Nobumitsu Obata, approaching. He had dark circles under his eyes, and he looked exhausted.

"Obata had to finish up the final proofs for the new magazine today," Shibata explained.

Riko nodded. That explained why he hadn't shown up earlier. Considering his connection with Agachi and the fact that his wife worked at the bookstore, he wouldn't have skipped the afterparty without good reason.

"I came straight from work . . ." he apologised.

Riko glanced towards Aki. She was standing a little way off, staring at her husband with a tense look. She wasn't making her way towards him, and he wasn't looking in her direction, either.

Riko let out a sigh and strode up to Nobumitsu. "It's been a while, Obata."

"Huh? Uh . . ." He looked flustered, caught off guard.

"Nishioka, the store manager. We met at your wedding." She smiled.

"Oh, right . . . Good to see you again."

"I just wanted to thank you for everything. I heard from Aki that you went out of your way to help with Agachi. It seems we caused your editorial team a fair amount of trouble . . ."

"Oh, no, not at all," he stammered, looking even more flustered.

Seeing them talking, Aki edged closer behind her. The other members of the editorial team, meanwhile, remained engrossed in their own conversations.

"I heard from Aki how much you've done to help us with this. I appreciate it," Riko said.

Behind her, Aki tugged at her sleeve. "Nishioka . . ." she murmured, clearly worried about what Riko might say next.

Riko, however, ignored her. "Aki was really struggling to set this up. I felt awful about it." She nudged Aki's arm with her elbow, a silent *leave it to me*.

"Uh . . . I see," Nobumitsu replied, sounding a little thrown off.

"Please don't be too hard on her. She may well have saved our store. Sales this month are up twenty per cent compared to last year. Hopefully, this will mean we won't have to close."

"Really? That's great news," Nobumitsu said, managing a small smile.

"But the best thing for a bookstore is having strong books and authors. That's what keeps us going. Agachi's work is amazing. I read all his books for the fair, and the pacing, the characters – it all feels so fresh. I see why young people love them. You were his editor for *Fly High!*, weren't you?"

"Uh, yeah. Well . . . I was his first editor, at least."

"It's wonderful. That book defined his style. It struck me as a turning point for him. I'm just an outsider, but I imagine that was thanks to his editor's influence. I'm sure you played a major role in shaping his career."

"Oh no, not at all. It's all about the writer, really," Nobumitsu murmured humbly – but his expression betrayed more than a hint of pride.

"Well, it's because editors like you put in the effort to create great books that we can do our best to sell them. Keep up the great work," Riko said, flashing him a dazzling smile.

Caught up in her enthusiasm, Nobumitsu found himself smiling back. "Yeah. You too."

"I'm looking forward to working together more." Riko gave a slight bow before stepping away.

Nobumitsu looked more at ease now. After exchanging a few more goodbyes with the others, Riko turned and headed towards the station.

"Nishioka!" Aki called, hurrying after her. "Why did you say all that?"

Riko stopped to meet her gaze. "I know I'm probably

meddling, but I don't want this event causing problems between you and your husband."

Aki's breath caught in her throat. She hadn't told anyone about the tension between her and Nobumitsu. How had Riko figured it out?

"Spot on, I see," Riko remarked. "You've looked off for a while now – distracted, not yourself. Even if work is going well, what's the point if it ruins your personal life? Sacrificing your marriage for your job isn't how we do things anymore."

"But—" Aki began to protest, but Riko cut her off.

"Don't be so stubborn. If you hold on to your pride too tightly, you risk losing something important. And from the look on your face, I'd say you want to make up with him."

"I do," Aki admitted, though her expression was still torn, like she might burst into tears at any moment.

"Marriage is tricky. You start off as relative strangers, so of course it won't always be smooth sailing. But that's why compromise matters. It's not like dating – marriage isn't something you just walk away from."

Aki bit her lip, silent.

"Then again, what do I know? I've never been married myself," Riko said with a self-deprecating chuckle. "Cheer up, okay?"

Aki started to say something but hesitated, then bowed her head. "Thank you."

"It's nothing." Riko gave her a firm pat on the shoulder, a gentle *hang in there*.

25

"Ah! Welcome back, Nishioka!"

Stepping out of the lift on the third floor, Riko ran into Ozaki, in the middle of swapping out the magazine displays.

"How'd it go?"

"Oh, well . . ." she mumbled vaguely before heading to the back of the store.

The right side of the floor was lined with magazines, while the left was dedicated to literary fiction. In the centre, directly in front of the register, was a large display table. This month's theme was works set in Kichijoji. It was a bookstore staple to feature books connected to the local area – but while most places leaned towards history and culture, Kichijoji was different. The neighbourhood was often voted the number one town young people wanted to live in, so naturally, all sorts of novels and manga comics had been set there. As such, they decided to launch a joint project across the third, fourth and fifth floors to draw attention to them. The third floor's focus was on literary fiction and magazines highlighting the local area.

To Riko's surprise, the line-up ended up being more diverse

than she had expected. Some books only made passing reference to Kichijoji, but others were deeply rooted in it. The line-up included classics like Yumiko Kurahashi's *Dark Journey* and Haruki Murakami's *Norwegian Wood*, alongside more contemporary works like Hideo Furukawa's *Route 350* and *Gift*, Mitsuyo Kakuta's *Drama Town* and Rio Shimamoto's *Little by Little*. There were also novels by authors like Hanamura Mangetsu, Eimi Yamada, Hitonari Tsuji, Yoshio Osaki, Eto Mori, Nobara Takemoto, Koichi Masuno and Eiichi Nakata. When they put the list together, they were amazed by how many famous writers had featured Kichijoji in their works. With names like these, they could have passed the event off as a publisher-sponsored fair.

But just stacking books on a table would have been boring, so they took excerpts describing the city and turned them into colourful display cards. Customers loved them. Kichijoji had a strong sense of local pride, and the books sold remarkably well.

Last month, they had gone all-in on Nao Agachi, drawing fans from all over Tokyo and the surrounding area, so this time, they wanted to do something that would resonate more with their regular customers. The local newspaper had covered the Kichijoji promotion last week, and it was attracting considerable attention. Many of their longtime patrons were thrilled, while other customers visited for the first time thanks to the publicity. For her part, Riko couldn't be happier to see so many people enjoying the store – the response made all their efforts worth it.

She moved away from the display tables and started checking the shelves one by one. The bestsellers were stacked on the front tables. Lately, headquarters had tightened control over what they could stock, and the number of new arrivals had dropped. Thankfully, other branches – Ogikubo, Okubo, and Iidabashi – had been helping by sharing some of their new stock. The managers at Okubo and Iidabashi had been Riko's trainees back when they first joined the company, and they still felt indebted to her. But it wasn't just that.

"It's not just your problem," Eto, the Ogikubo manager, had told her.

Everyone had the same fear – that headquarters would start axing underperforming stores one by one. Riko's branch was the oldest in the Pegasus Books chain, which made the anxiety even worse. Back when she had openly challenged Watanabe and Yamada at the store managers' meeting, many of them had secretly cheered her on. They couldn't publicly offer their support, but she knew plenty of them were rooting for her from the sidelines. That was how she had managed to keep the shelves stocked despite the circumstances.

"I'm heading off," a young part-timer called as he passed by. He had a large round badge pinned to his chest which read, *Ask me anything about mystery novels!*

That was part of a small initiative to make it easier for customers to approach staff. If an employee was confident in a particular genre – mystery, historical fiction, whatever – they could wear a badge like this. One of the contract employees had suggested it.

Riko believed in trying things out. If something didn't work, it was always possible to adjust course. A bookstore should evolve alongside its customers. She remembered the young man with the mystery badge complaining about being bombarded with obscure questions by hardcore fans, but instead of being discouraged, he had doubled down – and now, he was actively researching publisher trends and inventory. If anything, the challenge had motivated him.

The magazine section was also focusing on the local area. They had managed to collect a surprising number of back issues of town-focused magazines covering Kichijoji – *Tokyo Walker*, *Walking Guide*, *Hanako*, *OZ*, and even some mainstream fashion and lifestyle publications. The magazine team had been planning this for months, diligently researching and stashing away relevant issues.

Kichijoji really does get a lot of attention, Riko thought.

They had also put out back issues of *Vintage*, with a sign reading, *Featuring our very own bookstore!* It was the issue with the interview Riko had given, right here in the store. Embarrassed, she hurried past without stopping.

She started up the stairs. Ever since they had first used the stairwell as a makeshift gallery, it had become a permanent fixture. The walls were currently covered with excerpts from books that described Kichijoji, paired with enlarged manga panels featuring the town. Riko didn't recognise them all, but some caught her eye – like the scene from Yumiko Oshima's *The Star of Cottonland* where the tiny cat cries in the park in her apron dress, or the moment in Suzue Miuchi's *Glass Mask* where Maya dances in a fairy costume in the shopping district. She hadn't seen those since she was a kid. Nostalgia washed over her. Next to each illustration was a photo of the real-life location, along with a neatly written description. She didn't know who had provided the commentary, but it was surprisingly stylish.

Things had changed on the fourth floor, as well. The usually stiff atmosphere of the specialist books section had been softened with preserved flowers and fabric wall hangings.

Here, the local focus leaned towards history and culture, with books about the region's past, as well as books from local artists and works by university professors teaching nearby. It reminded Riko of how much this city attracted scholars and creative types.

As she absentmindedly flipped through a book, she overheard a customer asking a staff member a question.

"One moment, please," the employee replied, pulling out a small notepad.

That was a habit Riko had instilled – never rely on memory alone, always write things down.

She headed up to the fifth floor. There, a sizeable portion of the floorspace was dedicated to the Kichijoji event. They had gathered various manga series with clear ties to the town – Toru Fujisawa's *GTO*, Masanori Morita's *Good-for-Nothing Blues*, Hisashi Eguchi's *Stop, Hibari!*, Yumiko Oshima's *The Star of Cottonland*, Suzue Miuchi's *Glass Mask*, Masakazu Katsura's *Video Girl Ai*, Yuki Miyamoto's *Cafe Kichijoji*, Mine Yoshiaki's *Sgt Frog*, Kiyohiko Azuma's *Azumanga Daioh* . . . Some never explicitly named the town but were unmistakably set there. Unlike novels, manga comics rarely got this kind of local spotlight, so customers greatly enjoyed it. Manga fans tended to have very specific tastes, so Riko had been a little worried how it would be received, but sales were exceeding expectations. Perhaps the stairwell exhibit had sparked interest, or maybe people were just eager to revisit old favourites. In any case, the older titles were selling better than the newer ones.

Further down, the light novel section had been completely revamped. They had adjusted the selection, taking the advice of a bespectacled customer who always loitered there. Writers like Nisio Isin, whose work straddled both the literary and light novel genres, were now stocked in both sections. Meanwhile, they were using the rankings of his works on his light novel fan site to help them curate a small, impromptu mini-fair.

Over in the children's section, a small table and chairs sat on a carpeted area, decorated with plush toys. A staff member – wearing an *Ask me anything about kids' books!* badge – was reading aloud to a few children. They did this for about two hours a day on request. It was extra work, but the staff believed it would help create loyal customers. And of course, the hope was that if these children grew up loving books, they would want to keep coming back when they were older.

We've made a good bookstore, Riko thought. It had improved so much over the past few months. It was warm, lively, full of discoveries. The staff cared. If she were a customer, *she* would certainly want to keep coming back.

And yet, by the end of next month, they would be closing down.

Earlier that same day, Riko strode into headquarters brimming with confidence. Sales for January were up twenty per cent year on year – easily surpassing the target she had set in the store managers' meeting. At this rate, the store should still be viable even with the rent hike.

Now, in the same conference room where the meeting had been held, she was about to make her case directly to the president himself, at his own request, with Watanabe and Yamada in attendance. She launched into her explanation, laying out the store's situation in detail – how hard they had worked, how their efforts were reflected in the numbers. She wasn't nervous. She could confidently say she had done everything she could.

When she finished, she looked at the president. As always, he was smiling that warm, Ebisu-like smile of his.

"What do you think?" she asked.

"I have to say, you've done a great job," he replied smoothly, his expression unchanged.

"I can't believe you pulled it off . . ." Yamada began, but a sharp glare from Watanabe cut him off. Realising his mistake, he shrank back,.

"So," Riko pressed, "does this mean the store can stay open?"

The president didn't answer. Instead, he turned to Watanabe.

With a stiff expression, Watanabe delivered the verdict. "Sorry, but the decision stands. The store's closing."

Riko couldn't believe her ears.

"What? But you said . . .! You said that if we improved the numbers, we could stay open!"

"Did I?" The president tilted his head. "I believe what I said was, *Go ahead and give it a shot*. I never made any promises."

"Besides," Yamada jumped in to back him up, "you've been running things according to your own whims – scrapping uniforms, appointing contract employees as floor supervisors without approval, starting some kind of supporter system that drags customers into store operations. Just because sales are up a little doesn't mean we can tolerate that kind of behaviour."

Riko's patience snapped.

"If that's how you feel, why didn't you give us more full-time staff?" she shot back. "I never wanted to put that much responsibility on contract workers, but we had no choice! We were short-staffed! And I never eliminated uniforms – I just made them optional for new hires. That was a last resort, a way to cut costs. You have no idea how much we've saved, how much everyone has sacrificed. Do you know how hard my team has worked to achieve these numbers in just six months? You've never even set foot in our store – how could you possibly understand?"

Yamada faltered, shrinking back. "I'm sorry ... But it's out of our hands now." He glanced nervously at Watanabe. "Honestly, with results this strong, maybe we *should* reconsider—"

Before he could finish his sentence, Watanabe shut him down. "It's done. There's nothing we can do."

Riko clenched her fists. "Why? I need a real reason. After everything we've done, I can't go back and tell my staff it's over without an explanation."

"That's something I should answer."

The president's voice was calm, his Ebisu-like smile still intact.

"Sir?" Watanabe and Yamada said in unison.

The president leaned forward. "I *did* say that, yes. But the retail landscape is changing. Your store's numbers have improved, it's true. But will they stay that way? Right now, labour costs are unusually low, and you've been running all kinds of promotions to bring in customers. How long can that last? Once the building renovation begins, those customers will drift away. Won't they?"

"But sales are up twenty per cent year on year! We're outperforming every other store! Construction will set us back, sure, but we can recover quickly with our current team. And once we reopen in a new space, we can push even harder for more growth."

"That's assuming your store will be part of the new

building," the president said. "But nothing's set in stone. There's talk of leasing out the entire space to a single corporation."

Riko bit her lip. She hadn't heard that before.

"And there's another factor," he continued. "A major bookstore chain is planning to move into the area. Their new store will be bigger than our Ogikubo branch. Kichijoji is about to become a battleground."

"I don't care how it happens," Riko pleaded. "Even if we have to downsize, even if we move to a different location – I just don't want the store to disappear."

At this point, she was willing to try anything – even begging. She *needed* to find a way to fix this.

"Why are you so fixated on that place? Are you afraid of losing your position as store manager? Because you've done well – I'd be happy to assign you to another store. Maybe somewhere more challenging. Right – like the Ogikubo branch. That one needs revamping."

Ogikubo was Pegasus Books' new flagship store – bigger, more prestigious. Objectively speaking, that would be a promotion.

"I appreciate the offer, but what matters to me is keeping our store in that neighbourhood."

"Why?" The president's tone grew sharper. "It's just one old bookstore. What's the big deal if it shuts down?"

How could she make him understand? Saying she wanted to protect her employees' jobs wouldn't convince him. Calling it *her* store would sound sentimental. She needed something concrete.

Then, without thinking, the words came out. "Because that store is Pegasus Books' very first location. It's our history.

The founder cared about it until the very end. It's a symbol of everything this company stands for. Shutting it down would be—"

"So what? I don't need some outdated relic in my era."

Watanabe and Yamada flinched at the president's tone, both shrinking back into their chairs like they wanted to disappear out of sight.

Riko held her breath. She had never heard the president speak like this before.

"The old man was proud of that store," he continued. "He was ashamed of the fact he made his fortune running bars and cabaret clubs. He was a country bumpkin with no education – he had an inferiority complex. He convinced himself that owning a bookstore was somehow more *cultured*. As if that made a difference. Business is business, no matter what you're selling."

He pulled a cigarette from his breast pocket. Instantly, Watanabe and Yamada sprang into action – Watanabe flicking his lighter open, Yamada fetching an ashtray from a shelf in the corner. Even in moments like this, they were a well-oiled machine. Despite everything, Riko was impressed.

The president took a slow drag before continuing. "The truth is, he always wanted to pass the bookstore down to his favourite child – my sister, Mihoko. He figured my older brother would take over the restaurants, and Mihoko would marry someone who could run the bookstore chain for her. That was his dream. *I* was just an afterthought."

He let out a dry chuckle – but it was nothing like his usual warm, jovial smile. This was something different, something twisted. A glimpse into a part of him he usually kept hidden.

Riko, feeling like she had caught a peek at something she shouldn't have, lowered her gaze.

"But Mihoko went and married some lout he didn't approve of. Ran off, cut ties with the family, said she didn't want a single yen from him. So, in the end, there was no-one else left. And the useless second son got saddled with the scraps."

Riko had heard the story before. It was well known that Pegasus Books had originally been started for Mihoko. The company's founder had never recovered from the disappointment when she left.

"At first, he stuck me in that store to do grunt work. That was thirty years ago. My manager at the time had orders to give me the worst tasks possible – deliveries, cleaning, running errands, you name it. All day, every day. No handling customers, no stocking shelves, nothing that required thinking. I wasn't allowed to use the lift during working hours, so I lost count of how many times I ran up and down those damn stairs."

His voice dripped with resentment.

It suddenly hit Riko – she had never once seen the current president visit their store. The founder used to drop by at least once a month, since he lived nearby. But the new president? Never.

Of course. He didn't want to be reminded of it.

"And after all that, after making me go through hell, the old man still wouldn't hand it over to me. Even on his deathbed, he clung to control. No matter what I wanted, he opposed it. I had no choice but to obey him. Him and his stubborn pride."

Somewhere along the way, his father had become just *the old man*. And every time he said it, there was pure hatred in his eyes.

How had things got so bitter between them?

"Well, he's gone now. And I'm going to do things my way. I'll accomplish what he never could."

People always said the president was just a figurehead, that he lacked his older brother's business acumen and relied entirely on his right-hand men.

Looking at him now, Riko realised just how wrong they were.

"So, you're really going to shut us down?" she asked quietly.

For the first time, she understood. This wasn't about Watanabe or Yamada. They were just pawns in his game. The president himself wanted to be rid of the store.

"That's right." He crushed out his cigarette in the ashtray.

"But . . . after everything we've done, after all the effort we put in . . ."

The words slipped from Riko's lips before she could stop them.

All because of a grudge against his father? *That* was why he was throwing it all away? It was ridiculous. A store with more than thirty employees, a place where hundreds of customers came every day – none of it mattered to him?

"I'm sorry," the president said suddenly. "Back then, when you spoke up – I was curious. I wanted to see how far you could push yourself."

Riko felt the strength drain from her body. She had hoped – expected, even – that the president, at least, would understand them. That he wasn't like Watanabe or Yamada.

But in the end, she was just another pawn, too.

"You did better than I expected. No wonder they call you a star bookseller."

Was that sarcasm? An honest compliment? His tone gave nothing away.

"That's why – look, the store is closing. But I've got a new job for you. Something more meaningful than just managing a bookstore." He leaned forward, locking eyes with her. "How about heading up our ebook sales?"

"Ebooks?"

"That's right. Physical stores are on their way out. Print books, too. They're heavy, they take up too much space. Stocking and selling them in brick-and-mortar stores is hopelessly inefficient. You need shelf space, employees, security against shoplifters – it's a waste of resources. The future is digital. People will buy their books online and read them on their devices. Simple as that."

Riko wanted to argue that convenience wasn't everything, but she bit her tongue. There would be no getting through to him – not when he was this excited.

"We're already setting things in motion. I'm launching a joint venture with a major tech company," he said, casually dropping a big-name corporation. "It's going to be huge. At first, I thought I'd put my nephew, Nojima, in charge . . . But you're the better choice."

Nojima – the manager she had replaced. So that was why he got pulled back to headquarters.

But would ebooks really take off that fast? Publishers already had a head start in digital sales, and they owned the content. A bookstore chain had no leverage. How could they possibly compete?

She was still lost in thought when the president leaned in closer. "Well? What do you say? Sounds like something you'd want to take on, doesn't it?"

26

Riko sat alone in the izakaya bar – Momokichi, her usual hangout near the store. They had gathered here just the other day for the afterparty following the Nao Agachi fair, but this was her first time coming alone. Still, she was a regular, so the staff quickly guided her to a seat at the counter.

Tonight, all she wanted to do was drink by herself.

She had just handed in her resignation. After rejecting the president's personal offer to lead the company's new business venture, staying on wasn't an option.

Earlier, she had told everyone about the store closing. Most of them were in shock. Some had started crying. It was painful to watch. After all the effort they had put in, after everything they had built together, *this* was how it ended? A lump of cold frustration welled up in her chest. *She* felt like crying, too.

But she had no regrets about quitting. She had done everything she could. For the past five months, she had given it her all as a bookseller. And if she was being honest with herself, they had built a great store. If that still wasn't enough, then there was nothing more she could do for Pegasus.

"I thought I'd find you here."

A voice from behind made her turn around. It was Aki.

"Mind if I sit?" Without waiting for a response, Aki took the seat next to her.

"And here I was, trying to drink alone."

"Sorry," Aki said lightly, but she showed no sign of leaving. Instead, she flagged down a passing waiter and ordered a beer. "Aren't you eating anything?" she asked, noticing that Riko only had a plate of salad in front of her.

"You think I have an appetite at a time like this?"

"Well, *I* do. Excuse me! I'll have the rolled omelette with natto, the spiced grilled chicken, cold tofu and the shrimp and avocado mayo salad."

"You sure can eat," Riko muttered, a little taken aback. She knew Aki must be just as upset about the store closing as she was.

"Can't fight on an empty stomach."

"Fight? Fight what, exactly?"

"I handed in my resignation, as well. So, it's time to start job hunting."

Aki spoke so nonchalantly that it took a second for Riko to process her words.

"What? Why?" she practically shouted.

"Shh," Aki hushed her, putting a finger to her lips. "I don't know. Maybe I just got caught up in the moment. We all worked so hard to make the store great, and if they can't recognise that, then what's the point? A company like that has no future."

"You're being stupid. Every company has its share of unreasonable nonsense. You're going to quit over that? You're such a child."

"Well, if that's the case, then what about you? I heard the president wanted you to lead a new ebook division."

"You heard? I want to sell *real* books, in a *real* store. Digital books aren't for me."

Besides, she had already told everyone she would leave if the store went under. They all believed her, and they all worked hard because of it. She couldn't be the only one to jump ship, could she? Not that anyone would blame her if she did . . .

"Right. A bookstore is special because it's a physical space – real books on shelves, staff and customers coming in and out. Like a showroom for books. They just look better when they're sold in a store."

Aki was right. Ebooks weren't real books – they were just data. A completely different thing. A bookstore wasn't simply a place where books were sold – it was a space where customers, publishers and booksellers met, where conversations happened, sometimes even clashes. That was how you ended up with something new. It was a place where people connected through books – *that* was what a bookstore was, and that was why she loved them.

"So, what are you going to do now?"

"I'm not sure yet. I have some savings, so it's not like I'm in immediate trouble. I'll take my time to figure it out. Actually, I've already had a few job offers."

That part was true. As soon as word got out about the store closing, people started reaching out to her. She would probably end up choosing one or the other of them.

"I mean, I *am* a so-called star bookseller. I'll figure something out," Riko joked.

"Of course. The way you fought till the end for us has made you an industry legend. As long as you're not too picky about the details, you'll be fine."

"I hope so."

A waiter set a beer and some chilled tofu in front of Aki. She lifted her glass, so Riko picked up hers, and they clinked them together. A crisp, clear sound rang out, and Aki downed half her beer in one go.

"Ah, that's good."

Riko sipped hers in silence.

"You know, this is kind of strange," Aki said.

"What is?"

"The two of us, drinking together like this. There was a time when I couldn't stand the sight of you."

"Well, the feeling was mutual. Speaking of which, how are things with your husband?"

"We're doing fine. I mean, if we have kids, I'm sure there'll be plenty of things to argue about again, but I'm working on brainwashing him in advance," Aki said with a smirk.

Riko was genuinely happy for her.

"That's the way to do it." She laughed. "Train him bit by bit."

"Still, a lot has happened, huh?"

"Yes. But it was fun. Honestly, if you hadn't been our manager, I never would've had the experiences I did. I appreciate everything you did for us."

Hearing that, Riko felt a pang inside her heart. She didn't feel like she deserved that level of trust.

"You know . . ." she began, stopping herself when Aki turned her full attention to her. Unable to maintain eye contact, Riko looked down. But she had to say it. "I owe you an apology."

"Now? What for?"

"Well . . . Actually, you know those wine glasses you got from Shibata? From Hitotsuboshi? I *was* the one who broke them."

"Huh?"

"I'm sorry. I didn't do it on purpose. I just . . . I wanted to know what was in the box. I was curious about what Shibata had given you. I planned to put them back after peeking, but then I got startled by a noise, and . . . well, I dropped them."

"Why? Why would you do that?"

"You probably already know this . . . but I used to date Shibata. Before he met his current partner."

"Yeah, I've heard the rumours."

"The first present he ever gave me was a pair of Baccarat glasses. And then he sent you the exact same ones. I just . . . I had to know. But that's no excuse. It doesn't matter what the reason was – I had no right to open something that was addressed to you. I crossed the line. I'm really, truly sorry."

She bowed her head, bracing herself for Aki's response.

"So . . . *Were* they the same?"

"Huh?"

"The glasses he gave me – were they the same as yours?"

"Oh . . . Yes. That's why I panicked."

"What an idiot."

"What?"

"Oh, not you. I meant Shibata. Men really are hopeless, aren't they? They don't understand how we feel at all. I wouldn't be surprised if he gave his wife the exact same thing."

"Maybe," Riko murmured.

That *did* sound like something Shibata would do.

"He's good at his job, but he's clueless when it comes to women. Honestly, you're better off without him."

Is she . . . trying to comfort me?

"Well, I guess it can't be helped. I mean, I *did* like the glasses, but whatever."

"Actually . . . I went and bought replacements. I was going to swap them before you found out, but I didn't make it in time."

"Seriously? You should've just told me. It really wasn't that big a deal."

Aki shrugged it off like it was nothing. She wasn't mad. She wasn't trying to blame Riko for what happened.

Riko let out a breath of relief. She had been carrying that guilt for so long.

"Not exactly the kind of thing you just say in the moment, you know?"

"Yeah, I get it. Still, looking back, why were we always so on edge?"

"I honestly have no idea."

It was funny how things had changed. Now, Aki felt closer to her than anyone else. Compared to their battle with headquarters, their past fights seemed so petty. Aki probably felt the same way – which was why she could laugh about the wine glasses now.

"Anyway, let me know when you decide on a new job," Aki said.

"Huh? Why?"

"Because I'll apply there, too."

"You're kidding." Riko nearly dropped her glass.

"Wherever you're going, I bet it'll be interesting."

"You haven't changed. You know work isn't just about having fun, don't you?"

"Of course. But come on, wouldn't it be better for me to come with you than to have to start again from square one?"

She had a point. Maybe starting something new with Aki *would* be fun. But that wasn't what came out of Riko's mouth.

"Not happening. I'm finally free – I'm not dragging any baggage from my past around with me."

"Baggage, huh?" Aki pouted.

Riko smiled. "But if you're *really* struggling, I suppose I can consider it. I doubt too many places would want to take in a troublemaker like you."

That probably came off as harsh, but Riko wasn't the type to say, *Best friends forever!* – not at her age.

"Still talking down to me, huh?" Aki grumbled. Then, suddenly remembering something, she pulled a slip of paper from her pocket. "I almost forgot. A customer – that Hoshino guy – called before I left. He wants you to call him back."

"Hoshino? What for?"

He was a regular at the store and one of the five customers who had attended the Supporters' Meeting. And of course, he had helped Riko out of a tough spot once. But they had never spoken outside of the store.

"I had better call him before I get too tipsy."

With that, Riko grabbed her phone and stepped outside.

A few minutes later, Riko returned to her seat, looking dazed. She sank into her chair, almost in a trance.

"What happened? Did he just ask you out or something?" Aki teased her, noticing how out of it she seemed.

"What? No, nothing like that. Something even more incredible just happened."

"Incredible? What do you mean?"

"I got headhunted."

"Wait, what?"

"There's a plan to bring a big bookstore chain from Kyushu to Kichijoji. You know the one."

"Wow! Seriously? And?"

"According to Hoshino, they're opening a large street-level storefront in that new building by the station. The second and third floors will also be part of it, so it should end up being the biggest in the country. It turns out, Hoshino works for them – he's the project lead. He said he's been visiting bookstores in the area for research, and he was really impressed with how we run things."

". . . And?"

"He asked me to be the store manager."

"Are you serious? That's amazing!" Aki practically leaped up in excitement.

"And he said I can bring as many staff members as I want."

"*Now* we're talking! The universe hasn't abandoned us after all! You're saying yes, right? We can all move there together, can't we?"

Aki was already celebrating, but Riko hesitated, watching her carefully.

"I don't know . . . It almost sounds too good to be true. I agreed to meet with them next week to discuss the details."

"If it's the company I think you mean, you don't have to worry."

"Maybe, but I haven't heard anything about the terms yet."

"What does that matter? Ozaki, Mami, Anna – we'll all get to keep working together! That's the most important thing, right? Everything else will sort itself out. And if there's a problem, we'll deal with it then."

"But still—"

Just as Riko was about to voice another doubt, a loud voice interrupted her from behind.

"Found you!"

"Hey, no fair! You two were drinking without us!"

They turned around to see the staff – Mami, Ozaki, Mita, Yamane, the Kurata brothers, and just about everyone else who was working today – standing there.

"What's going on?" Riko asked, surprised.

"*What's going on?* You tell us! We're all drinking together, that's what!" Ozaki practically scolded her.

"If it's a farewell party, we're doing it together. We're a team, remember?" Mami added, throwing her arms around Aki from behind.

"Excuse me. Do you have a private room available?" Mita asked the restaurant manager.

Luckily, there was an open space, so the manager led the group further inside. One by one, they all followed.

Riko and Aki grabbed their glasses and went after them. Just before stepping into the room, Riko leaned close and whispered in Aki's ear, "Don't say anything about the job offer yet. I don't want to get their hopes up for nothing."

Aki just nodded silently.

Inside, everyone took their seats. Riko accepted the space in the centre. Once everyone had settled down and placed their orders, Ozaki stood up. The room quietened down, waiting for her to speak.

"We all came here tonight because we wanted to thank you, Nishioka."

"Thank me?" Riko blinked in surprise.

"These past six months have been an incredible experience. We've grown so much. No matter where we go next, we'll be able to handle just about anything thanks to what we learned with you."

"But . . . I couldn't save the store . . ."

"That doesn't matter. We all saw how hard you fought for us. You even left the company because of it. Sure, it's sad the store's closing, but we're grateful for everything. Thank you."

"That's . . ." Riko sat there stunned, not sure what to say.

A moment later, Yamane stepped forward, holding a bouquet. "This is from all of us. A token of our appreciation." She handed Riko the flowers.

Riko took them silently, too overwhelmed to speak.

"You did a great job," Mita said.

"Thank you," someone else added.

"Really, thank you," another voice joined in.

Riko looked around at everyone, struggling to find the words. She lowered her gaze.

"Thank you," she finally managed, before her tears spilled over.

Someone started clapping. Then another. And another. Soon, the whole room was filled with applause.

"I only made it this far because of all of you," she said hoarsely. "Thank you."

The applause grew louder. Riko couldn't stop crying.

Just then, their drinks arrived. The room was abuzz again as everyone took their glasses. Once everyone had a drink, someone called out, "Aki, you should do the toast!"

She stood up.

"Nishioka. Everyone. These last six months have been tough, but they've also been an invaluable experience. Like Ozaki said, no matter where we go or what we do, we'll be okay. That's how much we've grown. So, let's raise our glasses – to an amazing manager, and to all of us, the best team ever."

A round of applause followed.

"That's not how you lead a toast!" Mami teased.

Aki chuckled, then lifted her glass high. "Alright, alright. That's just how I feel about all of you. Now, enough talking – let's raise our glasses to an incredible team and an even brighter future. Cheers!"

"Cheers!"

Their voices rang out together as glasses clinked high in the air.

Everyone was smiling. Aki, Ozaki, Mita, Yamane – every single one of them. Even in the middle of all this uncertainty, they were beaming as they raised their glasses.

As Riko looked around at each face, a thought settled in her heart.

This wasn't the end. It was a new beginning. Starting tomorrow, she would keep moving forward.

So that one day soon, they would all be able to laugh like this again.

"Cheers!" Riko called loudly, downing her drink in one go.

KEI AONO was born in 1959 in Nagoya, Japan and studied at Tokyo Gakugei university. After starting her career at an anime magazine, she worked as a fiction editor at a publishing company. In 2006 she made her fiction debut with *The Reason I Won't Quit*. *Bookstore Girls*, published in 2012, sold 200,000 copies in Japan and was adapted for television after the third book in the series won the Grand Prize in the "Book I Want Made into a Movie" category at the Shizuoka Bookstore Awards. It was followed by six sequels, with sales of more than 600,000 copies in total.

HAYDN TROWELL is an Australian translator of Japanese literature whose work has appeared in *Granta*, *Electric Literature* and *Words Without Borders*. He has translated fiction by major prize-winning authors such as Yasunari Kawabata, Maki Kashimada and Rie Qudan, and he has worked extensively with publishers in Australia, Japan, the UK and the US. Haydn holds a PhD in translation studies from Monash University and has a background in both translation and creative writing.